BAD APPLE

After completing a psychology degree, Alice Hunter became an interventions facilitator in a prison. There, she was part of a team offering rehabilitation programmes to men serving sentences for a wide range of offences, often working with prisoners who'd committed serious violent crimes. Previously, Alice had been a nurse, working in the NHS. She now puts her experiences to good use in fiction. *Bad Apple*, and her previous novels *The Serial Killer's Wife*, *The Serial Killer's Daughter* and *The Serial Killer's Sister* all draw heavily on her knowledge of psychology and the criminal mind.

By the same author:

The Serial Killer's Wife
The Serial Killer's Daughter
The Serial Killer's Sister

BAD APPLE

ALICE HUNTER

avon.

Published by AVON
A division of HarperCollins*Publishers* Ltd
1 London Bridge Street
London SE1 9GF

www.harpercollins.co.uk

HarperCollins*Publishers*
Macken House, 39/40 Mayor Street Upper,
Dublin 1, D01 C9W8
Ireland

A Paperback Original 2024
1

First published in Great Britain by HarperCollins*Publishers* 2024

ISBN: 978-0-00-866281-3

Set in Sabon Lt Std by HarperCollins*Publishers* India
Printed and bound in the UK using 100% renewable electricity at CPI Group (UK) Ltd

For those who've experienced, or been affected by, sexual violence. To the survivors and in memory of those lost.

Content warning:

BAD APPLE, although fictional, tackles many issues
that some may find distressing. There are mentions of
rape and sexual assault, self-harm and suicide, physical
and mental abuse throughout.

Prologue

She shouldn't be driving.

The roads were narrow, unfamiliar; each bend took her by surprise as it appeared like magic through the ominous entrails of mist hanging a few feet from the ground. Not a quicker route back after all. Her mother's voice filled her mind:

Calm it down. Take your foot off the accelerator.

She took her tear-blurred eyes off the road, threw her head back and let out a frustrated cry. 'Whhhy?'

The Mini swerved dramatically across the lane and she fought to regain control.

So typical for her mother to be right. She said he was stringing her along, that he was a good-for-nothing layabout with dodgy mates. A lowlife druggy.

But no, as usual, she'd argued the toss: 'He's not in with that crowd. You don't need to worry, Mum. I've cleaned up my act for Oakley's sake.' And the last sentence she uttered as she flew out the door. 'I'll be careful, Mum.'

Her stomach griped. When she walked back into the

house, returning far earlier than she'd said, what would her reason be? Perhaps she should just drive until the early hours, go back when it seemed enough time had passed so to avoid the critical analysis. She looked at the petrol gauge and her shoulders slumped. Nope. She had to go home now. She could be light and breezy – all, 'Silly me, got the wrong night. Thanks for babysitting again though.' Yeah, that could work, actually.

Anything but the truth.

Anything but the sour-faced, reproachful glare her mother would give if she were to give the real reason.

Her self-pitying thoughts came to an abrupt halt as lights filled the car. She squinted into the rear-view mirror, her mouth agape at the closeness of the vehicle behind.

'Dickhead!'

She put her fist up but lost control on another bend, wrestling with the steering wheel before righting herself. Jesus, that had been close. She swore at the man behind. It *had* to be a man. She put her foot down, trying to get some distance between them, stop him blinding her with his headlights. *I should've got a taxi* crossed her mind just as the yellow glare of lights changed to blue. Her heart juddered.

'Oh, shit.' She took her foot off the accelerator, knowing it was too little too late. As the Mini slowed, her thoughts sped up. She'd swerved all over the road. She'd been drinking. She'd probably fail a breath test. Her mum was going to kill her.

Don't panic. You can talk your way out of this. Blame the weather conditions.

But if the copper dragged her into the station, did her for drink-driving, how would that look to social services?

They'd already been far too involved in her life in the five months since Oakley's birth. She was already on her last chance . . .

She could floor it. Lose this idiot. She'd only swerved because he was too bloody close to her. It was his fault. Her sensible head, the one she now wished she'd had on for the entirety of this past week, told her to pull over. She might be lucky – it could even be as simple as a brake light being out.

Relief swept through her. Yeah. 'Course – this heap-of-shit car always had something wrong with it. Her guilty complex immediately caused her to jump to the worst scenario when the simple reason was more likely. Without further thought, she indicated and pulled into a wider part of the lane. And waited, both hands gripping the wheel.

Through her rear mirror, she followed the man's progression from his unmarked car towards hers, swallowing down the golf-sized-ball that had formed in her throat. He wasn't in a police uniform and took slow, steady steps. Not in any rush. Making her sweat, no doubt. There wasn't anyone else in his vehicle that she could make out, no movement from behind the dark windscreen.

He stopped alongside the driver's door. *Here we go.* He ducked down and motioned for her to lower her window. He smiled. There was a warmness to it, and his eyes crinkled as it reached them. For a split second, she relaxed, allowing herself to return the gesture.

'What a night, eh?' she said. 'Really hard to see the . . .'

'You know why I've pulled you over?' He placed one hand on the opened window while the other tapped on the roof of the Mini – the rhythmic drumming loud, but no

3

match for her heartbeat. His face was close to hers and she instantly panicked, turning hers away. *Shit, shit, shit.* He'd smell the alcohol for sure.

'No, Officer.' Best say as little as possible.

'This your car?' He cast his eyes around the interior, then stood back from the window and began walking around it without waiting for her answer. She saw him take out a notebook. How could she get out of this? She swung her door open and got out.

'Stay inside your vehicle, please.' He strode back around to her, an arm outstretched indicating that she should get in. But she stood, rooted to the spot.

'Look, I might've been driving a bit erratically, but it's the mist. And the lanes – I've not driven this way before. I'm used to the bright city lights.'

He nodded. Gave a sigh, then shook his head. Like he was weighing up whether to let her drive on without taking up any more of their time. 'Name and address, love?'

She blew out a breath. It wasn't over, then. Dammit. But, *love.* At any other time, that would annoy her, but right now she was taking it as a good sign. She reluctantly gave him her details, each admission feeling like a nail in her coffin. She shivered against the cool air biting at her skin. With her eyes averted, she pulled her fake leather jacket tighter around her, then looked down – her gaze travelling from her bare thighs towards her high-heeled boots. She'd borrowed them from her old roommate three years ago and failed to return them. As she raised her head, she locked eyes directly with the man standing in front of her, and something in her brain made a connection. Despite her thumping heart, the adrenaline racing through her veins, her mind cleared.

4

'What is it I'm supposed to have done?' She frowned at the officer. Why was he in an unmarked police car? 'Are you even on duty?'

'Was on my way home, actually.'

Braver now, standing upright. 'Then, I'll ask again, why did you pull me over?'

'A feeling,' he said. He took another step closer to her, his body a few inches from hers. 'Call it gut instinct.' Her own instinct flared, and she flattened herself up against the Mini, uncrossing her arms but putting them up to her chest, palms flat, facing the officer. If he even was a police officer. She'd heard about a bloke recently who'd pretended to be a copper, pulled a woman driver over and then attacked her.

Her bag was on the passenger seat, but even if she could reach it, she'd have to fumble inside to find her mobile. She gave a furtive glance around. The lane was in darkness, no sign of other vehicles approaching. There were hedgerows either side of the road. The lay-by she was in was muddy, but no evidence of a gate into a field, or any houses. There was nowhere to go – no one to hear any cries for help.

'Can I see your ID?' She heard the wobble in her voice, and as he smirked, she felt the wobble in her legs, too. He grasped hold of her, one hand on either shoulder. The thud of his notebook landing on the ground echoed in her head as if it were amplified.

'Woah. Careful now, love.'

Great. Now if he really was a cop he had more cause to think she was drunk.

'Look,' he said. 'You and I both know that if I breathalyse you, you'll be over the limit, yeah?'

She had to assume he was the real deal. For now, her

only concern should be making sure he didn't book her. She tried to remember her past experiences with coppers – if this one was off-duty could he even breathalyse her? She shook her head, the knowledge not coming to the fore. She couldn't chance it.

'Then don't,' she said, giving a shrug. 'I'm sure you don't want the additional paperwork. If you're on your way home, like you said.'

His smile returned. 'Come with me.' He stepped back from her, swiftly taking her car keys from the ignition through the open window. He locked the door and pulled her towards his car. The clacking of her boot heels sounded like rapid gunshots in the night. He told her to get in. Then he started the car.

'What the hell?' she said, glaring at him. 'I thought—'

'I'm not shopping you. Don't worry.'

A heaviness pressed down on her chest, expelling the air from her lungs. She gasped and grappled with the door handle.

'I'd like to get out. Let. Me. Out.'

'I'm afraid that won't be possible.' His eyes stayed on the road ahead. His calm demeanour evoked the opposite reaction in her.

'Why? I don't understand . . . where are you taking me?'

'Oh, not far. Just up here, in fact.' He made a turn onto a dirt track and the car bumped along it for a few minutes. All the while, her heart and mind raced frantically.

There was no radio in this car, nothing that made her think it was a cop car. But then, he did say he was driving home after finishing duty, didn't he?

If he's a police officer, everything will be fine.

6

She wouldn't come to harm. Surely.

The car engine died. He turned to her.

'You do something for me, I'll do something for you.'

Realisation made her insides freeze; her body went rigid, like rigor mortis had instantaneously invaded every muscle despite being alive.

'No,' she said. Didn't she? Or was the word trapped inside her head. 'Please . . .'

She closed her eyes, the tears squeezing from her lids spilled down her cheeks.

A sensation of falling as the back of the seat reclined.

A hand pushed up her skirt and thrust between her legs.

Her lower lip quivered, but the scream she desperately wanted to burst from her, remained dormant. He yanked her knickers down. Material ripped as her thighs were roughly parted. Why wouldn't her limbs move? Fight against him? The hair at her temples tickled as tears rolled into it. That's what she concentrated on when the pain started. She imagined the trail they were leaving, the path they were taking between her dark strands of hair and along her scalp towards the back of her head. She visualised the damp patch they'd leave on the headrest of the seat.

She imagined Oakley's baby face and wondered if she'd ever see it again. His tufty piece of hair that jutted from the crown, his gummy smile as he looked with unconditional love into her eyes.

An hour later she was home. She avoided any talk with her mother, heading straight for the shower. As she held Oakley in the early hours of the next day and he sought the love in her eyes, she turned away, afraid of just what he'd see.

7

One year later

It's your word against mine.

> God, you think you're untouchable, don't you.

That's because I am. No one'll believe you – not by a long shot. Not with your history. There's no CCTV footage, no evidence even if they were to go looking. Which they won't, of course.

> You're meant to protect people.

And I do. I'm protecting you right now, aren't I? You won't come to harm if you keep your mouth shut. I'm looking out for you.

> You're disgusting.

I didn't hear you complain when I was in you.

Her heart bashed against her ribs as the messages and conversations replayed in her mind. Over and over. He was right. No one would believe a long-serving police officer – a *detective* – over the alcoholic drug abuser she'd been painted as, whose kid was removed from her custody. A pitiful yelp escaped her. She should've known something wasn't right. Trusted her instinct instead and driven off. Stupid, stupid woman. And then to allow it to continue. She banged her fists against her temples. This was all her fault.

Through her tears, she reread her first journal entry – how he'd pulled her over that misty night, her relief when he offered an alternative to a drink-drive charge. Her despair when she realised his intention. How she assumed that was the end of the matter . . . Her life ended that night and her son's life was now someone else's responsibility. Death was all she deserved.

She added another entry to her journal, closing it with finality, then she took a screenshot of the phone message thread. She hesitated with her fingertip hovering above the send button. Would this even shake him? Cause him concern? Nothing had rattled him during the past year of her threatening him. But maybe this would if she told him she'd sent it to others too. Her mind paused, skipped, rewound, fast-forwarded. It was all too much. She stuffed the phone down the back of the sofa. Then took the journal back to its place.

Once she'd concealed that, too, she returned to the sofa, positioned the cushions and sat down. She shook the plastic bottle, spilling the cylindrical white pills into her shaky palm. She briefly wondered how long she'd be lying dead in her own vomit before she was discovered. It would likely be her mother who found her. She was the only one left who might question her lack of activity and finally pop over to check on her.

'Sorry, Mum. But you probably saw *this* coming, too . . .' Her hand slapped against her open mouth, depositing the fatal heap inside. For a while, she held them there, her cheeks bulging like the hamster she had when she was six. What was his name again? Jimmy. That was it. He'd lasted for three years – apparently a great age for a hamster. Twenty-four wasn't such a great age for a human. She snatched the vodka bottle and took a swig large enough to aid the journey of the pills.

It took several more gulps, and plenty of gagging, before she'd accomplished her task.

9

No going back now.

He'd won. That bastard would get away with what he'd done. If anyone did ever find out, they'd think she was weak, selfish even, for not fighting him. Both in the moment, while he raped her, and now – as she left this life. Other women would no doubt fall foul of his manipulation, his twisted and controlling ways that enabled him to get what he wanted.

Did she owe it to his past and future victims to stay and fight a battle that might destroy her anyway? Owe it to the child she let down so badly? She didn't have the strength. He'd made sure of that.

Leaning back into the cushions, awaiting death, she gazed around the room at the discarded, unplayed-with toys – the remnants of her life. Her head fell back. Staring at the ceiling, she hoped that he'd get what was coming to him one day. Then she closed her eyes.

Chapter 1

NOW

BECKY

The envelope propels through the letterbox as I'm three paces away from the front door. It lands face up on the patchy doormat, the name and address printed in large, black letters leaping from it. I stop dead, staring at it like it's a stand-off. A rush of warm air passes through my dry lips. Licking them would be futile; the moisture's instantly been withdrawn by anxiety.

Mrs Rebecca Lawson

A cold sensation alights my nerve endings and I shiver myself into action, tentatively taking the final steps and sucking in a lungful of air as I swoop my hand down to grab the envelope.

As I run my fingertips across the top line, I wonder how these three little words could possess such power to cause goose bumps on my arms. How they can provoke a deep ache within my belly, the beginnings of a familiar

11

nausea. If it were junk mail, I'd find it easier to brush off the offending string of letters. I'd immediately tear it into tiny, unintelligible strips of nothingness. Obliterate all record of that person.

But given the 'Greater Manchester Police' stamp mark on the envelope, I'm confident it's a communication I've been expecting – and if my pathetic begging has worked, it contains hope. A means of digging myself out of the depths of despair I've languished in this past year – the rut I've been neck-deep in since moving to this shit area of Salford five months ago. Destroying it right this second will be cutting off my nose. I take a few unsteady strides through to the kitchen, shimmying around the stacked boxes I've yet to unpack, place it on the table and lean over it, my frown deepening. I haven't used that name for a while and certainly not since the official final order came through. Strange that Marcus has chosen to address me like this.

Did he think I needed a reminder?

A blast of tinny-sounding music erupts from my mobile – a rarity these days. I get the odd text or WhatsApp message but can't remember the last actual call. I ignore its insistent tone. I need to read the letter first. Deal with one thing at a time.

It's the only way I've managed to see each day through since finding out what he did. It's a coping mechanism that the counsellor I saw after the death of my parents taught me. Seems a lifetime ago, but it's only been ten years. How different my life would've been had they not taken that trip. Had my dad not been driving on the road at the exact moment the best man from a wedding party – who'd chosen to jump in his car fully aware he was hammered – turned down the one-way street and hit them head-on. I'd have continued on at Falmouth Uni, close to where I'd grown up – qualified as a psychologist and found a picturesque cottage by the sea to live my happily-ever-after in. I always imagined I'd meet and marry a Cornishman, have children and then work from home in an adapted summerhouse in the garden, my doting, loyal husband bringing me cups of coffee with custard cream biscuits on a plate to keep me going between clients.

Instead, here I am. Divorced and living alone. Desperately attempting to salvage something from the mess the man I ended up marrying made. My mobile pings with a voicemail notification. My attention drifts to it and my muscles twitch with the urge find out who could be bothered enough to stay on the line once the standard greeting cut in.

'No! Just get on with it. Open it now, open it now.' I pull my gaze back to the letter.

My breathing shallows and I press my hand against my thudding heart. I need Chief Inspector Marcus Thomson's words of praise that are contained within this envelope, to increase my chances of securing the psychological assistant job and enable me to move forward with my life. He was the only senior rank I felt able to ask. It's not as though I left with my head held high. Heat invades my cheeks as the memory of my last day on the force shoots unbidden into my mind, and I place my cool palms against them.

'Sorry it had to come to this.'

My eye roll was automatic and clearly didn't hide my contempt – but I added an audible "humph" to make sure there was no room for misinterpretation. I was standing with my feet hip-width apart, back rigid, hands balled into fists at my side as I faced the day I'd been dreading. I listened to the final, shallow words of someone who'd been promoted

13

above me more than once despite not deserving it.

'If there was any way around it, we'd have found it. But . . .' DI Wallis paused and scratched his shiny head '. . . you've put everyone in an awkward—'

A familiar tide of anger rose. I physically pushed it down by pressing the heels of both hands into my stomach.

'*I've* put this team, this force, in an awkward position,' I said, in a more controlled way than in previous discussions with those higher up. 'You're not serious, are you?'

He shuffled papers on his desk, then lined up several pens and pencils. He cleared his throat. 'It's gone to the top. Right to the top, you know that. Face the facts. You were wrong, and you've caused them to make an impossible decision.'

'Yeah.' I sucked in my cheeks and shook my head. 'And turned out that the not-so-impossible decision was *me*. You're all going to live to regret that choice.' I watched as Wallis's straggly, dark eyebrows shot up. He started to stand, so slowly it was like watching a predator trying not to startle its unsuspecting prey.

'Don't make it worse for yourself, Lawson.'

'Don't. Call. Me. That.' I backed out of DI Wallis's office, not breaking eye contact with him until the door slammed closed. 'Wanker.' I turned slowly and headed back to my desk, collected the box containing a cactus – my thirty-fourth birthday gift from my team – a coffee mug, and all the stationery from my drawer whether it was mine or not, and without glancing at my now ex-colleagues, I strode towards the lift.

'Hey, Becks!'

I bit down on my lip, kept my gaze forward. 'Come on, come on,' I mumbled, willing the lift doors to open before he could reach me.

'Wait up.'

Charlie Harris, energetic, friend to everyone, bounded up beside me. I waited for a sarcastic comment – his usual dry-witted one-liner, but it didn't come, instead he offered an apologetic smile.

'I'm sorry. I have to escort you . . .'

'Oh. I see.' I forced a tight-lipped smile then turned around. 'Don't trust that I'll hand in my pass? Wouldn't want me coming back causing more trouble, would you?' My voice travelled across the office floor, garnering looks of pity from what had been my team. Charlie cleared his throat with an awkward cough, but said nothing.

The silence in the lift spoke volumes. Charlie held his hands clasped in front of him, his head bowed. The atmosphere was heavy with guilt, sadness, regret. He hadn't put his career or reputation on the line for me, and although he wasn't alone in that, it was his lack of support in particular that stung the most. And a part of me hated him for it. The other part had to accept he didn't feel he had a choice in the matter and I shouldn't hold that against him. His inaction wasn't driven by malice, it was due to misplaced loyalty. It was driven by a fear of the repercussions. Had I considered those a little more deeply myself, I might still have been a detective. I might still have had the means and the ability to make a difference. Protect lives. Uphold the law.

The lift doors swished open and I shot out and across the foyer, my mug jangling against the ceramic plant pot within the box as I stormed off. I heard footsteps close behind and after swiping my pass to get through the barrier for the final time, I chucked my ID card back towards Charlie without looking at him. 'See ya.'

'Becks,' he said. 'Don't be like that? All this, it doesn't mean we can't still be mates—'

I turned in his direction, but kept walking backwards, away from him. 'Honestly, Charlie?' I forced myself to make eye contact. 'It might.'

He hung his head. For a moment, I stopped, my only thought to drop the box containing my stupid items and give him a hug, tell him it was fine and of course we were still mates. That it didn't matter that I'd lost my job, my husband, and would likely lose my home. That it was okay that I hadn't gained support from my colleagues when the shit really hit the fan. That I understood. But we both knew none of it was okay and if I uttered any of those things, Charlie would know them to be lies. And I wasn't the liar in this situation.

And so, with nothing left to say, Charlie turned and headed back to the lift, and I left the building for the last time.

The hairs on my neck prickled with warning as I walked towards my car. I was being watched. While it could be any number of people, my gut told me the identity of my observer, and there was no way I was giving him the satisfaction of letting him know I'd felt him. With my eyes down, I lowered the cardboard box onto the back seat, then climbed into the driver side. I risked a glance into my rear-view mirror as I drove away, but could only see a shadow in the window on the top floor.

I knew it was Detective Sergeant John Lawson who'd watched me leave the staff car park. Leave my profession, the job I'd grown to love, behind me.

And it made my stomach knot realising he'd be smug in the knowledge that he'd just won the battle.

Chapter 2

NOW

BECKY

The once-white, now-yellowing kettle boils so violently it moves a few inches across the laminate worktop. I flick the switch before it takes a dive off the edge in a bid for freedom . . . or death. To be fair, it could do with being put out of its misery. As with the majority of my possessions in this pokey, ground-floor flat, it was either a bargain charity shop find or an item donated to me by a concerned friend. Of which I don't have many anymore. I don't even want a coffee – in fact I could do without the caffeine; I'm shaking enough.

More delay tactics.

What if Marcus Thomson *hasn't* written a glowing reference? He might've only told me he would, just to get me off his back. I pour the still-bubbling water into my mug, stir the spoon until the clinking against the ceramic becomes annoying. Looking out the window, mug held tightly between my hands, I watch the magpies gather in the courtyard. It's a four-foot square, concrete block with a hole in the middle – I assume for a rotary line. Not that I own one – no need to wash many clothes for one person. I tend to hand-wash my underwear and few items of clothes and hang them over the three small radiators. At home, I'd had a washing line running the length of the garden. I blink the image away. Well, that's not my home anymore, this is.

'Right, best get on with it then.' I place my mug down without even taking a sip of the instant coffee – the usual shot of resentment that John took the filter machine rearing its ugly head – and snatch up the letter, quickly flipping it over to avoid looking at the name again. I slide my thumb beneath the envelope's seal, tearing it open with a swift movement. The crisp white paper is folded with the sender's address showing. My mind slows to a stop, unable to comprehend what I'm seeing. Then it registers. It's not from Marcus.

It's from John.

'What the . . .?' I skim-read the letter. None of the words make sense, but the sentence 'If you continue to harass me, I'll have no option but to apply for a non-molestation order' is enough for me to gather that my ex-husband is attempting to stop me from continuing my 'grossly inappropriate' behaviour.

I throw the letter and grab my mobile, pacing the tiny area of kitchen like a caged lion as the dialling tone goes on and on. How dare he. What a bloody cheek.

'Put me through to Chief Inspector Thomson,' I snap when the call is finally picked up. He's bound to know what's going on. Maybe John even went to him to discuss this ludicrous action.

'What the hell is going on, Marcus?' There's a pause, and for a moment I think I've been put through to the wrong person.

'Ah, Becky,' he says, clearing his throat. 'I'm sorry you had to hear it like that, but I thought it best if you found out about John's upcoming promotion from me before the rumour mills begin to grind.'

I reel. 'Wait, what?'

'I left you a voicemail. I presume that's why you're calling.'

'No. I was . . . I got a letter,' I stumble over the words, my thoughts rushing and colliding in a big blur in my mind. Christ. It was bad enough before, but *promotion*. The point had been to get him off the force. Stop him from abusing his power – not increasing his ability to use it. He's going to be a detective inspector? How?

'A letter?' he asks. But John's threat of an order against me has already melted into insignificance.

'He can't. Marcus. He can't. How are you letting this happen?'

'It's a good move for him. A fresh start.'

'*What?*' My head swims. A fresh start? Is he actually saying this? 'But . . .' The walls of my kitchen close in even further. I smack the palm of my hand against the closest one, push against it as though it's about to physically crush me.

'In a roundabout way, you got what you wanted. He's leaving Manchester. I know it comes a little late for you . . . ' He sighs. 'Rebecca? Are you there?'

I take a huge breath in, slowly release the air in an attempt to reduce the pressure that's in my head, to ensure I make my next words calm.

'You *know* what he is, Marcus.' The accusation comes

19

from my mouth as steadily as a hiss of air from a slow puncture. My face burns, anger and shame filling every blood vessel.

'Oh, dear. Please don't start this again. It wasn't . . . he wasn't . . . ' Marcus bumbles down the line and the fire within my gut reignites as I think about John; talk about him.

'I can't believe this. I saw for myself, Marcus. I know—'

'You're fully aware of the law and how the chain of evidence works – how someone is innocent until *proven* guilty.' I envisage his deeply furrowed brow, his face flaming red as he spits the words he's repeated a dozen or more times to me over the past year.

'And *you* know the system can sometimes let justice down.' With a lightning-hot rage swirling in my gut bringing tears to my eyes, I realise in this moment that the intensity of my feelings didn't lessen; they were only ever hiding beneath the surface. That these past few months I've kept them at bay . . . just. It's obvious that unless this gets sorted once and for all, I'm never fully taming the anger he's caused.

'You can't keep dredging this up. It's over.' I hear him take a few shuddering breaths as though he's recovering from a sprint. A pang of regret sweeps through me. He's endured a lot lately with his wife's illness and I don't like stressing him out; he's been good to me. But then the words from the message on John's burner phone flash back into my mind.

'It's not over for his victim, Marcus.'

And it's not over for me either.

Chapter 3

THEN

BECKY

Everything ached as I lifted my arm up, key in hand, to open the front door. The past twelve hours had been busy from the off, but the shift hit another level when a call reporting a gang-related stabbing on the Ordsall estate came in. After emergency response had dealt with the initial incident, together with paramedics, our team attended. The lad had lost a lot of blood, they said, was barely conscious when they stretchered him off. *Treat it as a possible murder scene,* Wallis directed. A heavy lump sank down into the pit of my stomach. If the teenager didn't pull through, the toll would be seven dead this year in Manchester. Seven lives wasted. Outside of those stats, over fifty young stab victims had ended up in the ER. The numbers were horrific, and each homicide took a little bit more from me.

With a grunt of effort, the blue front door swung open, and I stepped over the threshold. As I did, a memory flashed through my mind – John swooping me up into his arms, banging my head on the doorjamb as we laughed and entered our new home. I remembered my comment about blue being apt for two coppers, the shrill laughter as John collapsed to the beige carpet with me on top of him. How we'd made love there and then without even bothering to close the door.

I stared at that area of carpet – the beige colour somewhat darker now, and in need of a good clean or replacement – then shrugged off my jacket and hung it over the banister, smiling. I felt my eyes crease, like paper, and touched my fingers to them. Swollen with tiredness. If I looked into the round hallway mirror right now, I'd likely look ten years older than my actual thirty-three years. I turned away, deciding not to confirm my theory. Sometimes ignorance was bliss.

Muted sounds of the telly reached me, and so I followed them to the lounge. Without speaking, I slumped down next to John on the sofa. We sat in silence for a while. No words were required. The good thing about being married to another detective was the understanding. There were bad things, too, of course – not least the near-constant fear of one of us being killed. But in that moment, a sense of knowing not to speak was what I needed most.

Ten minutes passed. The shift's weight had now lifted enough to let me breathe freely again.

'You're going to be late,' I said, turning my head to the side to look at him. I reached out and ran my fingertips down his sideburns, then back up, over his sandy-coloured hair. 'You really are going for the Seventies Gene Hunt look. I thought you were losing those?'

'What? You don't like them?' He feigned shock.

22

This was the same kind of back-and-forth banter we'd had following our respective shifts for the past week, but I still managed to laugh. Routine, comfort, was enough to blur the edges of the horror just enough to carry on turning up each day.

'If they were the stick-on kind for fancy dress purposes, maybe.' I finally found the strength to kick my shoes off, then stretched my legs out and placed my feet on the glass table.

'What do you think this is?' John stared at my black-socked feet. 'Resting after an early shift? There'll be none of that, Mrs Lawson. Now, make your husband dinner before he has to leave to catch bad guys.'

'Sod off,' I said, giving his arm a shove. 'You should've made me something ready for my return.'

John gives an exaggerated 'humph' as he lifts himself off the sofa. 'Good job you bagged the best-looking detective *and* best chef on the force, then, isn't it?' He disappeared into the kitchen, and moments later, returned with a tray. I smile at the single red rose in the bud vase that was accompanying the plate of steaming food and an ice-cold bottle of Bud.

'Ah, you're too good to me. Thanks, babe.' I quickly made myself comfortable and balanced the tray on my lap. 'Hmm . . . stew. Excellent,' I said, immediately shovelling in a mouthful.

'Jesus, really?' John straightened, shooting me an incredulous look. 'How long have you lived here now? Five years? Bloody stew my arse.'

'Hah! Sorry,' I said, quickly swallowing. 'It's hotpot, isn't it.' I screwed my nose up at him, attempting to be endearing. He crossed his arms, the contour of his muscles visible through his white shirt.

'I don't bloody know.' He shook his head. 'Thought I'd made a northern lass out of you, then you let me down. My granny would turn in her grave. *Lancashire* hotpot, Becks.' He wandered off towards the hallway, muttering as he went. I couldn't contain my smile. If I'd had the mental energy, I'd have argued for the merits of the Cornish pasty and said how I'd take one of those with chips over a hotpot any day of the week. Just for shits and giggles. But I carried on, stuffing my mouth like I'd gone several days without eating. I always came back from my shift ravenous, even if it'd been a relatively quiet one. Which was a rarity at Salford Criminal Investigation Department.

When we'd first met, I was shiny new, naive, filled with enthusiasm and had the unshakable determination I would make a difference; help change the world. John watched me from afar for a few weeks, not saying much, interacting as was required to carry out our roles. I watched him, too. He had a certain vibe; a charisma that up until then I'd only seen on TV. He seemed aloof in an interesting way, intriguing as though he had something delicious hiding beneath the surface that only the chosen one would be capable of uncovering and devouring – he was a mystery that required solving. I found that undeniably alluring – like a drug. When you'd had a hit of John Lawson, you had to keep returning for more.

One we'd connected that warm, summer evening at The Crown pub – ending with sex standing up against the wall around the back of the premises like a couple of horny teenagers – I was hooked. I wanted him. Longed for him. Needed him. I had assumed him to be forbidden fruit, but thankfully relationships between two serving officers weren't prohibited. And that was that. A done deal.

Now revived, albeit temporarily, from that injection of calories, and with my mind firmly thinking of another form of injection, I called to John.

'Sorry, m'lady – did you require another service?' His eyes flickered as they met mine, and his breath hitched. 'Ah. You *do* . . . ' He unbuttoned his shirt, and to save time, I undressed myself, flinging my work clothes over the back of the sofa. His eyes were wide as I lowered my bra straps. Still seated, I pulled John by his belt towards me and undid it, unzipped his fly and released him. He groaned as I ran my tongue along his length, then took him fully inside my mouth. His hands squeezed my breasts, his thumbs flicked over my erect nipples. I was close to coming when he pulled away, and with his trousers around his ankles, he pushed me down onto the sofa and spread my legs wide.

'Hurry,' I breathed.

He pinned my arms behind my head with one hand, used the other to guide himself in. His thrusts were slow but hard and my body jerked with each forceful plunge. Then he held me tighter, drove himself in harder, slamming into me with all his might. Had I not been about to orgasm, I would've had to tell him to stop. This level of aggressiveness was unusual. But then I reminded myself, I *had* asked for it knowing he was about to leave for work, *and* I'd told him to hurry.

Soon after, John left in a rush, saying something about an emergency. I didn't like the sound of it, a creeping sensation starting at the nape of my neck. I wished we worked the same shift pattern more. At least if we were together, I'd know what was happening. But although John was great at being part of a team, he enjoyed being out on his own – and I know he often orchestrated such situations. Sometimes I wondered if he had a death wish.

After I clicked through at least twenty channels, and mind-numbing boredom was threatening, I finally settled on a new rom-com to watch. Anything to distract my thoughts. As I lay back and attempted to relax, a pain shot through my left shoulder; I rubbed it, trying to release the knotted muscle. It was no good – I needed another diversion. Snacks.

I rummaged in the lower kitchen cupboard for sweets. Nothing. I knew John kept anything remotely snacky in the highest cupboard. Away from temptation, he said. Fitness was important – especially in our job. He liked us to keep track of calories. I dragged the dining chair across the floor, stood on it and stretched to reach something that felt crinkly. Crisps would do if there was nothing else.

I retrieved my hand, and in it was a flattened, but in date, packet of chocolate footballs. 'Yes. You beauty.'

Pleased with my find, I reconvened on the sofa in front of the telly, chocolate on lap, eyes on Channing Tatum.

I awoke with a jolt and sat up so quickly that I knocked the packet from my lap. I must've dozed off – the credits of the film were on. Not wanting to leave any incriminating evidence, and always the detective, I went about collecting the chocolate balls that had rolled everywhere. As I swept my hand down the back of the sofa, my fingers hit against something hard. Grasping it, I pulled it up.

A mobile.

Not one I recognised; a cheap, prepaid type.

My mouth dried as intrigue immediately turned to concern. I rubbed the back of my neck, where the hairs prickled with unease. It was a brand-new sofa when we bought it a few months back. We'd had zero visitors to the house and it wasn't mine.

Why did John have a burner phone?

For a long moment, I stared at it; turned it over in my hand. Then I placed it on the glass table, where I stared some more. My initial thoughts – that it was someone else's or borrowed from a mate – didn't stick for longer than a few seconds. The more worrying thought crowded those out: Did John have this phone for another reason? Like for drugs? I shook my head. No. John was one of the best in the force. I knew him. He wouldn't take bribes; he certainly wouldn't break the law. We were part of the same division, but he was often on different cases, and we worked opposite shifts a lot. Maybe the phone was something to do with a case I wasn't aware of. Was he undercover? No. Of course he wasn't. We're CID.

With a sharp intake of air, I snatched up the phone, quickly stabbing the on button before my thoughts could catch up with my actions. And I waited. Suspended in time – my body still, while internally my blood pumped violently, and my heart banged loudly in my ears.

It's just a phone.

So why did I feel so apprehensive?

The phone slipped in my clammy hands as I tried to fight the uneasy sensation. I knew this feeling, and having worked in the police for five years, instinct, even if it appeared out of place like now, was a remarkably accurate indicator. A warning that should at least be considered, not disregarded simply because it didn't seem possible. Some of the old-school brigade, John included, swore by gut instinct.

A tinkling notification sounded. It had turned on. My scalp tingled.

Please be nothing.

I pressed some keys, my hands trembling. There was

bound to be a password, so I waited for the inevitable block. But it didn't come. I frowned as I easily scrolled through the display to find logged calls. Surely this was a positive sign. If John was using this phone for something illegal, he wouldn't leave it unprotected, at risk of someone else seeing it. The last number dialled was to an unnamed contact from a couple of weeks ago. It was looking likely this could be an informant of John's. My shoulders lowered, the tension ebbing. He hadn't spoken of being in the process of gathering intel and being a handler, but it was a delicate balance protecting sources' safety and preventing corruption – sharing too much could mean jeopardising the relationship. He was likely meant to take this to work with him and it'd slipped from his trousers when we were having sex. I should call him, let him know it's safe. I pushed another button to get me back to the home screen. My breath caught in the middle of a relieved sigh as a screenshot of a message thread filled the screen, with the text reading: You're not the only one I've sent this to.

Cold tentacles of dread wrapped themselves around me, squeezing the air from my lungs.

Chapter 4

NOW

BECKY

The single beep, followed by silence, signals the termination of the call. I keep it against my ear for a few seconds, unable to quite believe that Marcus hung up on me. He hadn't even given me details of John's promotion. When exactly was it happening? Where? When I last spoke to Hannah, knowing she was one of my few remaining contacts in CID, I'd tiptoed around the subject of John. I'd asked that sort of nonchalant, general question about the old team – 'The A Team' as I used to think of us prior to someone pointing out that was the name of a crime gang responsible for a spate of shootings in Salford – about who was doing what, how everyone's families were. Of course, she saw straight through my attempt. 'Don't be a time-waster, Becky,' she'd said. 'Just ask.'

With no use pretending further, I'd got to the point. 'Is John still pulling the wool over everyone's eyes?'

She had sighed and shrugged, avoided telling me anything that could lead to her breaching any form of code. Always-by-the-book Hannah. But she had, in a rather vague kind of way, hinted that changes were on the horizon. Until today, I'd assumed any 'change' would entail a sideways move, or with any luck, a downward one. Not a bloody promotion. I look at the letter again. Why is John threatening an injunction against me when I don't even know where he's living? Surely no court will conclude there are grounds to protect John from *me*. It's an empty threat. A pre-emptive strike because he thinks I'll create a fuss as soon as I hear his news.

The ceiling lights vibrate violently at the same time as thudding footsteps and screams filter through from the upstairs flat. I instinctively cover my head with my arms and duck.

'Jesus! Now what?'

I've let the blaring music, slamming doors, rowdy visitors coming and going all hours, ride for the past five months – kept myself to myself. Live and let live and all that. But they've picked the wrong day today. A distraction from thinking about John is just what I need. I jump up, swipe my keys off the hook by the fridge and swoop through the lounge and out the front door in three seconds. It's only four o'clock, but it's perpetually dim and shadowy here in this five-storey concrete block because of the construction of the flats above mine. I stride out and along the front of the building to reach the door that'll take me to the steps. Taking two at a time, I fly up the stairs to reach the second storey and stomp along that floor's external corridor.

Before I even consider what I'll face, I hammer on the door – so hard that the wood rattles in the frame. Had I taken time to think through my actions, I might've grabbed something I could use as a weapon. Just in case I'm not welcome. Which, of course, I won't be. I cast my eyes around now, searching for a suitable item and quickly bend to reach for the broken-off piece of a terracotta plant pot – its live content long since deceased and now used for cigarette ends. I slip it partway up my sleeve as the door flings open.

The large-framed, white male, his face puce with barely suppressed anger, pushes his sweat-stained, vested chest against me.

'Yeah?'

'Can you keep the noise down?'

'What noise?' He sniggers.

'Come on. I—' My attention falls from his ruddy face as a high-pitched yell rings out from inside the flat. Despite the urge to barge straight past him, I stay put, years' worth of police training superseding my emotional reaction. Given my defunct status, rushing in wouldn't be good for anyone. All my senses are on high alert as I evaluate the situation. 'You okay in there?' I shout past the oaf blocking the doorway.

'Do one,' he says, shoving me. I stumble backwards, my pulse picking up rapidly as my fight-or-flight response kicks in. I regain my balance and begin easing the ceramic shard from beneath my cuff. He frowns and takes a step back to retreat into his cave. Has he seen something in my eyes? The flicker of the 'don't fuck with me' attitude I'm feeling right now?

'I'm not leaving until I know she's all right.' I step forward. 'It's the neighbourly thing to do, eh?'

He gives a cruel laugh, shakes his head. 'The neighbourly thing to do would be to never come 'ere again. No one gives a shit about the noise. If you do, you should give yer head a wobble.' He throws his hands up. 'See where you are?' He gives me a look up and down, then spits. A large glob of it lands on my shoe. With a glinting line of saliva still hanging to his chin, he juts his lower jaw forward, squinting at me in a way I imagine he thinks is menacing. 'Tamsin! Ai – come tell this posh twat to wind 'er neck in.'

Movement to his left catches my attention, and I hold my breath as I wait to see 'Tamsin' – expecting a bloody face, a blur of dark bruises, cuts, maybe evidence of past broken bones; a timid, fearful middle-aged woman. But she doesn't come into sight.

'Don't worry,' a voice says from the shadows. 'It's not what you think.'

'I'd like to see you, Tamsin. So I can assess that for myself, please.'

'What are you? A fuckin' social worker? You 'eard her. She's fine.'

I hear a whimper.

'Shut yer skriking,' he shouts over his shoulder into the darkness. Then his head whips back to focus on me. 'An' you. You mind yer own fuckin' business. Got it?' He goes to slam the door, but I whack my foot into the gap. The wood hits hard against it, the pain shooting up my ankle and I bite my lip to repress the yelp. The man's eyes narrow, his nostrils flare and I realise there's every chance I could get a smacking here and there's no one to assist me in this situation. But I've made my move now, and I'm not backing down. If I did, he'd smell weakness and any slight advantage I think I have now will be gone.

'Perhaps I should call for assistance . . . ' I raise my eyebrows and give a knowing smile. 'I'm sure there'll be some willing types in the vicinity.'

He shakes his head, looks down at my foot, and then back at my face. He's weighing me up. 'Nah,' he says, leaning close enough I can smell a putrid mix of stale cigarettes and alcohol on his breath. 'You ain't got the connections. Look at ya, pathetic bint. Only good for one thing.'

He's a foot taller than me – a head-butt wouldn't land, so I ball my hand up and jab it hard and fast into his solar plexus. He jerks forwards, eyes bulging, a hiss of air escaping his mouth. I duck down, making sure my eyes meet his. 'Leave. Her. Alone,' I say. 'If I hear one more fucking noise from this flat, there'll be trouble.' I slap him on the shoulder. 'And wipe the spit from your face, you vile, misogynistic piece of shit.'

I walk away, for now. But I'll watch and wait. He'll have to leave sometime and then I'll go and check on Tamsin. I've a feeling she'll have something more to say when that bully's out of the way.

Chapter 5

NOW

BECKY

Most of the coffee granules scatter on the worktop, my hand too shaky to administer the full heaped teaspoon of it into the mug. Almost a year off the force means I'm less accustomed to these kinds of adrenaline spikes and today there's been two in quick succession. The last hour has been the most stressful since the one leading up to reporting my own husband to the police.

I don't bother wiping up the mess beside the kettle, and after gazing at it for what feels like an eternity, I turn my back on it and take a few steps into the lounge. Sitting on my too-big-for-this-place armchair (which was the only item of furniture I fought for from the house when it sold, because it belonged to my mum) I sip my drink and try to order my thoughts. The altercation with the unpleasant man from the flat above has done two things. Firstly, it's made me realise how much I miss my job, and secondly, it's reignited my desire to fight for justice – specifically women's. I need to devise a plan. I can't sit back and do nothing. I might not be able to change things in an official capacity anymore – although even when I *was* a detective, my report and subsequent complaints about John weren't properly investigated as far as I'm concerned – but I can make a stand, be an advocate for victims of abuse. I can still make a difference. And I *will* make it my business to stop John from using his new position to create more victims. Because he will, I'm sure of it.

It's gone quiet upstairs. I stand up and move to the kitchen, my head tilted up, ears straining. Silence isn't always a good thing, in fact it's probably a bad thing. There's a very real chance that by poking the bear, I've aggravated the situation and potentially made things worse for 'Tamsin'. I hope she's okay. With any luck, the arsehole's drunk himself into a stupor and she's getting some peace. I haven't *seen* people going in and out of the flat – just heard the commotion. Maybe she doesn't live there, she might be one of the visitors. That's not the feeling I get, though. The occupants of the other flats aren't known to me either. It's weird living in close proximity to people who you've never met. It's alien to me. In Cornwall, community was everything. Not only did I know our immediate neighbours well, but I could name every person in the village, who they 'belonged to', how long they'd lived there. That's the Cornish way, I guess. Manchester was somewhat of a culture shock, but mine and John's home was in a street where at least we recognised our neighbours. We said hello, had chitchats with them, knew their names. They were pleasant.

I sigh, my shoulders heavy with the knowledge I won't be experiencing that same warmth here. Although, I must be grateful – renting anywhere was tough, I had several knockbacks and was ready to give up when Hannah spotted this place and the landlord here gave me a chance.

The letter from John lies on the side, the words of warning glaring at me like they're daring me. John's voice, harsh and threatening, rings in my mind as if he's speaking them. Whipping the paper up, I take it to the hob, ignite the burner and hold the corner to the gas. A smug satisfaction grows in my stomach as I watch the orange flame take hold and engulf the letter. I drop it into the sink just before it's fully consumed and turn the tap on, covering my nose with my sleeve to prevent breathing in the smell. After opening the window, I look at the mush of ashes and acknowledge that while it was a bit futile, to me, it's a small win. It represents me taking a 'fuck you' stand. And now the determination to stop John is back, I know it's the first of many. With renewed vigour, I make a call.

'Hi, Charlie,' I say as soon as he answers. I cringe at my overly 'gushy' tone, but before he can put up any barriers, or make an excuse to not speak to me right now, I quickly add, 'I think I'm finally getting my life back on track, and I think I owe you an apology . . . '

'Oh, er . . . Becks. This is a surprise . . . ' Charlie stumbles over his words; I've caught him off-guard with the offer of an apology. He'll come across as a right dick now if he doesn't give me the time of day.

'The call? Or me acknowledging I need to say sorry?' I laugh, hoping it doesn't sound as forced as it is. A twinge of guilt tugs at my conscience. It's only a little white lie, as my mum would've said – I would like to put things straight between us even though I wasn't in the wrong.

'Well, both, I guess. Good to hear from you though,

Becks. Really.' I hear muffled voices, the dull beats of music in the background. I check my watch. He's at the pub. Which means he'll be with other off-duty detectives. The usual suspects, no doubt. Minus John, I'm guessing. Or, maybe I'm hoping that's the case. It hurts to imagine those I used to consider friends mixing with him knowing what they know.

'You with Hannah by any chance?'

'Nah, mate – she's still doing admin, you know her. A few of us are chillin' out at The Crown—' His voice cuts off, then muted words filter through what must be his hand covering the phone. Whoever he's with has just cursed him for telling me where they are. As if I don't know. Christ, they're so predictable – The Crown's been the preferred pub for years.

'Hey, Charlie . . .' I wait for him to come back on the line. 'Tell them not to get their panties in a twist, eh? It doesn't take a detective to figure out where you are.'

He gives an awkward laugh. 'Nah, it wasn't that. Just . . .'

'Doesn't matter. Really. Do you fancy a catch up? I feel so bad about how I left things.' I hope the edge of desperation in my voice sways the balance.

'Sure.'

I envisage the congregated team all rolling their eyes or making slicing action across their throats with their fingers. Most of them would walk over hot coals before seeing me after the shitstorm I supposedly created for John. I suck in a deep breath as I recall some of the responses to me reporting him – hold it before slowly releasing. Keeping my cool is paramount from here on in if I'm to get Charlie onside.

'Great,' I say. 'Thanks, Charlie. Tomorrow any good for you?'

'It'll have to be early. Coffee at Hamley's Café, say eight-thirty?'

'Perfect. I'll see you there.'

If I'm to have any success in putting a stop to John's promotion, which will undoubtedly see his power and control increase, I'll need insider knowledge of his whereabouts so I can begin my campaign. My tactics failed spectacularly before, and I was the one to suffer. This time, I'll try a different way to take my ex-husband down.

Chapter 6

NOW

BECKY

With the result of a disturbed night's sleep camouflaged with the most make-up I've worn in a year, dressed in my casual-but-smart navy linen trousers coupled with a cream top, cropped jacket and wearing stylish boho wedge sandals, I stride confidently into the café and wave to Charlie who's sitting at a table in the far corner. Away from prying eyes. Or, more to the point, away from anyone from the team who'll cast judgement on him for being with me if they happen to walk past and spot us. I mentally bat the unwelcome twinge of hurt away. I know what I'm up against, no point being upset. I order an iced latte, and before swiping my card, ask the barista to hold a second while I catch Charlie's attention.

You want another? I mouth, while needlessly shaking my hand to indicate drinking. He hesitates, then puts up a thumb and I return my attention to the young, tattooed man waiting patiently for me. 'A large latte, too, please.' Charlie's never had anything different the whole time I've known him. Not even when Christmas rolls around and the menu is awash with delicious-flavoured coffees, including my favourite, the gingerbread latte. He always sticks to the norm. I'd hazard a guess it was him playing safe, but from what I've seen over the years, that doesn't seem to stretch to how he plays in other aspects of his life. I don't think his taste buds have ever experienced anything outside of his comfort zone. Or, at least, not outside his cooking capabilities. A few of the female team have, in the past, attempted to mother him – I, too, invited him around to the house to eat with me and John on a few occasions. Maybe he knows precisely what he's doing.

I close my eyes and breathe in the aroma of *real* coffee, savouring it. There's something reassuring, joyful about it, and along with the smell of freshly laundered bedding, it's my favourite. With my first month's wages of my new job in Psychological Services if – no, *when* – I get it, I'm buying a coffee machine. The best you can get; superior to the one I had to part with. I hear a polite cough and open my eyes. I'm met with the barista's raised neat, dark eyebrows and a playful smile.

'I think you need this,' he says, gently pushing the tray towards me.

'You're not wrong there . . . ' I check his name badge, 'Elijah.'

'And here,' he says, pulling a card from a holder. 'Take this loyalty card.' He stamps it and hands it to me. 'You get one for each hot drink, then a freebie once you hit ten.' I thank him, and as I pop it on the tray and walk towards Charlie, I note he's doubled the stamps. A warm sensation fills my stomach; there's still those who extend small acts of kindness, and for a second at least, it restores a little of my faith in the male species. Here's hoping that's a sign.

Charlie looks up from his mobile and slides it to the side of the table when I set the tray down. I give my brightest smile.

'Really good to see you,' I say, sitting opposite him. 'I'm sorry I left it so long. I was mad-busy trying to sort out the new place, you know?'

'God, yeah. Completely understand,' he says, his eyes leaving mine. I can almost feel the hurt oozing from him. He'd sent a few messages after I left, which I mostly ignored. I was hurting too. 'You settled now then?'

'Er . . . well.' I screw my nose up. 'It's not the *best* place.' Charlie looks alarmed. 'Oh? Where?'

I rattle off the address, quickly adding that taking the flat was a last resort, having run out of options. Charlie gives me a sympathetic look and I turn away as a little bit more of me breaks.

'Oh, Becks,' he says.

'It's fine. Really. When I get the new job I've applied for, I'll be able to afford something less dodgy.' I offer a weak smile, unable to cover the real emotion – the anxiety – continuously bubbling inside my gut.

'Well, if you need any *backup*,' he says using air quotes, 'you give me a call.' He reaches across and taps my forearm, his expression serious. Isn't it a bit late to offer that now? I bite the inside of my lip, swallow down those words and say instead:

'Cheers, I appreciate that. Actually, I've already had a bit of a run-in with the bloke in the flat above.'

'Oh, God, Becks. Is he all right?' He laughs.

'Damaged pride, maybe. Deserves more than that, though.'

'Be careful, eh? Don't go getting involved in something beyond your control; it's not like you've a team behind you ready to step in and diffuse an unsafe situation.'

My pulse whips against my neck and I have to clench one fist beneath the table. I had a team behind me last year, after all.

What little that did for me. But, pushing my emotions aside, I know this line gives me a handy lead-in to bring up the subject of John, and I'm about to use it when I spot Charlie's jaw tense and I know he's thinking the same. For now, I'll change the subject. I don't want to alienate him this early on in the conversation; I have to warm him up before I ask him my favour.

'How's your love life?' I grin.

Charlie relaxes, but then groans dramatically. 'The same as when you left, pretty much. Plenty of offers to cook meals for me, but no follow-through sums it up, mate.'

'Take some bloody cookery lessons – impress them. You're attracting the wrong kind of attention oozing all those needy mothering vibes!'

'Hey! You said it was endearing – even you fell for it.'

'Er . . . yep. That kinda proves my point.'

We share a laugh and for a blissful moment it's like old times. Before my world collapsed around me. My heartbeat skips as the image of the burner phone with that message pops into my mind. The first great big, waving red flag. *That you acknowledged*, an unwanted internal voice adds. I shake my head to displace it and return my focus back on Charlie. He's draining the large latte. He's going to make an excuse to leave soon; I must move the conversation on now or I'll miss the opportunity.

'I don't just seem to fall for adorable, charming qualities, sadly. Nope – I go full in for the dark and detestable ones that are lying beneath the surface too.' I raise my eyebrows. Charlie breaks eye contact and shifts in his chair, but I have to keep going now despite his obvious discomfort in where this is heading. 'Talking of my ex – did you know he's going for promotion?'

Charlie's cheeks flush. 'Jesus, Becks.' He leans back and crosses his arms.

42

'Is that a yes?'

He doesn't answer, and I think I've lost him – all his barriers are up now. But he remains seated so I'm still in with a chance.

'I need your help, Charlie.'

'No, absolutely not. Do not be starting this again, please.' His expression is pained. 'I came today because I felt bad about the cloud you left under, how I contributed to it by not backing you up. But please don't use that as a way to emotionally blackmail me into giving you info.'

'A few minutes ago, you offered to back me up—'

'That was for your safety because you're living in a dubious block of flats in Pendlebury. Physical backup, Becks – not providing details of serving detectives. You know I can't do that.'

'He's threatened me with court. Says he'll take out an injunction if I go near him. What does that tell you, Charlie? The man is running scared because he has every reason to. Think about it . . . I don't know where he's living, which division he's moved to. How would I be able to steer clear of him if I don't even know where he is? How would I know if I were within three miles of him? He's using bully tactics again.' I take a breath. My heart is racing. I know I've only got one shot at this, and Charlie's flushed face is telling me he's close to losing his patience with me. I have to get this all out. I put my hand on his. 'I got his letter yesterday at my new address. I didn't tell him where I'd moved to. Don't you think that's concerning?'

Charlie moves his hand out from beneath mine. 'Wouldn't his solicitor have sent it? John probably doesn't know—'

'No.' I sit back, shaking my head vehemently. 'The envelope had the Greater Manchester Police logo for

Christ's sake. It was sent by John. So, tell me – who's feeding *him* info?'

A look of concern passes over Charlie's face. 'I don't know. He left GMP months ago, too,' he says. 'I mean, he could've taken a bunch of stationery with him I guess. Like you did.' He raises one eyebrow. I ignore the sarcasm. I've got him thinking now, which is good. And the fact he's mentioned that John's moved divisions is even better, because with some careful wording, I might be able to get him to disclose *where* he's gone.

'I spoke with Marcus yesterday. He told me about John's upcoming promotion. Seems he's doing well for himself despite the "hiccup" in his career.' I control the growing ball of anger by taking some deep, diaphragmatic breaths. I don't want to come across as unhinged – a word used several times to describe me during the worst part of last year – not just by John, but by senior members of the team. I close my eyes and grip the handle of my coffee mug. 'Strange he's moved from GMP though, don't you think? Why would he need to? It's not as though I'm around. He ensured they chose him over me.'

'Fresh start, I guess,' Charlie says, echoing Marcus Thomson's words. His gaze drifts to the window. 'But yeah, to be honest, I did think it was odd. He got what he wanted, then left anyway. Almost like he was running away from something.'

'Or because that was the deal he had to make.'

'What do you mean?'

'You know – as in: we've covered your back, John, now you need to lay low. Disappear, kind of thing.'

'But he hasn't really though – he's climbing the bloody ladder still. I guess it's out of the city, though – maybe more

44

of a sidestep than a promotion, really. I wouldn't fancy Lymworth – there's as much going on there as in my love life.'

There. I've got it. I know where John's new area is.

Charlie lets out a sharp puff of air as he realises he's slipped up. 'Fuck's sake, Becks. You're good, I'll give you that.'

I smile. 'I'm afraid I don't understand what you're talking about.'

'Why do you want to track him down, Becks? Haven't you been through enough?'

'Yeah. But why should I let him get away with this kind of manipulation again? I only want to confront him about the letter.' My pulse skips, knowing that part is a lie. I want far more than that and I'll need Charlie's ongoing help to get it.

'But you'll land yourself in court if he catches you near him. Can you afford that?'

'I've not got much to lose at this point. I'll be covert. It'll be like old times, Charlie.'

'It's not like old times if you're not a detective anymore. More to the point, it's not safe on your own.'

'Safe? So you think I'd be in danger from John?' I watch him intently. His eyes skitter around the café, then he fidgets with the sugar packets in the bowl on the table – like he's having an inner battle with himself.

'If he sees you, knows you've purposely gone against his wishes in that letter he sent, he ain't going to be best pleased, is he?'

'That's not what you're saying though.' I pause, allowing the moment of silence to stretch until it's almost unbearable.

'No,' he says. 'You know how bad I felt not backing you up last year when I should've. I was a coward. It's gnawed away at me ever since.' He looks straight at me now. 'I

45

believe, if push comes to shove, that he'd . . . ' He lets out a long, juddering sigh, scratches his head. 'He'd hurt you, yes. If you pursue him, try to find out where he lives, you'll be the only one standing in his way – not only of his career progression, but of his new relationship, too.'

Charlie's face goes out of focus; the oxygen sucked out of the room and my body shakes.

'What? What . . . ' I put my hand to my chest, feel the erratic beating. 'His what?'

Charlie pales. 'Ah shit. I'm sorry, Becks. Didn't you know?'

I'm like a fish out of water, gasping for air. I push my chair back and bend my upper body over my legs. Tears sting my eyes.

'Is everything okay?' I hear the barista, Elijah's voice, above me.

'She's fine,' Charlie is saying. 'Just a bit of a panic attack.'

A few moments pass, and then I hear Elijah's retreating footsteps. And Charlie's hand is on my back. 'Shall we go to yours?' he says.

'What for?' I sit back up, look into his kind eyes. 'It's just a bout of anxiety, I'll be fine.'

He offers me another sympathetic smile. 'I want to help, that's all.'

Despite the episode zapping my energy, his words reinvigorate me. 'Great,' I say. 'The best way you can do that is to find out more about what the hell my ex-husband is up to. And help me get the son of a bitch once and for all. We can't let him ruin another woman's life, Charlie.'

Chapter 7

THEN

BECKY

What I was looking at didn't make any sense at first. But as the initial shock subsided, I was faced with what appeared to be a personal message intended for John together with a screenshot of a previous conversation. Not from an informant. Or, if this woman was one, John had stepped way out of line for her to be sending him what was looking more and more like a threat to expose him for sexual assault.

I paced. Increasing anxiety and an endless slew of questions clouded my mind, and each step made me feel heavier. My hand cramped with how tightly I gripped the small mobile.

'Come on, you're a detective,' I told myself. 'Assess and evaluate the evidence, detach yourself and view it impartially.' Easier said than done. How could I possibly separate my emotions from something like this? I rolled my shoulders, sat down and placed the phone on the table again. While I massaged my contracted muscle in the heel of my hand, I started to mentally list the facts currently known to me.

I found a burner phone in the back of the sofa.

It wasn't mine.

John didn't tell me he was working with an informant.

The message was a screenshot of a text conversation between the sender and the receiver. John's initials were visible – he was the receiver.

The sender accused him of rape.

My stomach lurched. Rape. One of the worst allegations – a game-changer. A career-ender. A prison sentence if proven.

A wave of dizziness caught me off-guard and nausea hit me. I blew out my cheeks, lowered my head into my hands. A few hours ago, I had sex with my husband of five years, as we regularly did. Now, I'm considering if I've been sleeping with a rapist. If I'm the *wife* of a rapist.

It was gone midnight. But there was no chance of sleep tonight. I stared at the mobile, not wanting to look at the screenshot again, but knowing I had to. I couldn't bury my head in the sand. I unlocked the screen and heart hammering, reread the screenshotted text.

It's your word against mine.

God, you think you're untouchable, don't you.

That's because I am. No one'll believe you – not by a long shot. Not with your history. There's no CCTV footage, no evidence even if they were to go looking. Which they won't, of course.

You're meant to protect people.

48

And I do. I'm protecting you right now, aren't I? You won't come to harm if you keep your mouth shut. I'm looking out for you.

                              You're disgusting.

I didn't hear you complain when I was in you.

I stopped reading to regain my composure. My eyes burned with tears, but I blinked them away and carried on.

I was scared you'd hurt me. I didn't consent to sex. You raped me.

                    You didn't once say no. You said nothing.
                    Like you're going to continue to do if
                              you have any sense.

In continuation of my assessment of the facts, I added: John didn't deny having sexual intercourse with her. His argument was that she didn't verbally say no. Her argument was that she hadn't verbally agreed either.

John knows what consent is and what it means. He's dealt with rape and sexual assaults for years.

I began turning out all the drawers in the bedroom cupboards and then progressed to the wardrobe, not sure what I was looking for but determined to find something to either back up or refute what I'd read. Did he have more phones stashed away? Was this a one-off? My head and heart clashed. I've dealt with enough rapists, too. The likelihood of a single offence was low. That's what my head told me. My heart said otherwise. John's life has been in the police force, protecting the public. His career has been exemplary. Never has anything been said that contradicts that. I know my husband.

John is not a rapist.

I'd have known.

Chapter 8

NOW

BECKY

My emotions scatter like crisp fallen leaves on a blustery autumn day as I walk home from my meeting with Charlie. I'd convinced him I'd be fine walking back, and that knowing he was going to help did mean a lot to me. On the one hand, I've gained an ally, someone on the inside who can help me to build evidence against John. On the other hand, I've managed to gain unwanted knowledge and I'm unsure how to process the information that John is starting afresh with a new woman. Charlie couldn't give me further details because he said that was all he knew. But my mind conjures John with a young, naive woman who has no clue what she's letting herself in for. He's going to use her for cover, like he did me. I wonder if there are other similarities. Does she look like me, too?

As I turn the corner and approach the block of hell, I'm struck by something out of place. After a few more paces towards my flat, I realise what it is. There's red paint daubed across my front door. In bold lettering the word 'slag' stands out loud and clear. I don't need two guesses to know who's done this. It's the coward from upstairs. When I reach it, I touch my fingertip to the 'G'; it's still wet. I've probably only just missed him in the act. Damn it.

Something nudges against my calf and I gasp, jumping back. I'm not sure what I'm expecting it to be, but my heart is banging like a drum as I look down. I almost laugh with relief. It's just a cat. Then my chest fills with pity. An undernourished tabby cat, its fur damp and matted, looks up at me hopefully, its pupils dilated.

'Oh, poor baby. You're pretty neglected, aren't you?' I tickle it under its chin. Then I open the door and let it follow me inside. Its mews grow louder, and it rubs up against my legs back and forth continuously as I stand searching through my inadequately stocked fridge, then the cupboard of basic food items, for something suitable to offer it.

'Fancy some of this?' I pull out a tin of tuna and share it between two plates. I add some limp-looking salad to mine and chop some equally limp-looking cucumber and overripe tomato. I really need to go shopping.

'Here you go . . . er . . . ' I check its sex, and as it appears to be minus a set of testicles, I'll infer it's a girl. 'Let's call you Agatha.' Seems apt to name her after my favourite crime writer, although maybe Marple is more appropriate. No, she looks like an Agatha. I place the offering on the floor and she immediately tucks in. I'm about to fork my pitiful lunch into my mouth when there's a bang on my door. I freeze. Surely I'm not getting a visit from the upstairs bully? Unless he's had a crisis of conscience and is washing the offending graffiti off my door, of course. I scoff. Unlikely. I leave my food and tentatively pop my head around the curtain at the window. It's Hannah.

'I know,' I say, when I see her staring at the red paint. 'Don't say a word,' I warn as I open the door wide. She tuts, then steps inside.

'Good to see you're getting on with the neighbours,' she says. She heads straight through to the kitchen and I follow. 'Oh, my God. Have you read the book *How to Win Friends and Influence People*?' She stares at Agatha, who has not only licked her plate clean but has jumped up onto the worktop and snaffled mine too and is now looking expectantly at the new arrival.

'That'll teach me,' I say, shooing her off and putting my plate in the sink. 'She was at my door, looking forlorn and hungry. What could I do?'

'You really shouldn't take in a stray. God knows what diseases it's carrying. Bound to have fleas.' She shudders. 'There are shelters you know. And besides, you're not allowed pets, are you?'

'Jeez. Have a day off, Hannah.' Tiredness swoops in, and all of a sudden, I want to lie down and go to sleep. I rub my eyes.

'See, you're allergic,' Hannah says. I glare at her. Her lips pout and she firmly tucks her loose jet-black hair behind her ear. 'Seriously, though, someone has to look at things sensibly, Rebecca.'

'Wow, I *am* in trouble. Thankfully you're not my landlord, then,' I say, giving a tight smile.

'You know it'll be difficult to get rid of it now you've fed it?'

I shrug. 'Agatha looked like she needed a rescuer. I simply stepped in.'

'You've *named* it?'

'I don't want to just say "it" or "cat". Anyway, it's not for you to worry about. Chill. What brings you here? I can't imagine it's the glorious scenery or scintillating company.'

'Actually, I thought it was time I checked up on you.'

'Oh, right.' I frown, my senses prickling. It's been a couple of months since Hannah came here. 'Any particular reason?'

'DCI Thomson was rather concerned after he received a call from you yesterday . . . '

'Was he now? Did he happen to inform you of the subject of my call?'

'Yes. Shall we have a coffee?' Hannah suggests, pushing the inquisitive Agatha away from her gently with her foot. 'Can you trap this thing in the kitchen while we sit in the lounge to talk?'

I make a drink for us both, then put a saucer of milk down for Agatha. I carry the coffees into the lounge, then, with difficulty, close the sliding partition door. I'm surprised it didn't break; it's the first time I've tried it, and it looks like it might be twenty years old. The yellowing colour matches my kettle. I decide in this moment both will have to go.

'Okay with you now?' I ask, before grabbing my drink and sitting down.

'Better. Honestly, Becky, you don't need to give the landlord any more excuses to evict you. Why has your door been vandalised? Who did you piss off?'

I roll my eyes. 'Ugh. Now that *is* a problem. It's the guy from the flat above.' I point upwards. 'Misogynistic bully. I was going to put a call in – he's most definitely abusing the woman he's got there. I hear him yelling at her, followed by her whimpering and crying. It's awful.'

'Domestics always are. I'm guessing you've had a

word, then.'

'You could say that, yeah.' I purse my lips, giving a coy look as I prepare for more jip from Hannah.

'Be careful. It's not like—'

'I have the backup anymore, yes – I know. I've had that conversation already today.'

'Oh? Who with?' She takes a sip of coffee.

I'm in two minds whether to come clean about this morning's meeting with Charlie. But we were the three musketeers when we were on cases together, and they are the only people, apart from Marcus, that I trust enough to share details with. They're my only remaining friends.

'I decided to try and bury the hatchet with Charlie,' I say, watching for her reaction. Her mouth forms an 'O' while she nods – I'm assuming approvingly – so I continue. 'I thought, seeing as I forgave you, that it was about time. I'd made him suffer long enough.'

'Good. Good.' Hannah's head lowers and she stares at the content of her mug. 'He told you then, I guess?'

'You knew?' I shoot forwards, my eyes wide. 'Why didn't you tell me? How long have you known?' I want to ask a load of other equally accusatorial questions, but the hot coffee that's slopped from my mug burns through my trousers. 'Ouch!' I jump up, put the mug down and wipe both hands down my trouser legs.

'Sorry, Becky. I didn't know how to drop it into conversation. I knew it would hit you hard.'

'I get that it must've been a bit awkward, but you really should've said something. I'd have shared info with you had it been the other way around. That's what friends do.'

'And I was being a friend. I didn't want to start you off on that path again after you'd spent so long getting straight.

You were moving on; I didn't see the benefit of putting a whacking great big barrier in your way. You deserve more than that after the shitty way you were treated by John and everyone else.'

My surge of emotion abates a little. 'Thanks.' I sit back down, my gaze on the dark wet splashes on the blue linen. 'Sorry, I shouldn't take this out on you.'

'I understand. It's a lot to digest. I get that. But you can't do anything about it.'

'But I can, and you know it.'

Silence. I've managed to get Charlie onside again – do I have any chance of Hannah going against the powers that be?

'Hmm,' Hannah muses. Then, it's as though a switch has clicked in her head and she stiffens, her demeanour suddenly irritated. 'If it were just her, then I'd say leave it, you know I haven't wanted to get involved in all this. But now there's a young kid involved, I'm not feeling so sure that's the right thing to do.'

A sharp, stabbing pain shoots through my head. Did she say a kid? Charlie never mentioned a child. This adds more fuel to the fire in my gut and I stand again and begin to pace. Hannah clearly thought he'd told me everything. Otherwise she'd never have divulged this additional info.

'You okay, Becky? You've gone awfully pale.'

'Bloody hell,' I say, ignoring her question. 'The right thing to do would be to warn this new woman of his that she's literally in bed with a dangerous rapist. I'm sure anyone would want to know that to protect their child.'

'Steady on, though, Becky. He's not a paedophile; he doesn't prey on young girls.'

Somehow, the thought it's a girl makes it worse and my

56

stomach cramps. 'So, you'd be happy to be in a relationship with a rapist and subject your daughter to him? Let him live under the same roof and interact with your little angel?'

'If I had one, then no, obviously not. Hell would have to freeze over before I allowed that.'

'Exactly. I – *we* – owe it to them to let her know just what type of man she's with.'

'Okay. Point taken.'

'Can you give me his address?'

Hannah's eyes close. Seconds feel like minutes as I watch her chest rise and fall rapidly while she considers my request. I know she'll be fighting her moral and lawful obligations right now, weighing up the likely repercussions of any action she takes. I lick my dry lips. Wait patiently.

'Give me your phone,' she says. I scramble for it and hand it to her. She concentrates while tapping in something, then she gets up. 'Thanks for the coffee. I'll see myself out.'

And as she leaves, she lays the phone on an unpacked cardboard box.

The door slams and I grab the mobile. On the screen, Google Maps is open, and a red pin marks the spot. I smile.

'Gotcha.'

My sleep is punctured with nightmares, and I wake up after one terrifying vision soaked in sweat, fear still gripping my insides. I reach a trembling hand into the bedside drawer, rummaging for the anxiety meds I was prescribed last year. My erratic breathing slows a little when my fingers find the container. I shake out a tablet and stare at it, small, round, and white in the centre of my palm. Tears spill down my cheeks. I stopped taking the tablets a few months ago. Felt I was finally coping without them; I could manage the odd bout of anxiety, like the one in the café earlier. With a renewed drive to do something about John, though, come consequences for me.

I roll the tablet with my fingertip. Close my eyes. I lost so much when I went after John before. My marriage, my job, my home – all gone. My security, my reputation, my sense of self-worth . . . ripped away from me in a matter of days, weeks.

I owe it to others – to the new woman in John's life – to see this through. And for me to do that, I must take the necessary steps to ensure I come through this without sacrificing even more of myself.

With a mouthful of water, I swallow the tablet.

Chapter 9

NOW

BECKY

The drive to Lymworth takes just under an hour. The sat nav states I'm currently ten minutes from where John is now living. I'm pleased I managed to control my urge to jump in my car immediately after Hannah left yesterday. The disturbing dreams last night gave me a nudge, reminded me that I had to take care of my own wellbeing, too. I eventually fell into a deep sleep and the second I awoke this morning, my mind and body were ready: itching to get on the road. I lasted until 7.30, then showered, fed Agatha a tin of tuna, packed a rucksack and walked to my car, keeping a wary eye out for signs of being followed. It was probably me overthinking things – but I wouldn't put it past John to have someone tailing me. That way, he would get early warning of me being near him and he'd be able to clock it up as some kind of evidence that I'm stalking him. Better to be overcautious. The coast was clear. I got in the car and, when the engine sputtered into life, I drove the opposite way first for a few minutes, checking my mirrors for a tail.

Now, as I park up on the outskirts of the village in a McDonald's car park and sit, my fingers drumming on the steering wheel, I realise I don't have much of a plan. And, I *need* a plan if I'm to outsmart John. He's keen to keep me out of his life, that much is clear from the threatening letter. It was his pre-emptive strike. He knew full well I'd find out about his new girlfriend, that he was living with her and her kid. And he wouldn't need a crystal ball to guess what I'd want to do. Driving right to his doorstep is exactly what he'll be expecting. He'll be prepared for it. I'll be walking into his trap. I've got to be less predictable; surprise him by acting differently to the old Becky. But how?

The smell of Maccies drifting in the air permeates my car and my stomach grumbles. I need food. An egg McMuffin will satiate me for now – and eating will give me some thinking time. Leaving my car, I head inside – regretting this choice as I step through the door. It's so quiet that I feel immediately conspicuous. With my nerves suddenly on edge I pull my jacket tighter around me. If Lymworth's a relatively small area, then those not from around here will likely stand out. It will be just my luck if John happens to come here for his coffee and carb fix; my cover will be blown instantly. I order on the digital screen to avoid speaking to the staff and tuck myself away – out of direct sight of the windows. As soon as my number is called, I'll scuttle back to the safety of my car.

My pocket vibrates and I fumble to get my mobile. No Caller ID shows in the display. Usually I'd ignore it, but for some reason I accept the call.

'Hello?' My breathing is shallow, my body reacting even

60

before I know who's on the other end.

'You need to leave. Now.'

Even with my heartbeat whooshing in my ears, the voice is loud, the tone clear. No room for misinterpretation; it's a warning. They, whoever it is, know I'm here – close to where John now lives. I push off the wall I'm leaning against and begin to walk around the restaurant.

'Yeah, you think?' I say while checking the toilets, and peeping into the kitchen – none of the staff look to be on their phones. 'Why's that?'

'Stop looking.' Now I'm accustomed to the adrenaline rush and my body is compensating, I can fully concentrate on the voice. It sounds male, but there's no way of ascertaining if that's the actual case because the person making this call could be using some kind of voice changer – even deepfake audio technology. Once I'd have thought that was far-fetched, but unfortunately, these days it's hard to trust that what you hear, or even what you see, is real. With the use of AI, believing your own eyes is becoming an outdated concept.

'Well, now – I think I will be the judge of that. I'm not keen on being told what not to do by a random stranger. Thanks for your concern, though.'

'Oh, I'm not doing it for you.'

They hang up before I can ask who it is. Not that they'd have obliged anyway.

'Number thirty-seven!'

I jolt at the voice directly behind me and swing around to see a pasty-looking teenager holding out a brown paper bag. It doesn't look like he's ever spent a single moment in the sun. This job, and gaming, are likely all he does with his life. Without speaking, I snatch the bag and head to the door.

61

'You're bloody welcome.' I hear the mumbled annoyance of the lad and a stab of disappointment hits me. When did I become so judgemental and rude? I turn, putting my hand up as thanks. I scan the area while walking back to my car. There are other parked cars, a few people milling around, but none that raise suspicion. I wait until I'm right beside the car before I hit the unlock button and quickly climb in and lock the doors.

My hands shake as I attempt to pull the McMuffin from the bag, the paper's crinkling noise increasing with my frustration. I finally jam the food in my mouth and chew viciously. The voice on the phone sounded somewhat familiar, but a name or identity doesn't come to me. I've changed my number three times over the past year – only a handful of people have it. Marcus, Hannah, my landlord, and more recently, Charlie. And, while each of them have my back and might well be concerned about me continuing to seek out John to bring him to justice, I don't believe any of them would resort to a weird, threatening phone call. And at least two of them have actively helped me get to this point. Why then warn me off?

The most likely culprit is John. He seems to have managed to get my address, I guess it wouldn't take much to obtain my number.

I gaze around the car park again, then at McDonald's. No one's even come in or out since I did. I stuff the last bit of muffin in my mouth, almost choking on it, then ball up the paper and get out. After tossing it into the bin, I walk slowly back to my car, then, checking around me to ensure no one is looking, I lower myself to the ground and stick my head underneath the chassis. With my fingers, I run along the underside feeling for anything that doesn't belong. I'm almost a hundred per cent certain no one followed me here, so if John or someone else knows where I am, perhaps it's because they've fitted a tracker.

Nothing here. I get up, go to the passenger side and repeat the process. No tracker.

Inside the car, I pull out the items in the glove compartment and door pockets, then get in the back and check the seat pockets and footwells. I sit on the rear seat, wipe the sheen of sweat from my forehead with the back of my hand, then let out a long hiss of breath. My mind swims with theories, but none of them seem to fit with the current circumstances.

'Face it, Becks – you're kind of enjoying this, aren't you?' I say aloud, laughing to myself. It's been a long time since I've had to use my brain in this way. I have to admit, I've missed investigating. I was always the first one to suggest playing Cluedo at Christmas – my mum and dad would pretend they were surprised, then would come the usual routine of teasing me, asking if I'd prefer to play Monopoly instead, but I always knew they were joking. It was an inevitability they'd grab the Cluedo board and set it up on the wooden dining room table. I loved it. I used to believe they always let me win, too. Dad told me, the day before he and Mum took the fateful trip, that not once did they let me win. There was no need, he said, because I always wiped the floor with them using my natural analytical ability. After they died, and I lost my way, I also forgot about those skills, instead choosing to put all my effort into psychology. I didn't regret that path, helping people was something I felt I was good at. Those words that my dad spoke came back to me one night, when I was in a particularly bad place emotionally, and at the same time, I saw a recruitment advert for the police force.

And voila. I ended up in Greater Manchester Police.

Sometimes, I think it was fate. Other times, I think it was simply a punishment; that meeting and marrying John was in some way a bad thing I deserved.

Right now, all I know is, I feel responsible for the lives of a woman and child; I don't want them to suffer like I have. What I know could save them from becoming victims of a man who has managed to stay below the radar for God knows how many years – a man who is manipulative and controlling and doesn't care about who he hurts as long as he gets his kicks. The law requires evidence – more than what I offered, apparently – to stop him from harming the public. I need to get that evidence, in whatever form it takes, and build an airtight case against him.

He's taken away my badge, but he hasn't taken my instincts, my skills as a detective, my moral values or who I am as a person. I will take John Lawson down. I will make sure justice is served for his victim, and I will make damn sure he is never in the position to create any new ones.

I get back behind the wheel and, ignoring the unknown caller's warning words, drive out of the car park towards my target.

Chapter 10

NOW

BECKY

Authorised covert surveillance under RIPA guidelines is one thing, even private investigators have to acquire a licence from the Security Industry Authority before carrying out any surveillance, but a civilian – like I am now – watching, recording any activity from outside a private residence, will result in legal action against me if I'm caught. It won't just land me in court for a judge to hand out a non-molestation order – it'll get me a criminal conviction. A prison sentence. A throbbing pain starts pounding my temples. I swipe my hand across my brow and stare at the moisture droplets; it's clearly not an effect of the cool March day.

I push my negative thoughts to the back of my mind and focus on the facts. I haven't been served with an order. Therefore, I'm not breaching a thing by being here, in the same village John is now residing in. All this boils down to is me ignoring a letter from my ex-husband. Who says I even received it? He can't prove I did; the post is terrible in Manchester most of the time. And while obtaining evidence of me being near his house might well mean that John does indeed gain an injunction against me, I'll still have some time between him applying to the court and the court granting it. Obviously, the best outcome is not to get caught in the act of watching him or his new girlfriend, work to gain the evidence *I* need, and then, turn the tables on John. Because he *will* trip up again, and I want to be right there to catch him out when he does.

He's the one who needs to be in prison.

The radio crackles at the same time the roads become quieter. The further into the village I drive, the greater the ball of anxiety grows in my stomach.

'Take the next left,' my sat nav instructs. My pulse quickens. The pin on the map is now only two minutes away.

Time to take a detour. I put my foot down and drive on past the left turn.

'Make a U-turn now,' the female voice demands.

I disregard her order, and with my chest against the steering wheel, watch out for somewhere convenient to park up for a moment to contemplate my next move.

'Recalculating.'

Up ahead, I spot a sign for a roadside café and indicate to pull in.

'Recalculating.'

'Enough!' I lean across and mute the sat nav. My tyres crunch on gravel as I manoeuvre behind the Café Shack. With the recording app on my phone switched on, I climb out of the car and make a meal out of stretching my legs as if I've been on a long journey, then make my way inside.

'Hiya, good morning,' I say, in what sounds remarkably like an Australian accent. I've no idea where it came from, or why I'm speaking this way, but, for some reason, I carry on using it. 'I wonder if you could help me.' The man behind the counter narrows his eyes. The ridiculing comments I received from my team whenever I attempted an accent now ring loud in my mind. Oh, God. I feel seen. Rumbled. I'd be a lousy undercover cop. 'I'm after a B&B in Lymworth, can you recommend one?'

He wrinkles his nose like he's smelled something bad. 'Doubt there'll be one round 'ere.'

'Oh.' I start swiping my mobile, offering a flustered look. 'Perhaps I've been given the wrong information, but my friend said there was . . .'

He turns away, busying himself with pouring a coffee into a cardboard cup. 'Your friend is wrong,' he says, pushing a plastic lid onto it. He turns back and slides the cup towards me. 'For the road.' His voice carries a finality, though his face remains neutral. He suspects I'm police. It's always an occupational hazard – like some people can tell a copper at twelve paces. Even though I'm not a serving detective, I no doubt have an air about me that can be sniffed out by those who've had enough dealings with the law. I wonder what skeletons this guy has in his closet for him to be this cagey.

'Well, thanks for your time.' I dig my hand into my jacket to find some change.

'On the house,' the man says with a firm nod. I return the gesture, pocket my phone, then grab the cardboard cup and walk out. I could've handled that so much better. What was I thinking? The gravel slips under my feet as I walk back to my car and I almost spill my free coffee.

'Hey! You.'

I instinctively turn. A woman, approximately thirty, with cropped hair, dressed in a black T-shirt and leggings with a brown apron over, leans against the side of the shack, cigarette in her hand.

'Yes?' I decide not to elaborate before she does.

'You're after a place to stay in Lymworth?' she says, in a strong northern accent.

'Yeah, just for the night.' I realise I've dropped my Australian intonation. Don't think I was fooling anyone anyway. 'I'm tired of driving, was going to pick up the journey again tomorrow.'

'The pub has a few rooms. No guarantee they'll be available 'course, but you could give it a go.'

'Thanks, that's great. What's it called?'

'The White Horse.'

'I appreciate it.' I'm too far away to make out the name on her badge. 'You're more helpful than your boss.'

She snorts. 'Not hard,' she says as she stubs the cigarette out on a tree stump and deposits it in a metal bin. 'He has a problem with women. More specifically, women cops.'

'Oh. I know his type.' I roll my eyes and give her a knowing smile. 'But I'm not a cop.' And I can say that with absolute honesty now. 'Shame you have to work for him.'

'Won't be for much longer.' She goes to walk back inside the Café Shack but stops short of the door. 'Might see you later at the pub then,' she says, before disappearing inside.

Sounds like that must be her usual routine. She could give me an 'in', but I'd have to be careful. Not exactly covert if I'm seen hanging around in John's local. Worse if I'm spotted talking to people, found to be asking questions. There's a possibility John himself doesn't frequent the village pub – you don't shit in your own nest. He's more likely to drink out of town now he's serving in a smaller area. I doubt he'd wish to become embroiled in local issues given he's a local detective. That could cause problems for him. Is it a low enough probability to take the risk, though? This troubles me as I get in the car and search Google Maps. I rack my brains for an appropriate course of action.

If I were a dog owner I could hang around on the village green and not seem at all out of place – and dog owners are always chatty, so it would be easier to suss out some useful info without appearing suspicious. But I'm not. I huff. Sip some coffee. It's bitter, but still better than my instant crap. While I wait, a car drives in and I watch the woman driver get out, open the back door and moments later take a baby out. I sit upright, whack the coffee in the cup holder. Of course. It's a weekday – supposing the new girlfriend's kid is old enough to be at school, I bet they attend the local primary. If so, she'd leave the house at around three, maybe, to go and collect her daughter. The thought motivates me. I have a plan, of sorts.

After some driving around to get my bearings and to build up the courage, I pull into The White Horse's car park and find a space as far from the entrance as possible. There's no reason John would know my car, it's a battered, second-hand one I bought after we split. Being a detective, though, he has access to DVLA and ANPR. Unless my vehicle's been flagged, ANPR would be a needle in a haystack job, but DVLA is another story. I'm banking on him not having gone that far. Yet. It pays to be cautious though. I still can't rule out he was my anonymous caller – and if that's the case, he already knows too much.

It's almost midday. I've got maybe three hours before I need to be close to John's address and it's a five-minute walk from here. I grab my rucksack, check there's sufficient cash in the zipped pocket, then head inside the pub. It's your typical village pub, having escaped the trendy makeover that a lot have succumbed to over the past few years. The one where everything's painted a pale sky-blue and looks uniform, samey and like every other bar. Totally stripped of its uniqueness and personality. I smile as I take in the deep-mauve, patterned carpet, the wood beams and dark-oak panelling. The smell of beer and pub grub greets me as I approach the bar.

'All right? What can I get you?' The woman in her fifties is a bit scruffy looking, her mousy hair hanging loose to her shoulders frames her square face, but she offers a warm smile. I cast my gaze around. There are a few older men gathered around a table on the far side, playing cards. At the pool table, two men in their early twenties are loudly mocking each other's skills at potting and a table in the restaurant side is taken by a large group of corporate types. None of the punters react to me entering, or when the bar person speaks to me. My muscles release some of the tension they've been holding.

'Might be a long shot,' I say, careful to keep my voice low. 'I was looking for a room for tonight—'

'You're in luck.' She practically pounces on me, reaching out and grasping my wrist. 'Don't tend to advertise, you know – we don't get a lot of footfall, so it's not part of the business as such. Just a word-of-mouth thing. I guess someone must've told you . . . '

'Er . . . yeah, actually. I stopped to stretch my legs at the roadside café, and I was kindly pointed in this direction.'

'Café Shack? Ah, that'll be our Nina, then. Bless her heart. Right, it's sixty-quid on the nose and that gets you a banging brekkie.' She grins, revealing a large gap where an upper incisor should be. 'I'll get you a key.'

I'm going to have to be careful about spending money, but for now I'm keeping my backstory about travelling through and that means going all in. I'll worry about dwindling savings later. I hand over the cash and I'm given the key. 'Can I get some food and take it to the room?' Despite the egg McMuffin and the stress of being here, I find myself craving food.

'Of course, my lovely.' She passes me a paper menu. 'Drink?'

'Diet lemonade, please.'

Within fifteen minutes I'm sitting in a room that looks to be straight out of an Eighties horror movie, with a chicken wrap and watching the world go by from the window overlooking the street. In the distance I can see rows of rooftops. I shiver. A cold sensation creeps over my skin, like someone is watching me. I convince myself it's tiredness. *I'm* the one doing the watching. Still, I scoot my chair back further from the window as a precaution. I don't want to draw attention to myself. After I finish eating, a thought hits me. *Shit.* I make a call. It goes straight to voicemail.

'Charlie, it's me. You know you said you'd provide backup when I needed it?' I pause, even though there's no one to respond. 'Well, I'm away . . . at an assessment centre thing as part of my interview for this new job—' I feel myself blush at the lie, as if I've never told one before '—and I completely forgot to leave food down for my cat. Don't ask.' I give an awkward laugh. 'Anyway, if you might be willing to use your *law-abiding* breaking and entering skills to pop in and give her a tin of tuna, I'd be eternally grateful. I realise this isn't the type of backup you were offering, and

71

I hate to ask, but I trust you and I know you like cats, unlike Hannah. Thanks, mate. I owe you one. She's called Agatha, by the way.'

There wouldn't have been any harm simply telling the truth. After all, he knows I plan to seek out John – but something held me back. I'll fess up when I next see him, but for now, the fewer people that know I'm here, on John's doorstep, the better. I realise it's also not a given he'll pick this message up, let alone carry out my instructions. If he does listen to it in time, maybe my line about me trusting him will be enough to swing it. I hope so, because I don't want to think about the poor cat going without food all night after I made a fuss about taking her in.

My stomach drops as I hear the sound of church bells chiming three; my inner voice questions me: *Do you really want to put yourself in this situation? Haven't you ruined your life enough trying to gain evidence of the truth?* Of course I have the option to walk out now, get in my car and drive back to my flat – attempt to properly rebuild my life. But will that life be something I truly want knowing I gave up the opportunity for justice purely because it was the easier option? I don't think I'd be able to live with myself.

I grab the room key, pull on my jacket and head downstairs. There's a rear exit, so I don't have to go through the bar. With my mind set on a new purpose, I begin the walk towards John's address. My heart gallops along to the sound of the Bee Gees, 'Staying Alive' as I strut the streets, my focus intent on the phone screen showing me the route. Every now and then, I look up to check my surroundings. The primary school is in the opposite direction. Assuming John's girlfriend walks to pick up the child, I'll surely see her heading towards me. If you lived in such close proximity, I doubt you'd drive. Unless, of course, you were on your way back from somewhere – work or something – or going to be setting off somewhere after the pick-up. My bet was on her walking. *If* her kid went to the local primary.

And then I see the sign. Woodlands Avenue. My lungs cease to operate adequately, and my legs stop moving. This is John's street. I'm here. I stand, quiescent, unable to form a coherent thought or perform a logical action. I've been immobilised by a road sign. I squeeze my eyes closed, blocking it out, while willing my bodily functions to return. I didn't want to draw attention to myself, but I'm going about it the wrong way. I open my eyes, give myself a shake, then internally yell, 'Pull yourself to-fuckin'-gether.' My body finally jerks into motion and I step forwards. My feet fall into a rhythm again and soon the house numbers get closer to thirteen. Typical he lives in a house with that number. I stop, duck down to tie up my Converse shoelace and take the time to scout it out. It's a semi-detached property, looks like it should be three-bedroomed by the size. It has a concrete driveway, not gated – and the garden is a neatly cut grass oblong. No car on the drive. I daren't spend too long here. I'll retreat to a safer distance and wait to see if there's any movement.

As I turn back, I see someone coming up the road I've just walked. I swallow hard. It's a woman, and she's holding a child's hand. They're ambling along, no rush. I can walk right past her on the other side of the road no problem, she's barely aware of anyone around her. As I take a deep breath and am about to stride towards her, I clock her black clothes under her open coat, and cropped hair.

No way.

My pulse leaps. It's the woman from the Café Shack. Surely it's not possible that she is John's new girlfriend. Not willing to chance it, I swivel on my heel and power walk in the opposite direction, back towards John's house. I can't be seen in this road by her if she is who I suspect. The urge to turn around to see her again is overwhelming. If I get a little further ahead, maybe to the junction, then position myself carefully out of her line of sight, I can wait and see which house she enters.

Even before she and her little girl turn into the driveway, I realise that she's the one. As soon as I saw her holding the child's hand walking up Woodlands Avenue, my heart knew. And now my mind knows it too. The woman's name is Nina. And she's living with a rapist.

I watch as they disappear into the house and a deep sadness washes over me. Poor, unsuspecting, innocent victims. Something inside of me screams that I must protect them.

Chapter 11

NOW

BECKY

Back in my room at The White Horse, a new worry springs into my mind. John's new girlfriend, Nina, has *seen* me. Not only that, but she knows I may have booked a room here. Her last words to me were: *Might see you later at the pub, then.* To knowingly interact with her could land me in the deepest pile of shit. There's no reason I can see why she would mention to John that she spoke to a random woman at the Café Shack. But if she were to run into me again at the bar, say, then I'm guessing she might strike up a conversation – and that *could* find its way back to him. He'll be on high alert at the moment, knowing I've likely received the letter and he'll pounce on Nina's info about a new face in the village looking for a place to stay for the night. Of course, another far worse possibility is her and John coming to the pub together. I can't afford to be caught this early in the game.

My panicked negative scenarios get drowned out by the noise level beneath me rising a notch – several different voices combine, and it sounds heated. Intrigued, I open my door an inch, but the subject of the argument is still lost in the muffled tones. Judging by the differing pitches, I think it's a woman and maybe two men. They abruptly cease, and I strain to hear what's happening now. Footsteps on the stairs catch me off-guard. Shit! I quickly, but softly close the door again, not wanting to be found eavesdropping. I jump back at the sound of a sharp knock. That was close. I tiptoe to the far side of the room then I call out to 'hang on a moment'. An awful jittery feeling erupts in my gut. The people were arguing about something, then immediately came to my room? Was I the subject of the dispute?

I plaster on a wide smile as I open the door. It drops as I'm met with a balding man dressed in a Manchester United football shirt and black jeans, holding out three twenty-pound notes to me.

'Sorry, love. My wife. She shouldn't have said this room was free.' His apology sounds sincere . . . but his face belies that. His eyes narrow as he focuses on mine, it's as though he's daring me to question this bizarre statement. I stand still, one hand on the door handle, the other firmly by my side while I contemplate whether to make a fuss, or to simply take the money and leave without question. My options aren't great. But I can't help myself. I frown, then turn to look back into the room behind me.

'No one else here but me,' I say.

He flusters, shaking his head in a cartoonish, comical way, that make his cheeks wobble. 'No, but there will be. It was already booked. Look,' he says, waving the notes at me, 'like I said, I'm sorry.' When I still don't make a move to take this 'refund', his nostrils flare and I wait for the ensuing rudeness that I imagine is on its way. 'I don't want any trouble,' he says, his eyes now widening.

Now, that's an odd thing to say. It cements the thought I had that the arguing voices were about me, and a growing sense of unease in my gut points to the possibility they know who I am. Did Nina spot me earlier, close to her home? I thought her attention was fully taken with her child, now I consider I was wrong. Had she been aware of me, it would strike her as being a huge coincidence for me to have been at her place of work, then in the street she lived on. If she called the pub, found out I'd checked in, she might've been compelled to inform John, because God only knows what he's told Nina about me. And what, in turn, he's told the pub owners.

'What trouble are you expecting?' I ask with a half-smile. It's met with an impatient huff. Sweat gathers above his eyebrows, his breathing speeds up. It's time to quit. I shake my head, lean forwards and take the money. 'Shame. I was looking forward to my full English in the morning.'

'If you could be quick,' he says, shrugging.

'Sure.' I slam the door, then go to the side of the window and peek out. There's no one hanging around. Am I being paranoid thinking it's personal? There really might have been a double-booking. It doesn't smell right, though. I stuff the items I'd unpacked back into my bag and pull on my jacket. In a sense, I've got what I came for – at least, the beginning of it. I know where John lives, and I know what Nina and her child look like. I've something to go on.

The woman who booked me in isn't anywhere in sight when I walk through the bar to hand over my key. I hope she hasn't been chastised physically as well as verbally. I catch

77

myself in this thought, my head dropping. It's sad that's almost always my first port of call in such a situation. That the woman has been, or will be, abused by the man. Even sadder that in 95 per cent of the cases where I've thought it, I've been dead right.

The other 5 per cent – well, I don't often think about those outliers. Better to be wrong but to have taken action, than right but too afraid to rock the apple cart and the result be a loss of life.

A niggling feeling gnaws at me, stopping me from driving straight out of the pub car park. I sit, hunkered down with the thumbnail of my right hand jammed between my teeth, biting down hard as I stare out my driver's side window at the rear entrance. The owner said my room was double-booked, that someone would soon be there to claim it and so my stubborn streak has dictated I hang around at least for a while to see just who materialises. If anyone.

Almost two hours pass, without any significant movements catching my attention. In that time, though, the sun has dipped behind the buildings and my shivering has increased. Rubbing my hands over my arms and legs is no longer creating warmth. The sky has become a dusky pink, the shades darkening rapidly as I sit and contemplate whether to get out and stretch my legs. I could chance a quick look around the front of the pub before driving back to the flat. A gut instinct is hard to ignore. I climb out.

With my hair tucked inside the hood of my jacket, hands shoved in the pockets, I make my way along the side of the pub towards the pavement that runs outside the front of it. When I drove in earlier I noted there were four wooden picnic-style tables, two situated either side of the main door.

I slow my pace as I near the end of the wall, listening out for conversation. It's not the sort of 'outside' weather where drinkers would likely congregate and chat after work, but smokers tend to brave any climate. John always hated the habit, it went against his idea of health and fitness, so I'm fairly certain I won't come face to face with him when I turn the corner. I wonder if Nina is forced to keep her own habit a secret.

My heart rate settles when I can't hear any voices and I step around to the front, breathing a sigh of relief when there's no one standing outside the pub. I give a quick glance up and down the street before walking briskly past the first two tables. From here, I should be able to pretend I'm on my mobile and use it as cover to peek in through the window without raising suspicion. I could be way off the mark, but the owner's behaviour was strange and I want to see if there is a reason for it.

I take my phone, dial my voicemail and put it to my ear ready for my fake conversation. I turn to look in the first window, but there's a plant and menu obscuring my view inside the bar. Hoping the other one has a clearer line, I wander along a bit, my focus seemingly on my phone. I side-eye the window, and my heart gives a jolt when I see a group of men in there. I pull the side of my hood a little more to cover my face, then when I'm confident, I take a good look.

My chest is raised high, caught in the middle of an intake of air and my legs lose power and give way like the muscles have liquified.

It's him. It's John.

I sit heavily on the bench of the wooden table, air releasing from my mouth in a loud hiss. *Shit, shit, shit.* He is the reason I'm here, so I'm not sure why I'm having this reaction – maybe it's the shock, the realisation that I'm within spitting distance of him. That man destroyed part of me – a part I can never recover. It was easier not seeing him while I attempted to put some pieces of my life back together. I suppose until the letter and subsequent news of his upcoming promotion, I could almost pretend he was dead. And, despite being adamant over the past two days that I need to put an end to his crimes, now actually seeing him again in the flesh, my old feelings of helplessness are right back.

My neck throbs with my racing pulse, my head is light, my eyesight blurring, and for an awful moment I think I'm going to flip into a full-on anxiety attack. I didn't bring the medication. Why didn't I think to bring the medication?

Stop. No. I shake my head, take a deep breath. *You're fine. You're safe. Breathe.*

I pull at my hood, desperate to lower it, to get more air. A sudden burst of deep laughter stops me. I blink to clear my vision, then turn towards the window, focusing in on the men inside the pub, propping up the bar, sipping pints of lager. And as I stand and watch my ex-husband, the adrenaline courses through me. My top lip is tight over my teeth, the muscles in my neck taut. *Look at him.* Laughing and joking as though he hasn't a care in the world. My stomach churns as anger bubbles and a memory of who this normal-looking, laughing detective *really* is, crashes into my mind.

Chapter 12

THEN

BECKY

John's key hit the lock at 4 a.m. My pulse was hitting one-twenty easy. I'd rehearsed what I wanted to say – had been going over it since I found the burner. I lay on my back, my hands crossed over my chest – each thud of my heart pained me as I waited for the bedroom door to open.

My breaths came fast, my lungs working overtime. His steps were steady, he wasn't in a rush to get into bed. Often his routine once he'd finished work was: food, shower, TV, then bed. If he followed that tonight, I had at least another hour, maybe even two before he entered the bedroom. The bottles of wine in the fridge door clinked together. He was in the kitchen. I swung my legs out of bed. Sat on the edge of the mattress, my hands clenched beside me. I couldn't wait any longer. I had to face this situation right now.

'Oh, hey, baby. Waiting up for me?' he said, when he caught sight of me in the lounge doorway. He had a sandwich in one hand, bottle of lager in the other. He took a big bite and smiled with his mouth full. Something in my stomach churned at the sight of the mushed-up cheese caught in his teeth. Every fibre in my body itched to run at him, push him to the floor and pound my fists into his chest until they were red and sore. Until all the anger and disappointment within me had been expelled.

But what if I was wrong. John, my loving, kind, funny, caring *detective* husband, could've been innocent of any wrongdoing. Just doing his job. I wanted, needed, to give him the chance to explain. An opportunity to tell me it was a sensitive case that DCI Thomson had put him on, that he was part of a team covertly monitoring a sex-trafficking ring. Anything I was able to wrap my head around other than the one theory I currently had.

I took a long breath in. Walked up to him and looked him straight in the eyes. Released it. 'Yeah, you could say that,' I said, my voice remarkably steady.

'If it's round two you're after, I'm afraid I'm done in.' He turned away from me, then plonked down on the sofa. 'Go back to bed. I'll be with you shortly.'

I heard it in his tone. He wanted me out of the way. He must've just worked out that his secret phone had dropped out of his pocket earlier. He needed to search for it.

'Hard night, then?' I asked. Without looking at me, he answered that it had been. I walked towards the bedroom. 'Don't be long, eh?' I said, leaving him. I stood outside the bedroom, closed the door so he'd think I was back in bed. And I waited with the phone inside my pyjama pocket, my breath held. After an age, I heard movement. I peeped out around the corner and saw John, his back to me as he ran his hands along the sofa cushions.

Please let there be a simple explanation.

Once I was satisfied he was looking for the phone, I stepped out from the shadows. John's face when he spotted me holding what he was looking for was a mix of 'caught red-handed' embarrassment, like his mother had just walked in on him having a wank, and complete horror; his eyes were wide like saucers, his mouth gaped open.

'Looking for this?' I said. I didn't even blink. Stared at him, waiting with bated breath for a confession. Hoping his admission would be that he'd taken a case without telling me. Gone deeper into it than he anticipated. I longed for the words: 'It's a big misunderstanding. I've been framed. I'm being blackmailed.' Anything.

He glared at the phone, then at me. Tried to gauge if I'd been able to access the content before answering me. I kept my mouth shut. It was the hardest thing, when my insides were boiling and my heart throbbed, and all I wanted to do was scream at him. Accuse him.

'Thanks,' he said, reaching for it. I instinctively pulled back.

And in that moment he must've known.

'Becks?' he said, softly. 'Can I have it, please?'

I stepped back further, all my senses alert. 'How come you have a burner in our house?' It was a simple question, but he didn't answer. 'What's it about?'

John shrugged. 'I don't know what you mean. It's part of this case I'm on, that's all.'

'I've not heard about a case. Who are you working with?'

'Becky! Just give me the goddamn phone.' His face turned beetroot red; spit flew from his mouth as he lunged towards me. I let out an involuntary scream and ran down the corridor, past our bedroom, panic finally setting in and

83

providing a rush of adrenaline. I headed to the back door. I didn't reach it.

John's hands wrapped around my middle and the air left my lungs with the force of being lifted off the ground, swung around and thrown to the floor. Gasping for breath but rage-filled, I scurried across the ground like a beetle, somehow keeping the phone in my clammy hand. Within a few feet of the door, John grabbed my ankles and my mind blurred, fear distorting any ability to fight. He yanked me backwards, the phone flying from my grip as I skidded along the floor.

John trampled over me to get to it.

There was a thud, followed by a crunching noise and I looked up to see John's boot squashing the black, plastic mobile like he was stamping out a cigarette end. Shards of plastic scattered.

'Fucking hell, Becky. Now look what you made me do.' He sighed, then hung his head. 'You shouldn't have interfered.'

I stayed on the ground, brought my knees up under my chin. Breathing hurt. But, through the overwhelming sense of shock and disgust, I managed to speak.

'What have you done, John?'

'Nothing,' he said, bending to gather the broken phone pieces.

Tears sprung to my eyes. I cursed myself. I'd been married to John for five years and finding a burner phone with alarming content was something I'd truly hoped was nothing to do with my husband, or at the very least, could be explained away. John's reaction stripped that hope from me like a lion tearing meat from its prey.

He knew that without the evidence on the phone he'd

just demolished, he was safe. But he also knew that if I'd seen it, which I think he believed to be the case, this wasn't over. What was the best way to manage the situation now? Should I say that I'd forwarded the messages to my own phone – or even to one of our colleagues? Make it clear that the evidence wasn't destroyed at all. Or would that make the situation worse? I got to my feet. My legs wobbled, so I used the wall for support as I walked. The atmosphere darkened even further, the sense of being watched by him causing my skin to prickle. I entered the kitchen with John following closely. He strode past me to reach the fridge, opened it, popped the cap off two lagers and held one out. He shook the bottle when I hesitated. I frowned, but accepted it. What was his game?

'We need to talk,' he said, clinking his bottle against mine as though we were celebrating. Bile rose into my mouth. I swallowed it down with a gulp of the cold drink. I knew the look on his face, I'd seen it often enough. It was his interrogation expression. The chill of the lager ran the length of my oesophagus, down into the pit of my stomach and I shivered.

We were in for a long night.

Chapter 13

NOW

BECKY

After sidling away from The White Horse and driving back with my mind spiralling, I feel completely on edge walking in the dark from the row of garages towards my flat. The strange episode with the landlord at the pub and wondering if John was behind it, then actually seeing him, gnaws away at me. I don't think he noticed me watching through the window, but what if someone else did and told him?

My eyes dart left to right, then every few seconds I look over my shoulder. The streetlights leading up to the block are out again – this is the third week and my multiple complaints to Manchester City Council have led to absolutely zero action. The lighting coming from the buildings ahead at least offer some illumination, but I open the torch app on my phone and wield it like it's a magic wand, swishing it this way and that. Pathetic, really, but there's something about the dark that's innately scary. Bad things happen at any point in a twenty-four-hour period, however, it's the night-time that brings with it the shadowy horror to heighten every fear. It was bad enough prior to my career choice. Now I have actual, real-life reasons to be wary. In my other hand, I clench my key in my fist ready to stab at any assailant, and I walk with the longest strides I can manage. At five foot two, I don't cover a great distance quickly unless I'm running.

When I'm close enough to see my front door, I'm relieved and pocket my phone, then release the key from its attack position. I catch my breath as I stick the key in the lock. Something is different. The red graffitied slur that had been there when I left this morning has gone. I touch my hand to the panel, now covered with a fresh coat of green paint; it's still tacky. 'Uh-huh,' I say aloud. I don't hang about any further, getting inside and swiftly locking the door behind me. The flat is eerily quiet. No noise from other flats, but more notably, no meowing either.

'Agatha?' I call before resorting to the standard kiss-calling that all cat owners seem to do. I move slowly through the flat, making the high-pitched kissing noises while half crouching and checking behind the boxes and under the futon, then, still in that position, progressing into the kitchen. Where is she? I stand upright, deposit my rucksack on the worktop and check the cupboard. A tin of tuna has gone, so I'm guessing Charlie got in and fed her. The plate is spotless – licked clean as though it's been through a dishwasher. Charlie obviously took it upon himself to paint my front door, but he wouldn't then have taken Agatha with him. So where is she? I give him a call, but it goes to voicemail.

'Hey, Charlie. Thank you, mate – really appreciate you

feeding the cat . . . and for redecorating,' I say with a laugh. 'Did you actually see Agatha when you were here?' And then my stomach sinks. He would've had the front door open while he painted it. Agatha must've escaped. 'Oh,' I say into the phone. 'I wondered if you might've taken her with you, but I think she probably just got out while you had the door open. Never mind. Thanks anyway. Speak soon.' I hang up and yawn; my entire body is weak. During the last twenty-four hours I think I've been through every emotion listed in the emotion thesaurus and my energy is zapped. The cat's not mine, so why am I feeling a crushing sense of emptiness?

A huge thump comes from above my head. Raised voices start, then grow louder, more intense, until the crescendo ends abruptly with a slammed door. I let my eyelids close gently, and I stay still, my breath held for a few moments, straining to hear further noise.

A yowling.

My eyes spring open and I look up to the ceiling as the long, drawn-out meowing continues. It's Agatha, I know it, and she's clearly in distress. What the fuck has he done to her? Tired or not, I'm not staying put here. I snatch the keys back up from the hook and make my way to the upstairs neighbours. I'm confident he's gone out, but I imagine the woman, Tamsin, is still there. I reach the door and put my ear to it before attempting to gain entry. Definite whimpers – both from Tamsin and Agatha. The hot ball of fire in my chest threatens to explode as visions of them both beaten, hurt and scared, fill my mind. I don't knock, instead I open the letterbox and duck down to speak through it.

'Tamsin, hi. I'm Becky, I live downstairs? Are you able to get to the door, sweetheart?'

The whimpering stops, the yowling, though, carries on. I breathe more rapidly; I must keep it together – I really don't want to frighten her by coming across harshly so that she doesn't feel safe opening the door to me. One bully is enough for anyone to contend with.

'Is your cat okay? She doesn't sound too happy,' I say, trying to keep it light, keep the focus on the cat, not Tamsin. That way, I might gain her trust enough for her to let me in. I try to see inside, but it's too dark. I step away, brushing my hands through my hair. Then I lean over the edge of the wall, check if he's around; I can't see him, but then, without the aid of the streetlights, he could be lurking and I'd be none the wiser. There's a shuffling noise behind me and I swing around to see the letterbox open halfway. I rush back.

'He . . . ' She gives a convulsive gasp and I have a dreadful feeling I know what's coming. 'He kicked him.' She breaks into sobs and every inch of my skin feels like it's ablaze. What a bastard.

'I can get a vet to look at the cat. If you open the door—'

'No. No. He'll be back in a minute. You don't want to be here, then.'

'Let me deal with him if the need arises,' I say, determination overtaking any fear I have of what would happen if he returned. I'm tempted to tell her I'll call the police, but experience has led me to the conclusion that doesn't work in these situations. 'I could take Ag—the cat, if you like. You don't have to tell him. I'll sort it.'

'You don't . . . you don't know . . . what you're getting involved with,' she stutters. And she's right, but I have enough of an idea that means I can't simply turn a blind eye.

'I've known men like him, Tamsin. I want to help. Please?'

Tamsin doesn't say any more. Even the cat's cries have

89

ceased. What a mess. If I can't coax her to open the door to me, what is my next step going to be? Charlie isn't answering his phone, although I'm not sure what he could do even if he did. Domestics are reported so frequently, and the perp isn't even here.

My thoughts are interrupted by the door opening and Tamsin's tear-stained face appears. I catch my breath. I feel my bottom lip quiver, my eyes stinging as they pool with tears.

'Shit,' I say, then blink rapidly and pull myself together, my professional demeanour automatically taking over. 'Do you require medical assistance?'

Tamsin's eyes are wide and imploring. She stands, in a dirty, white oversized sleeveless shirt, her bare arms held out to me like she's offering herself to be handcuffed. Her right forearm is scored with multiple horizontal scars, some from past cutting going by their keloid appearance, some more recent, the red inflamed lines still raised and angry. I swallow hard, my heart breaking. And that's the other shock. I'm not facing the middle-aged woman I anticipated. Tamsin is around twenty years old. I want to take her in my arms, hug her, tell her everything will be okay now. But life's not that easy. I do take hold of her hands, though, and I gently pull her out from the flat. If he comes back, we need to have an escape route.

'I don't need it,' she says, turning around. 'Can you help Punch, like you said?'

Punch? What the . . . 'I thought it was a girl,' I say. 'I guess you didn't name him.'

'Vince got him for me. Said he would help me adapt.'

I don't have time to unpack that statement, I need to get in there, grab Agatha and get us all to my car double-quick. 'Stay there,' I tell Tamsin. Inside the flat, the smell – a heady mix of stale alcohol, food, piss and vomit – makes me gag. I cover my mouth with my sleeve and, careful where I'm stepping, walk towards the kitchen where I hope I'll find Agatha. Nerves pull at my stomach, and I silently beg that she's still alive. I haven't heard any miaowing for a bit. Something knocks into my legs and, forgetting the awful stench, I lower my sleeved arm and take hold of Agatha, lifting her and quickly assessing for injuries. I can't see anything obvious, but if Vince has kicked her, she could have internal bleeding. She needs a vet, now.

I'm acutely aware he will be back any moment – he won't be able to leave Tamsin alone for long – he'll absolutely need to regain control of the situation he's just caused. Back outside, Tamsin sits on the ground beside the broken plant pot, her skinny legs sprawled in front of her. I didn't notice track marks on her arms, can't see evidence of anything on her legs and feet, so that's one less thing to worry about. But she's clearly malnourished. I've so many questions which will all have to wait.

'Okay, sweetheart, let's go.'

She looks horrified at the suggestion. 'What? No, no. Not me. Just take Punch. I have to stay.'

'I'm not leaving you!' I shout, my ability to remain calm ebbing. 'I'll take you somewhere safe.' I tug at her arm while attempting to keep Agatha in my grip. 'Tamsin. We have to move. Before he gets back.' I know once he's on the scene, it'll be near impossible to control the situation. Trouble will ensue.

'I can't.' She pulls her arm back and begins to crawl back towards the door of the flat.

'I know you're scared, Tamsin, but there are people who

91

can help – you don't have to live in fear of Vince.'

I'm not certain if it was only after I found out about John that I started to see the signs of domestic abuse when arriving at scenes of crimes or investigating them. It must've been, I guess, otherwise I'd have recognised many of them in my own marriage. Or, had I spotted the red flags, the warning signs, but decided not to dwell on them, preferring instead to pretend there was nothing wrong, paper over any cracks quickly and give him excuses for behaving how he did sometimes. The night I waited up for him – the night I found the burner phone that changed everything, put an end to any kind of head-burying. There was no excuse I could think of for how he treated me then, or afterwards. Is this some kind of hero's journey I'm on now? Why I'm compelled to bring John to justice; why I feel I must warn Nina, why I want to 'save' Tamsin? I'd messed up before, during an investigation a few years back by putting off taking the action required, afraid to break a family up needlessly and that ended badly. I *could* be overcompensating. Whatever my personal reasons, one thing I feel sure about right at this moment – Tamsin is in imminent danger if I leave her here.

Before I can plead with her, Tamsin stands, and in a split second she's up in my face, her nose almost touching mine. My muscles tense.

'It's not him I'm afraid of,' she whispers, slowly.

The haunting way she speaks the words coupled with the intensity in her eyes, makes my blood run cold. Before I can even ask who she *is* afraid of then, I hear pounding footsteps and I turn my head towards the sound.

'Go. Now!' Tamsin pushes me away and runs inside. She closes and locks the door.

Fuck it. I'm out of time.

Vince's footsteps close in. I have about ten seconds before he turns the corner and sees me outside his flat with Agatha in my arms. I start running in the opposite direction and reach the end of the concrete corridor just in time. I pause, peep around the corner. He unlocks the door and goes inside.

I lean back against the stippled wall, my breaths ragged. 'At least . . . I've saved . . . one of you, for now.'

Chapter 14

NOW

BECKY

My heart had pumped wildly when I half-jogged back to my car, carrying a squirming Agatha. The last thing I'd wanted was to be out in the dark again but if I couldn't help Tamsin, getting to an emergency vet in the centre of Manchester was my priority. I returned two hours later, and eighty quid lighter, with a subdued Agatha.

Now, with a blanket draped across my lap, my eyelids heavy with tiredness, I sit with her and stroke her less-matted fur. As much as sleep is needed, my mind doesn't appear to want to play ball and goes over the events of the past forty-eight hours in minute-by-minute detail.

It was well over a year ago when I found John's phone but it took a while for the fear that it wasn't just a one-off indiscretion to fully take hold. It had to be a pattern of behaviour. After his aggressive response to my questioning and then him destroying the phone, I began to look deeper into things. Even though at that point we were still living under the same roof, our relationship was all but over. John refused to move out, and I had nowhere to go, so we settled into a stalemate – always working opposite shifts and staying out of each other's way as much as possible. As I had the means and opportunity, I searched the database at work during my shifts, looking into the details of locally reported rapes. Most often, the rapist was known to the victim; there were fewer cases of sexual assault committed by a stranger. There were even fewer cases that resulted in a criminal charge or summons. I remember the burning sensation in my stomach when I realised how grim the statistics were. The specialist sex crime unit had been disbanded and while there were officers in every district across Manchester who specialised in sexual assault case investigation, I had to wonder if it was as efficient as it could be. How many people had been raped or assaulted but hadn't even reported the incidents because of perceived lack of resources, or for fear of not being believed?

The knowledge of the content on the burner, despite it no longer being viable evidence due to John destroying it, ate away at me. I didn't sleep a full night, was unable to keep food down. I lost weight, my muscle mass diminished and colleagues began to worry. Ask questions. The vision of the screenshot the woman sent John flashed up in my mind every hour of every day until it became too unbearable to keep to myself.

The rest, as they say, is history. Stunned, appalled, and driven by a sense of belief in the system, I mustered the courage to report him, hoping justice would prevail. I can still see the shocked, disbelieving looks on the faces of both John's and my colleagues. The lowering of gazes as I walked by them, the shaking of heads and tuts. Apart from Hannah and Charlie, suddenly no one wanted to work with me. It got worse when an investigation was launched, but I naively believed that following it, John would be charged.

No hard evidence was found and John managed to evade charges. So much for the system's integrity. It didn't matter what I said, everyone believed John, not me. And that's when his gaslighting really went up a notch and my life began its plunge downhill faster than an Alpine skier.

The question then was, and continues to be, how do I gather the evidence if the force itself is allowing John to stay in the service? I was the one to lose my job. If things went on and I was able to see the links, surely others would've done. Even without solid evidence, you'd hope it would be enough to make them think twice about him. His behaviour could put the public at risk. No one backed me up, not really. Were those higher up protecting John? If so, why? Just how many people did John have in his pocket? He must've had something on them for it to have been swept so easily under the carpet.

The hard truth is, I lived with a violent rapist and I'm not the only one who knew it, but I'm the only one to attempt to prove it. It's a bitter pill to swallow. But then, everything's different with the benefit of hindsight. I hadn't connected the dots prior to that awful night. I'd allowed his moments of unreasonable behaviour towards me to go unchallenged, not realising at the time that he was manipulating me, flipping even the most minor disagreements to lay blame at my feet. Always deflecting attention from his short-comings and somehow making them mine. A forgotten dinner arrangement with friends – well, that was my poor memory, not due to him never having told me. 'Look, silly – it's on the calendar.' I bowed down on each similar occasion, accepting the blame without dispute.

'Bastard,' I say, my teeth gritted. I lay Agatha gently on the futon and begin rummaging in the boxes for the info I'd packed away when I moved out of the house. After the report was filed and John found out it was made by me, things took an even worse turn and while he was at work one day, I packed his clothes in two suitcases, left them on the lawn and had the locks changed. I fully expected a rage-filled outburst and him demanding to be let back in, but he stood in the centre of our lawn and laughed. Belly laughed, like it was the biggest joke in the world. Even now, I shudder at the memory. He calmly put the suitcases in the car, called up, 'See you soon, babe,' to me as I watched through the bedroom window, and he smiled and waved, leaving as though he was simply going on holiday. Even then he was thinking a step ahead – he was measured, ensuring he came across as the level-headed one of us. God, I'd felt so stupid that yet again I hadn't seen what he was doing. Later, he'd used how *I* reacted that day as evidence of my unpredictable, unreasonable behaviour towards *him*. Once left alone in the marital house, though, I quickly turned the second bedroom into an incident room. Months of dead ends left me deflated. Everything suffered: my physical health, mental health, friendships and work life. They were the darkest days, or so I'd thought.

I shake myself from the memories back to the present and carry on searching the boxes. In the last one, I find the cardboard folder – with the words 'Operation Lawless' penned in black marker across the front. My heart gives an anxious flutter, like it contains a trapped butterfly. Once I open this 'can of worms' as Marcus liked to refer to that time, there's no going back for me: obsession will take over again. Of course, the codename isn't one generated by GMP, the ones they use are random and nothing to do with the case – it's my own. As is this investigation. Because if not me, then who? I think I've got Charlie and Hannah onside, although can't rely on them too heavily, the last thing I want, or need, is to get them suspended.

With no other option, I tip the contents out and begin to sift through it; order it and then I take it to my bedroom. Using coloured push pins, I stick a photo of John in the centre of the wall. It goes in easily as this was one big room once and is only divided from the kitchen by plywood. The landlord is a cheapskate. Then, one by one, I pin other index cards I made, newspaper cuttings and photos of relevant places, around his. I'm weirdly void of emotion when I look at his image now, especially having glimpsed him earlier in the pub. The dragging, heavy weight of fear I'd feel if I saw him, or a photo of him, has thankfully dissipated. In a way, it's like I've received exposure therapy for a phobia – the things he put me through after I reported him, the many times I was afraid of what he'd do to me, have been compartmentalised, locked away. I may have been left with anxiety, I think, as I pop a tablet in my mouth, but I'm done being scared of him.

The horrifying truth remains, though – John *is* dangerous. He's a corrupt cop and a predator – and my overwhelming belief now is that John's reign of terror is ongoing.

Chapter 15

ISABEL

Why the hell did she walk home on her own?

It was two in the morning, what was she thinking?

Where were her friends? If they hadn't left her, she'd be okay.

She was blind drunk. She was so stupid to put herself in danger like that.

Isabel's tears dropped onto the newspaper, each one spreading until it became the size of a ten pence piece and blurred the black print. She'd read similar reactions to headlines in a dozen different papers over and over. Ingested the words strangers had given during supposed interviews. Evaluated, then internalised them. Taking today's paper in both hands, she tore a strip off, followed by another. Slowly at first, controlled. Then with her heart rate rising, she ripped the paper with increasing force, her breaths hard and fast – her cries coming in hiccupping waves.

What gave them the right to judge these women?

Why were *they* being blamed for what someone did *to* them?

Why weren't the accusatory headlines aimed at the rapist? Where was the outrage at how he'd been prowling the streets, hunting for vulnerable women in the early hours of the morning to target them? Attack them. She thought victim blaming was something that happened years ago, before her time. She refused to even log into any of her social media platforms – comments there would be worse. Unfiltered. Unmonitored. What kind of society *still* pushed the narrative towards females being the ones who should alter their behaviour and modify their actions.

Why hadn't he been found, arrested, and thrown in prison?

With the little energy she had left spent, Isabel collapsed onto the carpeted floor of her parents' lounge. If they could see her now, they'd assume she'd had a breakdown. And maybe she had. Her insides felt hollow after months of fighting to bring her attacker to justice had proven fruitless. He'd planned it all too carefully, and even if he had, by some miracle, slipped up – well, then he'd use his 'powerful connections' to erase any wrongdoing for him. His final words to her before he left her, naked and vulnerable, were that no one that *could* do anything *would*. By which he meant that anyone in the position to bring him to justice would be unable or unwilling to attempt it. No one of any benefit would believe her, and only those who were as weak and powerless as her would listen – and they were of no help.

There's nothing worse than a hysterical bunch of women who all crawl out of the woodwork ages after the fact. They've no integrity.

100

The continued victim blaming she witnessed regularly in the media was proof that if she even tried to tell her story to a journalist, it would backfire. Before all of this, Isabel believed society had made good progress where women's rights were concerned. Now, it seemed nothing much had changed. The same old narrative was being perpetuated, the same powerful and controlling men continued to get away with poor behaviour. What must the woman in today's headline be thinking, feeling?

Isabel wept as she traced a finger along the zigzag pattern – the carpet she remembered her mum buying despite her dad announcing it was hideous. 'You have to hope no one comes here after they've had a skinful – it's vomit-inducing.' Then he'd laughed as he added, 'Not that you'd notice puke on that abomination.'

They'd divorced the year after.

The carpet remained.

She rolled onto her back, staring at the ceiling while her thoughts scudded like storm clouds. This is what he wanted. What he expected. For her to lie down, play dead. Do nothing.

Isabel Booth was not giving up.

She shot up, her stomach muscles pinching from the sudden movement, and began rummaging in the desk. Her mum always kept a good stock of stationery in there, not willing to join the twenty-first century and use its technology, preferring the art of letter-writing instead. She took a pen and flowery piece of paper and made herself comfortable. For a few moments her mind was blank. Months of pushing the unwanted thoughts away; compartmentalising them, resulted in a fuzzy memory of the events. She relaxed her shoulders, imagined herself sitting in the bar that night after her shift had ended. Recalled the sense of hopelessness after Lola had dumped her. She watched herself order a vodka. Straight, no ice. Then another. The smell of it cloying in her nostrils as a few hours later she ejected the liquid mixed together with the remnants of the cheesy chips from lunch, in the women's loos.

Then, even later, *his* face. Kind. Smiling. Close to hers. Offering assistance.

The memories she'd suppressed since last year flooded back. She wrote with ferocity, the words scrawling across the page. A new piece of paper, then another. She stopped only to rub her cramped hand. The last time she'd written this much, rather than typed, was during her A levels. Her laptop was in her bag, but somehow she knew that putting pen to paper was better – it flowed from her mind to her hand like she was being used as a conduit – a medium, automatically writing what the spirit was telling her. Her memory finally freed.

The room darkened, and Isabel flicked the lamp on. Her eyes finally went out of focus as the old grandfather clock struck ten. She slumped back, and with a sense of accomplishment, looked at the pile of paper. He'd say it wasn't evidence. And on its own, it wasn't.

But it was a start.

And she'd place a bet that she wasn't his only victim. She'd find others and together, they'd be stronger.

Chapter 16

NOW

BECKY

I wake up on my stomach, fully clothed and sprawled across the bed on top of the duvet cover, a pin sticking into my face. With a quick tug, it pops out and I rub my cheek. There's a large spot of blood on the cover, which I swipe at for some reason, even though I know that's not going to remove it. My neck's stiff, my head fuzzy as though I'm suffering a hangover. Did I take the anxiety meds too close together? Checking my phone for the time, I realise two things: I must've only had around two hours' sleep – if you can call it that, and I've got five missed calls. All from Charlie.

That can't be good.

Then I remember I called him. Twice, in fact, so he'll only be trying to return them. I need a shower and a decent coffee before I respond. There's a lot to discuss.

Feeling more alive following the shower, I dress and head

out – I'll grab a coffee at the place I met Charlie in the other morning. Hovering outside my flat, I listen for noises from Vince and Tamsin's. I dare not show my face there since taking Agatha last night . . . and leaving Tamsin. It's on my to-do list, though, because I can't just leave things as they currently stand. I'll never forgive myself if harm comes to her when I know how bad things are. Even if she is claiming it's not Vince she's afraid of. In fact, that makes the situation worse, really because what the hell else is happening in her life if he's not the one she's scared of? I tilt my head up to check if I can see anything along the balcony. No movement. Trying not to think anything negative, I jam my hands in my coat pockets and walk away.

The real coffee aroma immediately calms me when I walk into Hamley's café and join the queue. My phone buzzes in my pocket. *Yeah, I know, hang on, Charlie*, I think. I'm surprised to experience a rush of endorphins as I spot Elijah coming to the counter and taking over from the female barista. I feel my cheeks stiffen with smiling – it seems a while since I had that sensation. My hand unconsciously moves to the pinprick hole in my face and I touch it. Suddenly self-conscious, I flick my hair out from behind my ear so that it partially covers that side. I almost give myself an eye roll in response. What am I doing? The guy's at least ten years younger than me, and that's being conservative.

'Hey, you,' Elijah says as I reach the till.

'All right?' I fuss about trying to find the loyalty card, painfully aware he's staring at me. The last time I was here I left after having an anxiety attack – is that why he's looking at me this way? 'Caramel latte, please,' I say, handing over my card for him to stamp.

'Sure.' He takes it and starts to make my drink. Another

customer comes in and stands next to me, much closer than is comfortable. Don't people have boundaries anymore? I really thought after the pandemic, when two metres was the stated distance we should keep from one another, that when in queues people would naturally keep a decent gap forever more, even after restrictions ended. Seems that isn't the case. I shoot a disgruntled look at them, and make a deal of stepping further away.

They get the message.

I hear a cough and look back at Elijah's smiling face. 'Sorry, having an issue with the caramel, if you take a seat, I'll bring it to you in a sec.'

I narrow my eyes at him. 'Really? Don't worry, then, I'll have—'

'No, no. It's fine. The customer gets what the customer orders,' he says, then shifts his attention to the person next to me.

I choose the same table Charlie and I were sitting at two days ago and get comfortable. I may as well use this time to call him. But before I can, my mobile begins vibrating again and I hit accept.

'Finally!' he says immediately.

'Oh, hi, Charlie. Sorry for not picking up before – it's been a mad night.'

'I thought you were dead,' he says, his tone abrupt. He isn't being his usual sarcastic, funny self, I realise. He sounds completely serious.

'Why would *that* be your first thought? It's only been a few—'

'Because, Becks, in your voicemail you thanked me for feeding the cat and painting your bloody door!'

'Yeeah, and I meant it – I'm really grateful.' My sleep-

105

deprived brain is slow to figure out what Charlie's problem is here.

'Only, I didn't.'

'Didn't what?' I gulp down the dread as the implication of his statement sinks in, but it's as though I need full clarification before I allow myself to panic.

'I didn't pick up your message until really late, was too knackered to do it. It wasn't me, Becks. So who *was* in your flat?'

All saliva evaporates from my mouth; my throat tightens – no words can make it through.

'Here you go.' A large latte lands in front of me and I look up into Elijah's eyes, trying to say thank you. The garbled noise that comes out instead causes his eyes to widen. 'Oh, God. Are you okay?' He pulls out the chair beside me and sits, legs wide as he lowers himself to my level. 'Take a breath in through your nose,' he says, calmly. 'And blow it out slowly.' Even though I want the ground to open up and am embarrassed beyond belief, I do the breathing until I regain composure. Thankfully, it was a mild attack. This time. Elijah smiles, but jumps up, excusing himself as he has to get back to customers. I reach into my pocket for my anxiety meds.

Then I remember I've left Charlie hanging and I quickly pick up the phone.

'Your boyfriend did a good job,' he says.

I take a few sips of the latte to lubricate my larynx before swallowing a tablet and responding with a, 'Ha. Ha.' Then I look down to see that Elijah has left my loyalty card on the table. Stamped twice. 'Oh,' I say, turning around to catch Elijah's attention.

'What's the matter now?' Charlie asks in my ear.

'I haven't paid for my drink.'

'Freebies now, eh?'

Elijah slips behind the counter and out of my eyeline; I'll pay in a second. I focus back in on my conversation.

'It's nothing like that, Charlie.'

'Yeah . . . okay. Anyway, not to set you back into a panic, but speaking of your mystery knight in shining armour, could it be your new barista friend?'

'Well, he's never been to my place if that's what you're getting at.'

'I'm not judging, Becks.'

'I don't care what you think anyway. I'm just saying it wouldn't have been him. Are you sure you didn't ask Hannah to do it? I'll message her and check.'

'Don't waste your time. As I said, I didn't even get your voicemail until late, didn't get the chance to pass the buck. And anyway, Hannah was working a case last night – on what ended up being a homicide, actually. It couldn't have been her. Are you sure the cat had been fed? You're not jumping to the wrong conclusion?'

Charlie's questions throw me, and I mentally backtrack – I got home, saw the new paint job on the front door, went in and called for Agatha. She didn't come to me. I went into the kitchen, saw the empty plate, then checked the cupboard.

'Yes,' I say, having replayed my entrance into the flat. 'A tin of tuna was missing . . . as was Agatha!'

'Could you have miscounted the tins you had? Were any windows open that Agatha could've escaped from? Was she even in the flat when you left? She might've bolted out the door when you did?'

My mind scrambles and I begin to doubt myself as he bombards me with questions. So, this is how it feels to be

107

interrogated – and it's not even face to face. I drink some more of my latte, noting the tremble of my hand. This is also the type of thing John used to do. Confuse me by talking at me, not allowing me a word in edgeways, telling me I was wrong, that I must be mistaken. Like the time I couldn't find my phone and feared it'd been stolen. I'd looked for over an hour before he handed it to me, with what I thought at the time was concern plastered on his face. 'Found it in the fridge, babe. Are you OK? You've been very stressed lately,' he'd said. I'd been almost certain I did not put my mobile in the fridge, but the doubt had been planted. I disregarded the nagging suspicion that John had purposely hidden it. As I disregarded a number of other, more worrying things. I've become more attuned to gaslighting. Although, right now, I know that's not what Charlie's doing – he's merely attempting to work through the facts and his questions are all perfectly reasonable. Maybe he's right.

Did I know how many tins there were? *Had* I inadvertently let Agatha escape when I left early yesterday morning? I screw my eyes up, take a deep breath before changing the subject.

'I met John's new girlfriend.' I get the words out quickly, before I bottle it.

'What do you mean you met her?'

I can envisage Charlie's stunned face. 'It wasn't intentional,' I say, defensively. 'I stopped at a roadside café on the outskirts of Lymworth and she happened to be working there.'

'Jeeesus – what were you doing there? I thought you were at some interview thing?'

'I didn't want to worry you. I needed to see where John lived. Wanted a glimpse of her. I didn't realise it was Nina

108

to start with.'

'First name basis.' I hear the exasperation in his voice.

'But then I saw her walking towards John's address, with the kid.'

'So, *that's* where you stayed the night? Without telling anyone where you were? Not only that, but you decided to feed me some bullshit about an assessment centre somewhere totally different?'

'Yeah, sorry. I wanted to keep it low-key—'

'Don't ever lie to me again, Becks. Understand? Especially not when you're asking for my help. That's not on.'

'I know. Again, sorry. But, I called you last night, so you know I didn't stay in the end. I was asked to leave.' There's an intake of breath on the end of the line as Charlie takes this in.

'How come?' The lilt of his voice hints that he's cautiously curious yet dreading my answer.

'That's the thing, it was weird. A woman at the pub said the room was free, but then a man knocked on the door a little while later and claimed the room had been double-booked, but his body language was off. He seemed like he was lying.'

'Great. I guess that means John knew you were there and fed the bloke some story to get rid of you.'

I want to retort by saying now he was the one jumping to conclusions, but that won't serve my purpose. 'That was my first thought, too,' I say. Then carefully consider if I should let on that I spotted John in the pub afterwards. I'm about to tell him, but Charlie speaks first.

'Right. What's your next move, then?' he says.

'Um . . . I don't really have one yet.' Which isn't entirely a lie as I've only got a few ideas of where to go from here.

'When you do know, make sure to tell me this time, mate? I don't want to read about you in a bulletin.'

My ear is hot when I hang up. I finish up my latte, take my loyalty card and stand by the counter. Elijah isn't serving. There are two different baristas there now: one taking orders, one making the drinks. How long had I been talking to Charlie? I raise my hand like I'm back at school and manage to make eye contact with the woman preparing drinks.

'Is Elijah still here?' The noise of the frothing and steaming drowns out my question. I wait patiently for it to stop and then ask again.

'He's finished,' she says, before placing another cup beneath the steaming wand. I tilt my chin up in thanks. I rummage in my pocket, find a pound coin, pop it in the tip jar and leave. The two times I've met Elijah I've had inconvenient stress-induced episodes and he's pitied me by giving me free coffee. What must he think of me?

Chapter 17

NOW

BECKY

Dark clouds converge, casting large shadows on the ground as I walk back to the flat after trudging around town to kill time. I pick up my speed as a gust of wind whips my hair and I feel the first drops of rain spatter my face. I still stand and stare at the front door for several minutes, though, properly taking in how it looks; I'd been too distracted first thing. It's clear now, under the scrutiny of daylight, how rough the paint job is. The colour isn't matched, it's a paler green, which leads me to think it can't have been the landlord as he'd have known the paint shade, maybe even had some left over from the original work. It's also quite messy, as though someone only half-heartedly did it in a rush: anything to cover up 'slag' as quickly as possible. Vince? I don't *know* him – although I've already made my mind up about him – but who's to say whether he has a conscience. After he daubed it in the first place, maybe in anger, perhaps he felt bad. No, anyone who beats their girlfriend definitely does not have a conscience.

Charlie's worried admission that *he* wasn't the one to paint the door or feed Agatha niggles me as soon as I step over the threshold and a shiver runs down my back. Shaking it off, I go straight to the bedroom, grab a pen and some index cards and stand in front of my investigation board, tapping the pen against my chin as I try to put some of the things together and figure out my next move. As I said to Charlie, Nina is my key person of interest right now – she's the one with up-to-date knowledge of what John is doing. I write her name on the card and pin it close to John's picture. I need to search reports of sexual assault and rape that have occurred over the past year or so in and around the Lymworth area. Then see if Charlie – and Hannah if I can convince her – will be able to check if John was on duty, where and with whom, on the dates of the incidents. I'm not sure when John shacked up with Nina, or when he moved divisions, so the exact dates would be good to know. Although, as he's not relocated a great distance away, the parameters aren't necessarily a key factor. Given John's knowledge of policing, he's maybe going further afield to carry out his attacks to limit the risks of being caught. Or, he's being particularly ballsy, believing himself to be untouchable, as the messages between him and the unknown victim allude to. Hidden in plain sight. When I think about our relationship at the start, how wonderful I perceived it to be, how John appeared so loving and caring – right up until the night he was caught out – I realise how clever he'd been. How controlled.

My stomach twists, like a hand is inside of me scrunching it up as I would to an empty crisp packet. Gaining solid

112

evidence is going to be a challenge. If I thought it was hard before, when I was in the best position to investigate, then I'm facing an uphill battle now I have fewer resources.

Agatha brushes up against my legs and mews, letting me know she wants attention. I've been in here neglecting her for hours. I bend to stroke her.

'Hello, my little one.' I catch myself – she's not mine. She's Tamsin's. I'm merely safeguarding her; I must remember that. Poor Tamsin, Agatha – or should I say Punch – was her only companion. How must she be feeling without her? It's been quiet upstairs since my last visit, or at least it has been while I've been at home. I need to go and check up on her, without making a big deal of it – I don't want to gain the wrath of Vince. For either of our sakes.

A rap on the front door shocks me from my thoughts. I quickly grab Agatha, holding her tight to my chest. The sudden thought it's Vince coming to collect her makes my skin tingle. He wouldn't though, surely? Hopefully if he's even bothered to ask Tamsin where his 'Punch' is, she's told him the cat ran off after he hurt it. My blood boils at the very fact he named a cat Punch – I wish someone would give him a good hammering. I know that's not how justice works . . . but sometimes . . .

I relax as I peep out the window and see Hannah standing there.

'Don't you ever work these days?' I ask once she's inside.

'This is work,' she says.

My pulse picks up. Is this an official visit where she informs me John's made a complaint against me for harassment or something?

'Should I get my bag and join you at the station?' My attempt at making that sentence sound like a joke fails as I

113

catch the shake in my voice. But Hannah rolls her eyes.

'Loosely speaking, it's work *related*.'

'Ah. Right. Phew. You had me worried for a minute.' I take a seat on the armchair, while Hannah sits stiffly on the futon. If her visit isn't in an official capacity and it's not serious, I wish she'd loosen up a bit.

'I'm well aware I've had a part to play in your actions,' Hannah says. 'I'm sorry. I was wrong – I let my personal feelings cloud my judgement there for a second.'

'Not like you.' I laugh. She doesn't crack a smile. I get the feeling Charlie and her have spoken, and now realise I'm in my planning mode again. Obviously my nonchalant comment about not knowing my next move didn't fully convince Charlie. They are concerned for me.

'We've come to the conclusion you're likely going to do this with or without us,' Hannah says, shaking her head. 'So Charlie and I agreed that together we'll use the resources we're able to without getting ourselves fired, to help you—'

'That's great, thank you.'

'On the condition you keep us in the loop, Becky – we have to put your safety at the top of the priority list—'

'Potential victims need to be at the top of that list, not me. I can look after myself. I know what I'm getting into. I doubt his victims do.'

'Okay. I know you felt sure the evidence you found on the destroyed burner wasn't likely the first, or last time John has abused his position. But have you managed to find anything concrete since?'

My shoulders slump hearing these words. It's like the same old response as before. *Where is the evidence?*

'Not as such, no. Nina is my way in, though, I'm sure of it. You know I was *evicted* from the pub? I think it

114

was because Nina saw me at the café then in her street—'
Hannah lets out a loud sigh, which I ignore and continue.
'I reckon she told John, who put two and two together and
made sure the landlord had me thrown out – giving some
jumped-up excuse about double-booking, but I know John
has to be behind it. He doesn't want me around and we
know that's because he's still up to no good.'

Hannah, her doe-brown eyes trained on mine, cogitates
silently until I can no longer bear the cessation of speech.

'I haven't got much in the way of alcohol and snacks,' I
say, my eyebrows raised as I anticipate Hannah's response
to my next question. 'But do you fancy staying for a bit? I
could do with some human company for the evening.'

I almost keel over when she shrugs and says, 'Why not,'
and she finally relaxes back into the futon.

'Great. Thanks, Hannah.' After the discussion we've had,
I'm thrown by the ease at which she agreed. 'In that case, I
can offer you a premixed gin and tonic, or . . .' I take a few
steps to the kitchen and duck down into the fridge. 'Ooh,'
I say, pulling out the bottle of wine she'd bought me as a
flat-warming gift, 'there's this!' I smile, holding out the five-
month-old wine.

'Wow. I'm surprised that lasted. But I'll just have the can
please. I've driven, don't forget.'

'Sure.' The bottle isn't exactly ice-cold to the touch. The
fridge, like everything else here, is a bit iffy. 'I'll put it in the
freezer for a bit,' I say. I remove the sad and lonely packet of
frozen peas from the small compartment and replace them
with the bottle and can.

While we wait, we talk about anything other than John.
And for a few blissful moments, I actually forget about the
situation and enjoy a normal conversation. We discuss the

115

latest true crime documentary that's just landed on Netflix, the state of the government and social care, the never-ending issues with drug-related crime, and, once we've started drinking and exhausted the negative side of life, we talk about music, her family and how she's looking forward to a get-together with her brother and dad at his nursing home. Her face darkens for a moment, and she crushes her empty can in one hand while looking distant. I'm about to ask her if there's something wrong, but she recovers and carries on talking.

'I'd better get going,' Hannah says, checking her phone. 'It's gone eleven thirty.'

'Do you change into a pumpkin after midnight?' I giggle, but I'm aware my words are slurring. I haven't had alcohol for a long time and I've all but finished off the bottle. Coupled with me starting the anxiety meds again, its effects are probably more potent.

'It's the carriage that does that,' Hannah says, correcting me.

'Oh, yeah.' I wave my hand. 'I always mix up sayings. Could do with a fairy godmother though.'

'Yes. Someone to wave a magical wand and transform everything into something far better than reality.'

'If only, eh?'

'Sadly, life's not a fairy tale for most of us.' She gives me a hug. Tighter than she's ever done before. 'Please be careful.'

'I'll try my level best. I really am grateful to you and Charlie for having my back. Even if it took a while. I can rest a little easier knowing you're both searching for evidence from the inside.'

I lock the door as soon as Hannah's left, pushing aside a pang of loneliness. For the most part, I'm fine living alone –

116

but I wouldn't want it forever. I miss human company; the knowledge that even if someone isn't always here, they will come home to me.

The light is so dim in the kitchen I feel as though I'm in a seedy sex club as I stand, swaying slightly, washing my wine glass. I focus on how it's been a positive evening, with real progress made – and I feel buoyed by it. Or, maybe that's the wine. I smile, placing the glass upside down on the drainer and turn to check where Agatha is. I keep forgetting about not keeping the front door open for long, in case she makes a dart for it and goes back up to Vince's flat. I'd hope she wouldn't want to return to her abuser's place, but, well . . .

There's a tapping noise, rhythmic, and for a moment I can't figure out where it's coming from. I lurch forwards to check behind the stack of boxes, in case it's Agatha playing with a mouse, or spider. God, I hope it's not. I can't be chasing creatures around the flat tonight, I just want to climb into bed and allow the effects of the alcohol to carry me off into a dreamless slumber. The tapping becomes more urgent, and I realise it's the front door. It's almost midnight. The words 'don't open the bloody door' scream inside my head.

Then I hear the squeak of the letterbox as it's lifted.

Chapter 18

NOW

BECKY

Adrenaline surges through my veins, the drink-blurred edges of my mind suddenly sharpening as all the toxins seem to leave my body. I peer out the window; there's not enough light outside to decipher the shadowy form, but they appear to be crouching. I half expect a firebomb to drop to the mat. On high alert now, I rush back into the kitchen and fill the kettle with cold water just in case, then creep towards the door, watching the letterbox intently. If I'm lucky, it'll just be a pile of dog shit. If a hand pushes through, I'll bash it with the kettle. I move closer, raising the kettle ready to smash it down.

'Hello?' A whispered voice filters through the rectangular gap. My heartbeat is whooshing so loudly in my ears, I don't immediately know if it's a male or female voice. 'Can I come in?'

The fairy tale about the wolf and the three pigs springs

to my mind . . . *please let me in, or I'll huff and I'll puff.*

'Tamsin?'

The kettle, held up using both hands, becomes too heavy and I lower it to the floor, relief of not having to make use of it as a weapon, or as a means of extinguishing a fire, so great that all strength seeps from my muscles.

I open the door to find Tamsin, dressed in the same shirt she was in before, her arms wrapped around her middle and her face streaked with old tears.

'Thanks,' she says, stepping over the threshold. I poke my head outside, check around to make sure Vince isn't trailing behind her, then close and lock the door.

'I'm really glad you felt able to come here. Go on in.' I indicate towards the lounge – a mere three steps from where we're standing.

Tamsin studies me cautiously, and with an uncomfortable sensation running through my body putting me on edge, I break eye contact. She's the one who came here, I didn't ask her to. Why is she wary of me? More to the point, why am I feeling awkward? I wait for her to walk into the lounge, then offer her a drink. She declines with a shake of her head. Still standing, she slowly looks around the room, then through to the kitchen. It's the same layout as Vince's flat, so I'm not sure what she's expecting to see.

'Looks nice,' she says, returning her gaze to me. She opens her mouth again, but doesn't add anything else.

'You can sit down,' I say. My thought process begins to speed up – now I have the opportunity, how am I going to help her? What if I make everything worse? Is she even here because she wants help? I sit, hoping she follows suit.

'No. I'm good.'

'Um . . . Tamsin, sweetheart,' I begin, without knowing

how I'm going to broach the subject of whatever trouble she's in, because obviously something untoward is happening to her. 'Did you want to talk to me about—'

'It's my fault.' Her eyes, large and glaring, fill with tears and I want nothing more than to stand up, and go and hug her, tell her everything will be okay. But I just swallow down my emotion and let her tell me what's on her mind.

'I took the cat. It's my fault he's dead.'

Ah. That explains her furtive glances around my flat. She was looking for evidence of Agatha. 'He is definitely a she, and she's fine. The vet sorted everything out.'

The look of relief on her pale face tugs at my heart. I should've got a message to her, let her know Agatha made it. Poor thing has clearly been guilt-ridden since.

'Where is he? She . . .'

'Probably hiding in my bedroom, you're the second visitor this evening and she's a bit jumpy.' I smart at my wording. Like the cat's mine and I know more about her than Tamsin does. Or that it's Tamsin's fault she's timid. 'I'll get her.' I stand, make a move towards my bedroom. Then I turn back, a sudden thought coming to me.

'How did you take her? I thought I left her inside here?'

'Sorry – I snuck out when Vince was at the shop, came down here to have a nose around. I saw you come out, hid around the corner, watched you turn to lock up, then Punch came shooting out. You didn't seem to notice him run towards me. I took him back. I thought . . . well, I needed him, you see? He was mine. Clearly, it was the wrong decision . . .' Her head drops.

'I've been calling her Agatha,' I say. 'But she is yours. Maybe I'll just look after her until you're in a better position?'

Tamsin's eyes screw up tightly. 'Sure,' she says, her voice

120

weak. Her entire body looks as though it will fold in on itself. Disappear from my view. Like she's been doing it her whole life and can shrink out of sight on command. My heart feels like it's being crushed.

'No. Really. I'll consider her on loan until then.' I desperately want to reach out to her, take her in my arms and make a promise that everything will be okay.

'Did you see anyone else near my flat?' I ask, realising she may have witnessed who painted the door. She frowns. 'Did Vince paint over the graffiti?'

She shrugs. 'What graffiti?'

'Didn't you see it on the door?'

'No. But I was focused on the cat, really.'

'Well, after I came up to your flat that first day and had . . . well . . . that *altercation* with Vince, I think he painted "slag" on my front door. But when I returned the other night, it'd been covered, but I don't know who by.'

'Doubt he would've been so subtle,' she says, a haunted look crossing her face. I see so many young victims in her – ones I failed: the teenager terrified of her father's aggression who ended up sleeping rough on the street because no one did anything; the girl who was being abused but keeping it quiet, her baby also a victim, a case where I missed the signs, and many more like those. If there is a way to somehow undo the resulting damage by 'saving' someone else, then I have to try.

And there I was thinking John was the only one who could play saviour.

'Does he hit you?' I ask, softly.

'When we argue sometimes, things get out of control.'

'I'm sorry.'

'It's fine.'

'It's not fine, Tamsin.'

121

'Mostly it's my fault. He's protecting me.'

I need to tread carefully here. I don't know the full facts. But waiting to intervene could spell disaster.

'If a man tells you they're protecting you by hurting you, then I'd hazard a guess they're only doing it for their own end goal.'

'I can't leave.'

Tears burn my eyes as I watch Tamsin's spill down her cheeks, and acid burns my stomach as hatred fills it.

'I had a rough time with my ex, too,' I say.

I tell Tamsin snippets about my life with John – mainly in the hope that some of it resonates enough and she'll feel more able to trust me and share what's going on with Vince, or more to the point, the other person she said she was scared of.

After a few quiet moments, I begin to wonder who could've covered the graffiti. Even though John likely knew I was at the pub that evening, had maybe overheard me leaving a message for Charlie, he wouldn't have had the time to take it upon himself to paint the door then get back to the pub where I saw him with my own eyes. But he could've sent someone else to do it.

Mind games. His favourite.

'Tamsin – have you seen anyone suspicious hanging around the flats at all?'

'I barely go outside. The other day was the first time in ages.'

'It was a long shot.' I'm not going to get to the bottom of the mystery painter anytime soon. 'I just have this odd feeling my ex is playing games with me.'

'What does he look like?'

'I've got a photo, actually. Hang on.' I go into the

bedroom, approach the wall to unpin John's photograph. 'Were you behind it?' I whisper as I stare into the eyes I once loved. I turn and gasp at a shadow in the doorway. 'Shit, you gave me a fright,' I say to Tamsin as she steps inside my room. But she's looking past me, her eyes scanning the breadth of my wall, her mouth slightly open. 'Oh.' I turn around. 'Yeah, I know how this must seem, but—'

'Were you spying on me?' She shoots me a sharp glance that makes me shiver.

'No. No . . . of course . . . No. I'm not,' I stammer, unsure of what's going on. How has she looked at the wall and come to that conclusion? 'This is my ex-husband, John,' I say, passing her the photo. For a long moment, Tamsin stares down at it, and my heart is in my mouth, waiting for her to say something like: 'He raped me.' She gives it back.

'As I said, I don't go out much anymore. Don't think I've met him.' Then she steps closer to the wall. 'But I've seen him.'

I'm curious, yet dubious when she points to another image – a cut-out from a newspaper article, showing an ex-cop-turned-gun-runner being arrested by Charlie three years ago.

'Oh? Where?'

'Here.' Her lips curl as she jabs a finger at the image of the club next to it. A link I was never sure of, but kept it on my radar.

'Did you work at Moods?'

Her eyes fill with tears and she nods.

The club has a terrible reputation – but no official reports have ever been made against the owners. Tamsin's fears may well stem from trauma she experienced there.

123

'Did something happen to you?'

'Not me. Not directly. My friend also worked there.'

'What happened to her?'

'She committed suicide last year.'

'Oh, God. That's awful – I'm sorry.'

'Someone – a woman – came to the club looking for Fran but her questions seemed to spark a chain reaction – starting with the boss, and because Fran wasn't around, she spoke with me. I didn't say anything, but the boss assumed I did.'

'Say anything about what?'

'Something bad happened, before Fran – you know – topped herself.'

'You mean bad enough that it was the reason she took her life?'

'Yeah.'

'What was her full name?'

'Francesca Withers. Before she died, she warned me about . . . ' Tamsin looks around, as though she's expecting someone to be behind her.

'It's okay. You can trust me, Tamsin.'

She huffs. 'I don't trust no one anymore. The whole system's fucked. They only protect themselves.'

'Who?'

'The fucking feds.'

'You're saying that Fran warned you about the police? In what way?'

'She was raped. Then she was threatened. She lost her kid and everything.'

Chapter 19

NOW

BECKY

Armed with what I believe to be new, although as yet anecdotal, information gives me a sense of determination and I've decided to go back to Lymworth today. While Tamsin hasn't supplied solid evidence, she has provided a massive link and enough to enable me to investigate further. I have a name, Francesca Withers, to pass on to Charlie and Hannah. I texted them both as soon as Tamsin snuck back to her flat after dropping the unexpected bombshell that she'd worked at one of the places of interest I'd come across during last year's Operation Lawless investigation.

I can't finish my breakfast, and it's not just because the cereal is stale. I pour the uneaten mush into the food bin and pick up Agatha's plate, popping it into the sink. A food shop is a necessity; I can't let myself become too side-tracked today and forget again. I sit in the lounge and pull on my boots, then, for the umpteenth time I check my mobile to see if either Charlie or Hannah has responded to my rather vague text asking them to call me. I hadn't wanted to chance texting the name in case someone saw it.

No missed calls, no texts.

With too much adrenaline rushing through my veins to sit still, I grab a few items, check that Agatha is safely inside, then leave the flat. As has become habit over the last few days, I look up to Tamsin's flat before walking away. The external corridor running along the front of the building means it's impossible to see much, but it makes me feel better somehow. The snatched time I had with her last night was valuable on a number of levels. I must keep in mind that she needs help, too. I don't know yet who was asking the questions at the club and what part they have to play in all of this. There was also no time to get to the bottom of just who it is that Tamsin fears the most. I get the feeling it's not the club boss – but maybe one of his heavies?

And while Tamsin didn't recognise the photo of John – I know he's involved somehow. The weighted feeling dragging in the pit of my stomach makes me think it was him who raped Tamsin's colleague.

The drive to Lymworth is fraught – not only due to the stop-start traffic jams going out of Manchester, but with images of the first night I challenged John: his angry and panicked face, the burner phone, the screenshot, and his foot stamping onto the phone and breaking it, all flashing through my mind. Timing wise, it would fit with when Tamsin said Fran took her own life. Was the message on John's burner sent by her moments before she died as her final act of defiance? I wonder just how many other women John has targeted in this way. If Nina doesn't already suspect she's living with a monster, I have to warn her.

Once the traffic breaks, and the dull, concrete landscape changes to green fields, I'm able to relax a little. With the window dropped, I breathe in the cool, fresh air. This is the closest to being home in Cornwall with its rolling hills and green space. It's just missing the sea and the smell of fish. But it's not long before the feeling of freedom begins to lessen, and a knot grows in my stomach. I'm going back into the thick of a tightknit village where everyone seems to know each other. Where it's harder to hide.

That works both ways, though.

I reach for my water bottle, sip some water to lubricate my dry mouth.

I head straight for the Café Shack in the hope Nina is working there today. I park to the side, so my vehicle isn't visible from the café windows and watch the door, my eyes wide and unblinking, my hands wringing on my lap. Coming here again is a huge risk for me. But not coming here would be an even bigger risk for Nina and any other female John has set his sights on. I need to – *have* to – do this. I've waited long enough and I can't wait anymore.

Time slows – almost seeming to stop entirely as I wait, my breathing shallow. Two customers exit, causing my heartbeat to skip before returning to the tachycardic rhythm it's been in since pulling up here. Just as I think maybe she's not working today, the door swings open and Nina appears, a hand dipping into her pinny pocket and bringing out a packet. She leans against the side of the shack, as she did the first time I saw her, and poised with a cigarette in hand, looks across and catches my gaze. The colour drains from her face and she pushes off from the wall. *Shit*. She's going to bolt back inside.

I leap from the car, calling her name, then run towards her.

'Nina! Can you wait, please?'

She stops, her back facing me, and I note the way her head drops. She's in two minds. She wants to avoid me, yet at the same time I sense she's desperate to know what I'm going to say, too. I've got one chance to get this right.

'Thanks,' I say as I reach her. 'I'm aware this must be a bit awkward for you.'

Nina turns slowly. 'I haven't got time for your nonsense.'

The difference between our first meeting here and this one – her attitude towards me, the way she's glaring at me – is stark, and confirms my suspicions that not only does she know who I am, but that John's fed her the narrative he wants her to believe, and that means she's unlikely to take any of what I have to say in, let alone consider it.

'Shall we start again,' I say, smiling. 'I'm Becky.' I hold out my hand to shake hers. Nina takes a step away.

'Yeah. I know who you are now. Why are you here again?'

'To put my side across. I imagine what you've been told isn't entirely built on facts.' I raise my eyebrows, waiting for her to respond. Her chest heaves with a huge intake of air, then she crosses her arms and looks off in the distance. I keep going, afraid to stop in case she loses interest. 'I'm unsure what you know, about his past – our past – but I'd really like to be able to chat with you about it. He doesn't have to find out we've spoken. I could arrange to meet you somewhere neutral.'

Nina's breath judders, then she snaps her attention back on me. Eyes blazing, she shoves her face close to mine. I unavoidably blink, half expecting her to head-butt me.

'John said you were a conniving bitch,' she says, her voice low. Something in me breaks. Of *course* I knew he'd have manipulated Nina in the time he's been with her. How he will have spun his story like an intricate spider's web so that he came out looking like the victim: the fly caught by the black widow's trap. To Nina, I'm the one who's in the wrong, probably falsely accused him of something and made his life hell.

I wish she could see right now how far from the truth any of that is. One meeting like this with her isn't even going to scratch the surface. It'll take far more to undo what lies John's fed her.

'Yeah, I get what you must think of me. You've only heard John's version, though—'

'And that's all I need. It took a lot for John to open up about what you did, how you belittled him, made him feel worthless.'

My mind freefalls for a second. 'Nina, no – that's not . . . Christ, I wasn't the one—'

'Do me a favour. He's told me all about your obsession and toxic vendetta. Look, I understand you must be angry at him for leaving you, but don't waste your time trying to split us up. We're rock solid.' She turns to go back inside the café.

My heart's beating out of my chest as I follow, battling the urge to grab her arm, pull her back to face me so I can scream at her that it's all rubbish – and that he didn't leave me, I threw him out. But all the old feelings of helplessness crowd in, the awful sense of despair and panic consuming me, squeezing the air from my lungs. If I'm not careful, I'll play right into John's hands and come across like the 'mad, mental, psycho ex' he's told her about. My hope that she'd at least listen to my side, even if only out of curiosity, is dashed. Acid rises into my mouth; I swallow it down along with my anger with John, and take a steadying breath. 'What exactly did he tell you, Nina?' I ask, slowly.

She turns sharply, her face set. 'I'm not talking to my boyfriend's stalker. You ruined his life. Now do one.' She pushes me so hard I stumble backwards but manage to keep on my feet. I watch, dumbstruck, as she strides away and goes into the café, not once looking back.

With little of the energy I had first thing remaining, I slouch back to my car. He's done a good job on her. Is she me, five years ago? Had someone come to me in similar circumstances when I first met John – would I have also responded in that way? I have to admit I probably would have. I was deep under his spell within weeks of meeting him. Was flattered by his compliments and near-constant texts and calls. Felt as though I was the only person for him when he declared I was his soul mate and that he needed me in his life. Felt warm and safe when he told me he loved me and wanted to marry me during our second official date. As far as I was concerned, I knew him better than anyone else; believed he was kind, caring, loyal – all the traits you dream of in a partner. How could you possibly think badly of someone so normal? I shudder now, thinking about it. How it was only after finding the phone that I acknowledged our relationship hadn't been a healthy one. When I finally recognised all of those traits as a sign of love bombing – a form of manipulation and emotional abuse.

'Damn him!' I slam my hands on the steering wheel as a wave of anger ripples through me. I allow it to ebb away, but a lingering sense of despair crouches in my stomach. It's going to take a lot more work if I'm to convince Nina of

John's guilt. I have to find out who Fran was, because if she was the woman who sent that screenshot to John's burner, that would be the biggest link to date. And if she had the foresight to send it, maybe she had other evidence about her abuser too. The thought she couldn't gain justice and felt her only way out was suicide is horrific. If I can do it for her, then something good will have come from her death.

If there's one victim of John's who has evidence, maybe there are more. My insides give a sudden jitter. With what Nina just said, I can be sure that John will do everything he can to stop me from finding any proof.

Chapter 20

ISABEL

Isabel was stone-still; only her eyes moved while she observed the car pull into the supermarket car park and slowly manoeuvre into the bay next to her red Fiat. She'd arranged to meet in a public place for a few reasons – one being safety. Over the past year she'd learned the hard way that her attacker had a number of people who were only too keen to extinguish any allegations of wrongdoing before any such reports could make their way to the police, or, as was increasingly the case – before the media got hold of information and ran an exposé piece.

Isabel waited, hardly daring to breathe, as the woman – a new contact she hoped would lend her story to the growing list of victims who'd fallen foul of the serving detective's cold, manipulative and controlling behaviour – killed the engine. Isabel's skin prickled with anticipation. She had to be sure this one, who'd she'd only spoken with over the phone, was genuine and not another corrupt officer, before breaking cover. From the corner of her eye she saw movement – a

132

waving of an arm – and she turned her head. The woman, young-looking, petite with light-coloured hair pulled back in a ponytail from what Isabel could make out, also had the kind of haunted look about her that she recognised. The mask of abuse.

The last woman she'd tried to speak with had later been targeted and the result had been catastrophic. Isabel couldn't let that happen again – it was a fine line, a balancing trick, to make sure she gained the attention of real victims of rape and sexual assault at the hands of John Lawson and not those put up to answering her online post who were ultimately attempting to cover it all up.

Chapter 21

NOW

BECKY

Although I wasn't expecting a miracle, I had hoped for a better reception from Nina. Coming here again with nothing to show was a mistake. My muscles, rigid with tension moments ago, loosen and my entire body slumps forwards. My head bangs against the steering wheel and I groan as a throbbing ache begins pounding my forehead. What a waste of time. All I've achieved is a stress headache.

Marcus said, during one of the many one-to-one chats he had with me after I reported John, that I took everyone's pain on board – via a process of osmosis or some such waffle. I dismissed his analogy, but now I think about it, he could be right. Maybe I've always done it. The crunch of gravel beside me goes almost unnoticed as snippets of childhood memories flit through my mind – like the times I cried for hours over injured birds; as a teenager when I sat up all night with friends who'd been dumped by their boyfriends, spending days afterwards feeling so sad I couldn't eat – a rush of long-forgotten memories now playing out like a montage of my life so far, akin to those I've seen played at funerals. Although, in those, it's the happy times on display. I have taken on others' grief, pain and discomfort as though they're mine to carry.

I sit upright and grip the wheel with both hands. 'Which is why I'm the one who has to do this!' I say, giving it a frustrated jolt.

A knock on the passenger-side window makes me start, and I snap my head around to see who it is, my heart clambering to get out of my chest. I've been sitting here, drawing attention for too long.

'You all right?'

I give a wary smile to the stranger staring through the window. He's got a beanie hat pulled down, so his eyes are obscured. With a sense of revulsion, I notice it's similar to one John used to wear on our walks through the woods on our days off. 'Yeah. Thanks.' I give a thumbs up, then without hanging around any further, start the car. I'm going to have to go back to Salford no better off than when I left. Another knock, harder, louder, stops me.

'You shouldn't be here,' he says, his face pressed up against the glass. Fear cuts through me like a knife through butter, and a shiver tracks down my back causing me to gasp. I turn away from him, whack the car into reverse, gravel spitting up either side of my car and hitting the metal. Pops, like gunfire, fill my ears as I fling the wheel around and speed out of the café exit back onto the main road.

With my nerves shot, my breathing shallow, I attempt to shake off the encounter. If I'd been anywhere else, I might've assumed the stranger simply meant that I can't stay parked there. That it was a friendly suggestion. Am I overreacting?

My mobile rings – the display on the dash of the car shows a withheld number and my instinct tells me to hit decline. I accept it, anger bubbling in my gut because I know the voice I'm going to hear before a word is spoken.

'Think you're clever, do you?' I yell.

'You were warned, Rebecca. Tut, tut.' I'm taken aback a bit because it's *not* the same tone of voice as the first call I received when I was at the drive-thru. As before, though, it'll be a voice-changing device, or maybe an AI. The origin will still be the same. John is behind it.

'To make it a level playing field, tell me who this is.'

'Doesn't matter who I am. Just do as I say.'

'Oh, right – so this is a game of Simon Says?'

'If you like. Simon says go home.'

'And if I don't play?'

'Oh, you don't want to know the consequences, Rebecca.'

My skin crawls hearing them say Rebecca – the smooth tone with an elongated second syllable, its sound as spine-chilling as the way I remember Hannibal Lecter saying the name Clarice in the film *The Silence of the Lambs*. Everyone knows me as Becky. My parents used my full name – they always said, 'You were christened Rebecca, that's the name we chose for you. If we wanted to call you Becky, that would be the name on your birth certificate.' If this is John, maybe he's trying to unsettle me.

'Threats are just that. You can't control me.'

'Stay away from Nina.'

'I'm not making any promises.' I lean forward to cut the call, but just before I manage it, the voice says:

'Tamsin's about to get a visitor.'

My blood immediately chills in my veins, but my mind stutters. What the hell? I stare at the display – I've terminated the call, there's no way of gaining clarification now.

Did I mishear?

It sounded like he was implying that because I didn't cow down to his demand, that something was going to happen to Tamsin.

Who *is* this person making threats?

I don't have time to figure out what it all means, and whether it was an empty threat; I can't afford to take any chances. Now is the time I wish I had a siren attached to my car. With the accelerator pedal pressed hard to the floor, I set off back to Salford.

Chapter 22

THEN

<u>Voice recording of phone conversation</u>
    'Oh, Francesca . . . You'd forgotten, hadn't you?'
    'No. No – I was given the wrong date . . .'
    'I understand you wanting to deny it was your fault. Of *course* you'd want to. It would be awful to have to admit to such a *faux pas* – what a terrible mother you'd appear to social services otherwise.'
    'You said you'd help.'
    'Please don't twist this around. I did everything I said I would.'
    'You did exactly what *you* wanted. Got what *you* needed. You let us down.'
    'You did that the day you put your needs before those of your own flesh and blood.'
    'It was all a lie, wasn't it? You used me from the moment you stopped me on the road that night.'
    'You've got it all wrong, love. It's okay – you're upset. I get that. You'll realise in a while, like you always do.'

'I don't know what you're talking about.'

'You'll remember, when you're not so hyper – that you're the one who did the using. You thought you could manipulate me, abuse my power because you believed I could prevent you from getting a drink-driving charge. I get it all the time. Women, men sometimes, throwing themselves at me, making it uncomfortable for me – anything to try and get off the hook. Now you're just realising you messed up and you're looking for someone other than yourself to blame.'

'That's not it . . . not what I'm doing.'

'I've got to go. I'm sorry it didn't work out better for you. Guess you can always have another kid. Try not to fuck the next one up.'

Chapter 23

NOW

BECKY

My focus is on the road ahead as I weave in and out of the lines of traffic, undertaking in frustration at the middle-lane hoggers – the heel of my hand pressing against the horn multiple times. I'll be lucky if I don't get pulled over for aggressive and dangerous driving offences. With that thought, I ease off the accelerator slightly – if I were to be stopped, I could arrive late to Tamsin.

Might I already be too late? My heart sinks.

Part of me is utterly convinced it's just scare tactics – a nasty attempt to gain control over the situation. A way of preventing me from getting to Nina and building a credible case against John by suggesting harm will come to another woman. Which makes me think whoever is making these calls to me, knows me – or at least knows *about* me.

If it's not John, it has to be someone John trusts – or who he has in his pocket.

I roll my shoulders, the pain of the increasing tension I'm holding in them becoming unbearable. The caller could be anyone. Next time they ring, as there undoubtedly will be more, I'll keep them talking, delve deeper and find out what they know. I should be able to tell if it's John – there must be things only he would know.

Turning off the dual carriageway, familiar buildings come into view, and I allow my lungs to fully inflate with the stale, warm air in my car. I hadn't even thought to turn up the air-con. My knuckles are white from gripping the steering wheel so tight, but I'm almost at the flats. Mustering all my self-control, I slow down – I don't want to alert the 'visitor' with a screeching tyre, drugs-bust-style arrival outside the block of flats, nor do I want to attract attention from anyone else that might ultimately aggravate the situation.

My eyes dart about as I drive into the road. There's no parking allowed, but I don't want to waste time going to the garages. I pull up across from the building, its heavy darkness even more depressing than usual; its oppressive quality presses down on me, crushing me. The sense of claustrophobia makes me want to jump out of the car straightaway, but I force myself to wait. Watch. There are a few people walking by, probably ambling towards the shopping centre, others milling about – no one takes any notice of my car. I don't immediately see anyone suspicious.

I lean forwards, my face inches from the windscreen, and look up towards Vince's flat even though I know it's futile – you can't see much from this angle; I need a better vantage point.

What if someone is already inside? Hurting Tamsin?

Her eyes – dark circles, haunted – flash up in my mind. The fear plain to see.

141

Could the person she's most afraid of be the same one making the threatening calls to me?

Checking my surroundings first, I get out of the car, leaving the hazards on in the hope I might not gain a ticket, then bolt across the road. Keeping close to the concrete walls, I edge up the external steps, and across the corridor towards Vince's doorway. A scream tears through the air and my heart plummets. I freeze. Shit. Did that come from the flat? I purse my lips, breathing gently through them to calm my jangling nerves, then close my eyes to concentrate. A burst of laughter erupts. I think it's originating from the road, not the flat. I attempt to swallow, but my mouth is too dry.

I carry on, edging closer and closer until I'm standing to the side of the front door, and press my back flat to the wall. My legs shake as I wait, unsure what to do. I'm unarmed, unprepared to face an aggressor. While I confidently handled Vince before, I'm less assured after the events of the past few days. There's a fine line between confidence and stupidity, I feel.

I shift my head, straining to hear any voices or movement. Nothing.

Forcing my legs to move, I take a step towards the door and stand in front of it. Every muscle is taut, my adrenaline surging as I prepare for fight or flight. If I had police backup, they'd use the enforcer to ram the door open, whoever was inside would be momentarily shocked enough to pause any wrongdoing and their own stress response would kick in, the most likely scenario being they'd attempt to flee the scene rather than get caught and arrested.

Without such a tool, I have to settle for knocking. Then I step back to the side again so I'm not directly in the path

142

of anyone making a bolt for it, or worse, flying out wielding a weapon. I heave a heavy sigh; there's no movement, no sounds at all coming from inside. Two things cross my mind almost simultaneously:

1. It was an empty threat, like I'd first thought.
2. Tamsin's dead, lying in a pool of her own blood.

I swipe my sweaty palms down my jean legs, take some steadying breaths, then chance knocking again. This time even louder, more urgent. Tamsin said before that she barely left the flat. Where the hell is she then? I try the door handle, but it's locked. I relax a little; that's a good sign. The upper flats don't have a back opening like mine does. Had someone broken into the flat, there'd be evidence of it. And the door would be unlocked now. My brief moment of relief is crushed with my next thought . . .

Tamsin, or Vince, could have let the attacker in. Then after the deed was done, they – or Vince himself – left and locked the door afterwards. My shoulders smack back against the wall, and I reluctantly pull my mobile from my pocket. I need help. My pulse thuds as the ringtone continues, each new trill taking me closer to the inevitable click of the voicemail message.

Come on, come on. It's not happening. Tutting, I lower the phone, about to hang up. Then I hear a 'Hello.'

'Thank God,' I say, quickly putting it to my ear again. 'Charlie, it's me. Remember your promise of backup?'

There's a pause, and I imagine Charlie quietly squirming, wondering how he can backtrack on his promise without coming off as a dick.

'Who is this?' a female voice demands.

Oh, shit. I've likely called at an awkward moment – now one of his female friends-with-benefits is assuming I'm some kind of love rival.

'Sorry, I was after Charlie. It's about a work thing?' I cringe at my pathetic excuse. 'Can I speak with him please?'

'There's no Charlie here.' They cut me off and I hold my mobile in front of my face, staring intently at the number until confusion blurs my vision. I scroll through the call log. There are no others logged. But this *is* Charlie's number. It's the one I've been using. The one I called him on when I was at the pub in Lymworth when I asked him to feed Agatha for me. And he *responded* to those calls.

A breath hitches in my throat as realisation strikes me:

He'd only ever rang me back *afterwards*.

He hadn't picked that call up, nor the ones since. The only time he'd directly answered was the call I made on the day I received the letter from John, five days ago. What the hell is going on?

Chapter 24

NOW

BECKY

I can't let my paranoia overtake my rational thought in this moment. There'll be an explanation as to why Charlie didn't answer, but now that my only option for backup isn't available to me, I have to admit defeat. With my shoulders low, head heavy, I retreat back down the steps letting out a relieved sigh when I note the absence of a ticket. My gut is telling me to put a call into the police – make an anonymous tip that there's drug activity in Vince's flat. At least that way, someone will check it out. And if there's evidence of a murder or kidnap or anything else suspicious, they'll begin an appropriate investigation.

After parking up in my garage, I approach my flat with a cascade of thoughts about what I should do next washing over me like a tsunami. Tamsin is currently 'missing' after a threatening call telling me she was about to get a visitor, and Charlie's phone seemingly *isn't* his phone. Could it have been cloned? That might account for the confusion surrounding who fed Agatha and painted my front door. Although, I know now that Tamsin took the cat, so it's only the mystery painter that's unknown. But, why would it be *Charlie's* phone that they targeted? I pull a hand through my hair and groan with frustration at myself and my scattered thoughts.

Agatha greets me eagerly as soon as I step inside. I pick her up and let her nuzzle against my neck, her warmth comforting against the chill of my flat. My sense of calm doesn't last, though. I can't be complacent. Popping Agatha on the throw laid out for her on the futon, I do a quick check of the flat. My eyes greedily scan every nook and cranny for signs that someone's been in here. Nothing is out of place in the lounge and kitchen. But this isn't the area I'd expect there to be evidence of an intruder. My heart gallops as I creep towards my bedroom.

I crack the door, my eyes widening with the squeak of unoiled hinges, then I continue to inch it open, scanning the entire bedroom to make sure I'm not going to get any surprise greetings, or someone bursting from my wardrobe. Once I'm confident I'm alone, I walk in, and my gaze falls on the investigation wall. It takes several seconds for me to clock them.

Three new photos have been added to the wall, pinned with red tacks in a circle around John's picture. I take a step towards them but am stopped by a sharp pain stabbing in my ribcage. I clutch a hand over my chest as my lungs paralyse and I struggle to inhale or exhale.

I can't believe what I'm seeing.

Tears smear my vision and I have to blink rapidly to clear the blur.

The noise of rasping gasps, like the death rattle of

someone leaving this life, fill the room. No one is here to help me through an anxiety attack this time. I force myself to move to the bed and sit on the edge, my hands beside me, arms rigid as I attempt to use my lungs. My mobile begins ringing. Will it be whoever left these photos? I'm not in good shape to deal with that. But it's the possibility it's someone else, the thought of rescue, or at least having a calming voice on the other end of the phone to talk to me, that spurs me on. With my hands shaking violently, I try to accept the call. I fumble, and it falls from my hand.

Jesus.

I can't breathe.

I shake my head, making sure not to look at the wall, and take a small, but relieving breath, then pick up the still-ringing phone and blindly stab the buttons in the hope one of them is right.

'Thought you were going to ignore my call.'

I screw up my eyes, concentrating hard on the voice. The tone of the sentence is light; breezy. Non-threatening.

'I . . . I couldn't—' I stop trying to speak, instead focusing on bringing air to my weak lungs.

'It's okay. I can ring back later . . . '

'No,' I say, recognising the voice. 'Stay.'

'Sure,' he says. Silence ensues while my breathing regulates. It feels like minutes have passed.

'Thanks, Elijah.'

'You're very welcome. Is everything all right, though?'

'Yeah,' I lie. 'All good now.' I refrain from glancing up at the wall. I need to be fully recovered before I begin to piece together what's happened here.

'Good. I hope you don't mind me calling you – I know it probably seems a bit . . . well . . . stalky. But—'

'How did you get my number?' The accusatory tone is strong, but I'm unflinching because it suddenly registers that I haven't given this number to many people, and certainly not to the barista at the coffee shop. I mean, yeah, I flirted a bit, but that's a huge jump away from passing him my contact details. Charlie's words come back to me:

'*Your mystery knight in shining armour. Could it be your new barista friend?*'

Is it a coincidence Elijah is calling now, the second I've returned to find someone has been inside my flat?

'Oh, look. Sorry. I've obviously misread everything . . . '

'Misread what?'

'I know we only met the other day . . . and . . . oh, God, I'm so embarrassed. I shouldn't have called.'

'Elijah – I just want to know how you got my mobile number. Please.'

'You left it for me. Wrote it on the back of the loyalty card. I assumed—'

My mind scrambles to remember the exact timeline of events when I was at the café last. I had looked for Elijah, I wanted to pay for the latte he'd given me. He put the loyalty card on the table alongside my drink.

'I don't recall doing that.' I get up and head to the kitchen, find my purse and pull everything out.

The card isn't there.

Did I give the card to the other barista before I left?

'You were a bit . . . preoccupied. Hah – perhaps it wasn't intended for me.' Elijah's awkwardness oozes through the line. Or is this all an act? I rub at my neck, frustration that I don't trust anyone making my skin itch.

'I've got a lot going on, Elijah. Can we pick this up again another time?' I spot the bottle of tablets on the worktop.

With my mobile on speaker, I shake a pill out and pop it in my mouth.

'Yeah, if you want.' Disappointment sounds in his voice, but I hang up without adding anything further. My mind needs to be clear before I talk more to him. Something strange is happening here, and I must get to the bottom of it. Right now, I can't trust anyone.

With a more settled mindset, and my respiration at a normal rate, I go back to the wall in my bedroom and stand, arms crossed, not daring to even touch the photos adorning my investigation board.

The images make no sense.

They do, however, look alarmingly real.

In the first one, a hand holds a knife to Tamsin's throat.

In the second, blood trickles out of an open wound at one side of her neck – her attacker's arm clamping around her, stopping her from moving.

In the third – and I have to close my eyes for a second before fully focusing on it again – there's a gaping wound stretching across Tamsin's throat from one side to the other, blood caught in the process of squirting from the artery like a Jackson Pollock abstract painting. The attacker holds Tamsin's limp, lifeless body up and with their face upturned, they smile menacingly into the camera lens.

Nausea sweeps through me, my stomach twisting violently.

I've seen awful images of death before. That's not new. I've even had to look at photos of people known to me, in the throes of their violent deaths.

But never before have I seen images where I know both the victim *and* the attacker.

Pushing aside my personal feelings for a second, I look

deep into the eyes of the person who's seemingly taken the life of another human. Then I take in the wider aspects of each of the images.

From what I see, there's no reason to disbelieve what's occurred in these grossly disturbing photos. There's just one thing that makes me question their authenticity.

But would anyone else question it?

I swallow, almost choking on the lump in my throat, and step away from the images; keep backing away until I hit against the opposite wall.

Then I stare, unblinking at the attacker with Tamsin in the photos.

Everything about them is recognisable. Real. This person has attacked and murdered Tamsin.

And the person in the photos is me.

Chapter 25

NOW

BECKY

The weekend passed in a stressed blur of worry that I wasn't safe in my own flat, theorising and researching how the photos of myself with Tamsin could've possibly been deepfaked, as well as obsessing over the alarming rate at which artificial intelligence is permeating the everyday. An article about it that I read on social media speculated that soon journalists would no longer be required, authors would be nonexistent as AI could easily replicate similar works and no one would know the difference, that artwork could be imitated . . . the list went on. It was pretty horrifying. My heart sank as I realised the article was also generated by AI.

The only time I left my flat was to sneak up to check on Vince and Tamsin's in the vain hope of spotting either of them – seeing Tamsin would've ensured I could've put the photos down to a perverse warning of what was possible. Of course, the worrying fact was, if someone had left the physical photos for me and then Tamsin were to show up safe and well, then I'd have evidence that someone – John – was playing games with me and I could take that to the police. So, for the threat to be taken seriously, the person behind the photos would require Tamsin to go missing for real. My recurrent thought all night was: Is Tamsin's life in danger? I kept coming back to the same conclusion: surely John wouldn't go that far? He's a dangerous man, a risk to women's safety . . . but, murder? Just to frame me?

Those questions are what brought me here.

Standing outside the CID building in Salford gives me a woozy, heady sensation, like I've just stepped off a rolling boat. My body sways a little as I lift my head to take in the upper-floor windows. The last time I was in this exact spot, John watched me walk to my car and drive away – leaving my job, career and friends. Knowing he had caused it all. Thinking he'd won. At least he's no longer here, there's no fear of accidentally bumping into him.

A sharp pain brings me back to the present. I look down at my palms where my nails have made a row of crescent-shaped imprints. I relax my hands and puff air from my cheeks. I won't allow him, the thought of him, or the memories of him, to hurt me again. I refuse to give him that power.

'Well as I live and breathe, it's The Beckster!'

I swing around and come face to face with Kyle Matthews, who was a cocksure, new DC when I left. He'd been assigned to me for his first case, and he'd been an arse-licker from the off. The Beckster wasn't a name I'd liked then, it certainly isn't now.

'Hey, Kyle. Still here?' I make sure to sound surprised.

He swings a rucksack over his shoulder, makes a show of

turning back towards his car, holding his hand out to press the lock on his key, then smirks at me. Of course I note the new-plate, midnight-blue Audi, but I don't want to give him the satisfaction of saying something. His ego doesn't require much more rubbing.

'DS now. Thanks to you,' he says, with a wink. I grimace, feeling my muscles tense. So, once a cocksure DC now an arrogant DS. How I'd enjoy bringing him down a peg or two.

'You're welcome.' I bite down on my lip to stop any sarcastic comments from emerging. Kyle begins to walk away, towards the entrance, then turns back to me.

'You comin' in then, or what?' He frowns, deep tracks that a tractor would be proud of, forming on his brow. I'm curious as to why this is his question, not 'why are you here?'

I don't want to give Kyle any information to go on, so I just shrug and catch up. We walk together in silence until we're inside the foyer. My stomach fills with butterflies as I take in the sights, sounds, smells of this place. It's hard to decipher if they're because I'm nervous about being inside this building again, excited to be back where I felt I belonged, or if it's because I'm afraid of what I'm going to come up against. No doubt it's a mix of all of those.

'All right?' Kyle's hand touches my shoulder. 'Gone awfully pale.'

'I'm fine. Nice to see you, Kyle.' I give a forced smile, walk away from him and towards the information desk. My legs tremble as I stand in line. In my head, I rehearse my lines – how I'm here to talk with DCI Thomson, that it's a personal matter and I need to see him now. I'm sure he'll agree to me going up to his office, or at the very least, meet me down here. I only need ten minutes of his time.

My eyes flit about as I wait. I know I won't see John, but it's as if my brain doesn't know that I'm safe and is expecting it anyway. I've no idea if Charlie and Hannah are here at this moment. If I see either of them, I'll have to grab them to speak with too. The tangled web of problems I've encountered over this past week is getting knottier by the minute and I could do with their help untangling it all. Some sense has to be made of all this.

Look what you've started again, Becky. Is this all happening because you couldn't let it go?

These, and many other accusations already fill my thoughts. Will I be blamed for opening yet another can of worms? Told not to rock the boat again. Didn't I learn any lessons before? But unless someone is brave enough to get the tin-opener out, things like this will never change. You only have to look at the celebrity culture, TV film etc., to know that people have remained silent for years, while knowing, or at least heavily suspecting, that abuse of power, sexual misconduct, sexual harassment and assault, misogyny has been going on under their noses. Silence is dangerous. In the police, it's even more so. You hear cases within the Met especially, the behaviour continues because they believe they're untouchable. Some of the reports of rape – if they're taken seriously, unlike John's – have proceeded to criminal cases, but then have been pushed back by a couple of years due to court backlogs. It's a joke.

I push down the rising anger as I reach the desk. I don't know the man standing in front of me. He gives an automated smile, together with a lacklustre greeting.

'How can I help?'

'I'm here to see Detective Chief Inspector Thomson.

154

Please tell him it's Becky—' I stall, my words sticking. In my rehearsed lines, I hadn't said my name. I'm not known here as Becky Gooding; the divorce came through after I'd left. Now, the thought of uttering the name 'Lawson' causes a blockage. The man raises his eyebrows.

'Just Becky?' He appears to be taking some odd pleasure in my discomfort. Maybe I'm overthinking that, though – after all, he doesn't know why I'm struggling to say it.

'Becky Lawson,' I say, quickly, my face flushing.

For an uncomfortable few minutes, I wait for the desired response – fighting back the negative thoughts of Marcus not being here today, or him being in a meeting for the rest of the day. When the man holds a finger up towards me to gain my attention, it's as though the world has lost its sound, and while his lips move, I don't hear his words. When was the last time I had a blood pressure check? It's like I've broken the surface of the sea after being in its silent depths, the noises from the building, together with the man's voice, flood back.

'Go on up. Apparently you know your way.'

I stare for a moment, wondering if I heard him right. He pushes an arm out, indicating towards the security barrier.

'Thanks,' I say. I take the proffered visitor's lanyard and head into the belly of the beast.

Marcus's office is a level below the CID which means I'm hopeful I won't run into old colleagues, but still I fidget as the lift rumbles upwards, praying it doesn't stop at each floor. The lights flash from one number to the next, my heart in my mouth waiting for it to stop. I check my reflection in the surrounding mirrors, slide my fingers through my shoulder-length hair to neaten it, dig my fingernails into the

155

corner of my eyes to rid the mascara gunk I'd forgotten to remove last night and attempt a smile to see how it feels.

I realise, with a jolt of shame, that I've let everything slip. I thought I'd been doing okay; managing – getting up each day, setting goals, seeking new opportunities and looking after myself. The latter has most definitely taken a nose dive. The fresh-faced, young detective that first walked into this building five years ago, no longer exists. I sigh. Is it possible to reclaim some of my former glory? Once this thing with John that's hanging over me has been taken care of, I'll be able to get on with my life and actually live it. There's a ping, followed by the automated voice – *Doors opening* – and I pull back my shoulders and stand tall.

The smell of coffee and recently cleaned toilets greet me as the lift doors swoosh open and I fight the urge to gag. Funny how certain smells can trigger a physical reaction. The last time I was on this floor was when I was told of the discharge decision. Marcus's office is at the end of the hall, so I stride with purpose towards it, eyes dead ahead. I'm not even tempted to sneak a look into any of the glass-partitioned larger rooms as I pass them. Best not to catch anyone else's gaze. The office door is already open when I reach it, and Marcus looks up from his desk, smiles and stands.

'Well, this was an unexpected diversion from proceedings this morning. Come on in and close the door.'

A part of me immediately relaxes: my shoulders give a little and the tension in my jaw slackens. My lungs release the held air and I manage a smile. Marcus, white-grey since I've known him, looks exactly as he had the last time I saw him. It's weirdly reassuring.

'I really appreciate you seeing me, sir.' I hold my hand out.

156

'Oh, come now. Let's drop the formalities.' He edges out from behind his desk and embraces me. 'I'm so sorry about being the bearer of unwanted news last week, Becky – I wanted you to hear it from me first, but I know it must've sent you spiralling.' He releases me from his grip and holds me at arm's length. I can't speak, emotion suddenly overwhelming me. I don't want to cry, so I blink rapidly and change the subject.

'How is Barbara doing?' Before I left last year, she'd been undergoing tests and Marcus was struggling to manage but keeping a brave face on things. That stiff-upper-lip British thing the older generation is known so well for. I'd been touched when he opened up to me during a team get-together at his house. Barbara's idea, of course. She liked to know who her husband was spending all his hours with and, additionally, enjoyed putting on a spread and getting to know the team. He took me aside, out of others' earshot, and was the first to ask how I was. At that point, rumours were running amok – how my marriage was failing, and that I was about to put in a report making an allegation against my own husband. When I wasn't forthcoming with information, not wishing to share too much with the boss, he shared the news that they'd found cancer. He was clearly devastated and I said I'd do anything I could to help.

'She's holding on,' Marcus says now, giving a firm nod of the head. 'A true fighter.'

'I'm glad to hear that. Please will you send my love?'

'Of course, of course.' He turns and sits back behind his desk. Points to the chair opposite. 'You remind me of her in that way.'

I'm taken aback by his sudden admission but can't

help smiling. Not sure how to react, I simply nod. Marcus ponders me further, his eyes glinting.

'You have something you want to share with me?'

My pulse bangs in my neck, his direct approach unexpected. 'Um . . . not exactly,' I confess. 'There have been some strange developments recently, though, and I think John is behind them. And I've found out some new information that I'm hoping will lead to hard evidence.'

'Okay,' he says. 'So, as I thought. You're not letting this go.' I'm pretty sure it's a rhetorical question, so I don't respond. 'Without another official report, my hands are somewhat tied—'

'Oh, I'm not expecting you to open an investigation or anything. Not yet.'

His eyebrows draw together, he steeples his hands on his desk and leans forwards. 'What are you here for then?'

'I wanted your help on a related matter.'

His jaw tenses and I feel a shift in atmosphere. 'I have a suspicion I'm not going to like this.'

'I don't like it myself,' I say, giving a nervous laugh. 'I've been out of the loop for a bit, obviously . . . I was wondering, what do you know about deepfake, or AI images, voices and the like? Have there been many recent cases where it's been an issue? Do the tech team have the ability to differentiate between real and fake photos, for instance?'

Marcus looks alarmed – not sure if it's the rate at which I'm firing questions at him, or the nature of them. I take a breath and wait for his response.

'If you're asking about this, I'll presume it's pertinent to the information you believe you have regarding John.'

'Yes. Although, currently, it's something I'm having a personal issue with. Linked to John, I'm sure, but nevertheless, it's me who's directly affected by it. Without giving all the details . . . '

'Sure, sure. I can't let you go walking around the offices asking questions, you understand and there's nothing I can tell you about ongoing cases . . . You're a civvy now.'

As if I needed to be reminded of that.

'I know, it's awkward and I wouldn't have come here if I wasn't desperate.' I flinch. That's the last word I should've used. It'll remind Marcus of the state I got in before. 'Feeling alone in all this has put a huge pressure on me. But I'm of sound mind – I can assure you of that.'

'You are still in contact with some of the old team, yes?'

A worrying thought snags inside my mind. *He's testing me.* Does he want me to unwittingly name-drop, so he can suss out who from the inside is helping me and then haul them over the coals? Or is he trying to catch me in a lie?

'A few people still speak to me, yes. Albeit reluctantly.' I attempt a light-hearted tone in the hope he doesn't ask who. He probably already knows. It wouldn't take a genius to figure out it would be the two people I was closest to when I was detective.

'Well, then.' He stands again, and I follow suit. Well then? He's brushing me off now, walking to the door and opening it for me to leave. He's said all he's going to. I've gained nothing. I hesitate at the door, my eyes imploring his. There's kindness in them and my disappointment ebbs as another thought shoots into my mind. When he mentioned me still being in contact with some of the team, was he giving his roundabout permission to seek their help under the radar?

'Thanks for seeing me today,' I say. 'I really do appreciate it.'

'It's fine. Do drop in to see Barbara, won't you? Maybe over the next weekend when we'll both be in? She'd love a bit of company.'

And, through the mixed signals he's giving off, I think I understand. 'Of course.'

Chapter 26

NOW

BECKY

Before I leave the car park, I put in a call to a locksmith. Whoever put those photos inside my flat is unlikely to have had a key, unless they somehow obtained a copy, but they could've got in by other means as the lock isn't exactly robust. Hence why I asked Charlie to 'break in' for me. I'd feel safer with a better door altogether, but my current funds won't stretch that far. A multi-point locking system is about my limit right now.

A swell of anxiety brings bile to the back of my throat as I think about my diminishing bank balance. It's taken a huge knock since the divorce; I didn't have enough energy to fight John for more from my share of the house sale. I dread to think where I'd be now had it not been for my parents' money. But guilt follows me every time I take from the fund because I know their intentions when they first took out the life cover were for me to put it towards my education and career in the event of their deaths. I draw in a long breath trying to ward off the tears. Letting them down is the worst feeling. I will make them proud. Soon I'll be able to focus on building a new career *and* the bank balance. It just has to take a back seat until I've dealt with John.

With several hours before the locksmith can fit me in, I decide now would be a good time to go food shopping. I drive away from CID without looking back at the place in my rear-view mirror. The burning swirl of acid in my stomach tells me this is probably the very last time I'll set foot here. There's nothing here for me anymore.

My mind is far from the task of choosing food items off the shelves at the supermarket; things pile up in the trolley and I've no conscious thought as to what exactly I'm placing in it. I glance at every woman in the store, willing one of the faces to be Tamsin's despite knowing this is the last place she'd show up. A griping pain, like a knife twisting my insides makes me catch my breath. While mentally I'm attempting to believe in the more positive outcome, my body seems to be resisting. I forge on – I'm no use to Tamsin if I buckle under the first real pressure John's put on me.

Back in the flat, while unpacking the bags, I realise half the shop is stuff I never usually eat. I shake my head as I place the jar of Madras in the cupboard, noting the four chillies on the label. That's never going to get eaten, then. Agatha nudges against my legs, and I have a sinking feeling that although I've purchased litter, I've not bought anything suitable for her to eat. I rummage through the remaining bags, and with a triumphant cry, I pull out a big pack of cat food.

'Well, there you go, Agatha – one of us has something decent to eat!'

Once I've fed her, I make a cup of instant coffee, take my mobile and sit on my bed, leaving the door open so I can hear the locksmith when he arrives.

My insides shake as I cast my eyes over the three photos depicting Tamsin and me. I touched on the idea of deepfake images with Marcus, anticipating he'd have something relevant to say on the topic. Really hoping he'd declare that it was easy to decipher whether a photo was genuine. But with him offering up nothing himself, I resign myself to having to research as best I can without any help for now. With luck, Charlie and Hannah will make contact soon and I can at least gather info from them. Given they're more hands-on than Marcus, I'm sure their knowledge will be useful, which is likely why Marcus covertly suggested I use my ex-colleagues. The minute I can prove the photos are fake, I can mark them as evidence. Of what, exactly, I'm still not sure.

As is usual when I'm searching the internet, I go down a rabbit hole. But this one proves to be worthwhile. I find fourteen reports of sexual offences occurring in and around Manchester over the past two years. There are months, but no actual dates – but I write each one in a notebook to fact-check later and ask Charlie to cross-reference with cases. If I'm armed with dates and times it'll make it easier to then look into any incident and try and link it to John. Once I compile a file of possible offences carried out by him, I'll move on to the next stage.

The news articles are pretty standard for these types of offences, some using emotive language, and even if not intended, they come across as sensationalist and, disappointingly, still focusing on what the victim was wearing, how they'd put themselves in a 'vulnerable' situation, implying it was the reason they'd been attacked. Will it ever change?

My coffee is cold by the time I'm finished, and that in itself reminds me about the call from Elijah. I write his name on an index card and pin it up on the wall next to the one stating 'anonymous caller'. I stick a Post-it with 'MOBILE NUMBER?' written on it over Elijah's. I stand back, tapping the marker against my bottom lip. I hadn't had a sense of unease when I met Elijah. And as far as I'm aware I'd never set eyes on him before that day I met Charlie in Hamley's.

Charlie chose there as the meeting place, didn't he? Does *he* know Elijah? I scribble this on a Post-it and stick it up too. I used to be so careful when meeting colleagues in a public place, never discussing cases for fear of being overheard. But my guard has since dropped – I don't know details about any live cases, so I don't self-edit what I'm saying. I can't even recall exactly what we spoke about in the coffee shop – whether we inadvertently gave details that could be used against me.

What possible reason would Elijah have for wanting to threaten me, though?

I rub at my eyes, sore from staring and lack of sleep, and leave the room. Still no calls from Hannah or Charlie, I note, as I scroll through my mobile. They're probably just busy, but a nagging suspicion pulls at my gut: *they're avoiding me*. Has Marcus warned them not to help me?

'Paranoid, or what, eh, Agatha?' Her fur is looking healthier, her eyes brighter as she surveys me from her position on the back of the futon in front of the window. I wonder if she's keeping an eye out for Tamsin. I go to her and smooth my hand down her back, starting off her engine-like purring. A shadow crosses the window outside and my heart leaps. The knock on my door makes my spine tingle with fear until I remember. The locksmith.

'Christ's sake.' I'm going to put myself into an early grave at this rate. The man, late fifties, carries an impressive kit and I recognise him from the photo on his website, so I relax and open the door. I make him a cuppa and pace the lounge holding Agatha while he does his job.

'Your landlord should've sorted this for you,' he says after I've paid him for the new lock.

'Oh, no worries. There wasn't anything wrong with the other one, per se, I just wanted—' I catch the look of concern on his face. 'What's the matter?' He sighs, and squints, then holds up the old lock.

'There is evidence of tampering,' he says, gently. Like he's delivering news of a death. I gulp down the rising bile. 'I mean, could be old, of course. How long you lived here?'

My vocal cords freeze, and I have to cough to clear my throat. 'Five months.' His lips push down at the edges, and he looks at the lock more closely.

'Well, it's difficult to say quite how recent the damage is, but good thing you've upgraded I'd say.'

I thank him and close the door, immediately locking it. I stand with my back to it and lean there, my mind whirring. I did know someone had been in here, of course, that wasn't news to me. And my suspicion was that they'd broken in and not used a key – but somehow, hearing it from the locksmith has cemented it and now, however much I'd like to deny it, it's clear that I'm at risk here. Maybe I should seriously consider asking to stay at Hannah's for a while. Even Charlie's – though that would be more awkward.

I call Hannah's mobile, no longer willing to wait for her

to find the time to respond to my other messages – I need her now.

Tears sting my eyes when the voicemail clicks in, the overwhelming feeling of isolation taking over all other emotions. I don't leave a message. Instead, I go into my bedroom, change into joggers and a sweatshirt and begin stripping everything off my investigation wall. Then I pack it up, together with a rucksack filled with a few days' worth of clothes and necessities, plonking it by the front door.

In the kitchen, I put out a row of plates and dishes filled with cat food and water, spread out paper around the kitchen floor and add additional litter to the makeshift cat litter tray. That should about cover Agatha for a couple of days. I could pop back to top up food if it's any longer.

'I'm going to be back, Agatha,' I say, giving her a tickle under her chin. 'And I'm going to bring your mummy back with me.'

To do that, I'm going to need Nina's help. And this time, she's not going to turn me away or refuse to listen. But with John, or people he's instructed, likely keeping tabs on me, I'll have to play it very carefully.

Chapter 27

NOW

BECKY

Every joint is stiff when I wake up on the rear seat of my car, cold and unrested. I check the time and realise I've managed to sleep a few fitful hours since I arrived at the local garage last night. Movement outside shakes me into life. After a vain attempt to make myself look presentable, I get out and head into Alan's Autos to pick up a courtesy car. Despite my unpleasant experience staying in my car all night – the fear of someone breaking into my flat outweighing any possible discomfort – I'm bolstered by the fact Alan agreed to the loan without me needing to bend his ear. Having only been off the force for a year, it appears I still have some contacts who are willing to help me out. With no questions asked, he hands over the keys to a dark-grey Toyota hatchback.

The relief as I drive off with a sense of anonymity lifts my mood and I flick the radio on and start singing along to Blur's 'Coffee & TV', smiling as I remember how I loved the video when I was around ten years old. Back when life was simple, happy and uncluttered by adult understanding. I purposely ignore the nagging voice in my head that's trying to interject – reminding me I've not got much to feel positive about right now with an ex who's threatening me, a missing neighbour and photos that depict me killing her.

I sing louder.

My plan is to drive to the outskirts of Lymworth, head to the closest car park, then take a bus into the village. From there, I'll make my way to The White Horse pub. That's as far as I've thought, but I've around an hour's journey to figure out the rest.

With my hair pulled into a ponytail and the khaki baseball cap that I found jammed in the driver side door pocket positioned low over my forehead, I walk towards the rear of the pub, stopping short of the exit door so I'm in a position where I can check who's around. With my back against the wall, I hover, pretending to scroll on my phone. I should be unrecognisable, even if they were expecting me to return, which I'm guessing they won't be. No one would be stupid enough to walk into a guaranteed trap. Nervous energy fires through my body – a mix of trepidation and excitement, a lot like the feelings I used to get when I was working on a case. When I'm certain no one is about to come out and see me up close, I move nearer to the exit. A small window is open and I'm able to take a peek inside. I almost fist-pump the air as I spot Nina.

Now all I have to do is either get her attention and hope she'll at least come outside, or, sneak in and take her by surprise and pray she doesn't make a huge fuss. If I go in, there's the risk of being cornered, though. While I'm mentally going through the pros and cons, the door opens. I quickly drop my chin and stare at my phone again, my adrenaline soaring. I can't see who's come out, and I daren't raise my head. There's a flicking sound, followed by the smell of cigarette smoke and then I remember Nina's a smoker and lift my eyes to check if it's her.

'Oh, for fuck's sake.'

Hearing her curse, and knowing I've been rumbled, I snap my head fully up. 'Hey, Nina,' I say, moving quickly to block her path back inside. 'You've nothing to lose by hearing me out. Please.'

She draws heavily on her cigarette, puffing the smoke out in a large plume, her gaze remaining on me. Dark circles under her eyes are prominent, there's no hint of make-up on her face, and as she asks what I want, I note her tone is flat. Despite sounding uninterested, she isn't riled by my presence like she was before. Something's altered. I latch on to this intuition like a dog clamping down on a bone, and run with it.

'I get how this looks and I'm well aware I'm not welcome around here. But, just for a second, will you please consider *why* John told you what he did. I honestly don't care about him not being in my life anymore—'

I stop speaking and take a step back as the door opens. The man coming out shoots Nina a questioning glance, but she smiles at him, so he continues on. Breathing a small sigh of relief, I carry on speaking, and although Nina doesn't interrupt, I can tell she's taking in what I have to say this time. I finish with the fact that not long after I found the burner and confronted him, I then took the difficult decision to report him. It was me who threw John out.

'You chucked *him* out?' These words are filled with

169

shock; anger. I nod, feeling a surge of relief to have got this fact across to her. She stubs out her cigarette, pulls a packet from inside her jacket pocket and lights another. She paces while she smokes, her head shaking every few seconds. 'I suppose I wanted to believe he'd chosen me over you. What a fool. I thought this time would be different.'

My pulse dips at her suggestion she's been through it before. 'This time?'

'Never mind that,' she says with a wave of her hand. 'Unbelievable. He said he split with you because he wanted to be a family. Live with me. With our daughter. What a . . .'

Nina's words blur, then mute as my brain struggles to comprehend the last bit and the sea-crashing sound in my ears prevents me interpreting anything further.

She just said *our* daughter.

Nina's eyes widen and she lurches towards me. Even if she's about to hit me, I'm powerless to stop her. It's like my software's glitching or I'm on a time delay. She's in my face, her mouth opening and closing silently. Then my hearing returns to normal, and I realise she's repeating, 'You all right?' again and again while shaking me.

'Sorry. Zoned out for a minute there.' I jiggle my shoulders, stretch. Like I've just awoken from a long nap.

'Seems we both have a few home truths to face,' she says. 'Come with me.'

Nina takes my wrist and pulls me towards the pub door.

'Oh, no. I can't go in there. John must've told the owner who I was because I was asked to leave . . . '

'It's okay.'

I tense, leaning back, my legs rigid like a stubborn mule. Is this what Nina wanted all along? To get me inside where she and the owners will lock me in a room to wait for John

170

to come and sort me out once and for all? But it's too late, I'm in the corridor. The woman who booked me the room, together with the man who lied about the double-booking, are standing, watching Nina haul me in.

'Top room's free,' the woman instructs.

The shock wears off and I regain my composure and my reasoning. 'I'm not sure you're going to want to do this – the police know I'm here.'

'You were dismissed last year, so I doubt that,' Nina says. 'Come on. You wanted to talk, so let's talk.'

A door slams behind me, the vibration sending a violent shudder up through my feet, into my legs and up my spine. I hear the click of a lock, then a bolt sliding across the pub door. The element of surprise I thought *I* had, has just been turned on its head.

Chapter 28

NOW

BECKY

I'm practically frog-marched to the stairwell, and within seconds I find myself back in the room I was in last week – the Eighties horror-style look now taking on new significance. My eyes dart around, half expecting to see John waiting in a dark corner. Maybe even Tamsin. The latter would at least alleviate my growing worry that real harm has come to her. But it's just me and Nina.

'Room not double-booked today, then,' I say, trying to hide my unease with a dose of sarcasm.

'I think we both know it wasn't before. You turning up here was just what John predicted.'

'Yes, he knows me so well.' I feel my lip curl as I spit the words. My hands clench at my sides.

'Make yourself comfortable,' Nina says, sitting on the bed and patting the area beside her.

In for a penny.

I sit, careful to position myself so I can keep my eye on her and the door. If the owners burst through, though, maybe even with John, I know I won't stand a chance at fighting them all off.

'The police really do know I'm here, Nina. I still have friends, despite John's best efforts.'

'We're only talking, Becky – and you are the one who came here.'

'And you're the one who dragged me inside with the owners locking me in!'

'We're not going to hurt you, if that's what you think.'

'Only got your word for that. They were only too keen to get rid of me last time.'

'I can assure you my parents were only acting on John's absolute conviction you were a psycho.'

'Your parents?'

'Yeah – they've owned this place forever. It's here I first met John.'

There's a slight give in my posture upon hearing this. And now I remember the woman saying 'that would be our Nina' when I mentioned the recommendation I had from the Café Shack. I'd assumed she'd merely meant 'our' as someone who worked for them, forgetting that up here 'our' often means a sibling, or family member. Now I feel more confident I'm not in immediate danger, I get to the point of why I'm here.

'There are things I feel duty-bound to tell you, Nina. And I understand your default will be to put up barriers and protest everything I have to say. But if you want to protect yourself and your daughter . . . '

My chest tightens at the mention of Nina's daughter. *John's daughter*. I want to know more about that. How, when, and more specifically why given his reluctance to ever even talk about having a baby with me. I'm aware though that there are more pressing things to cover, and I likely don't have long.

'Look, I wasn't best pleased seeing you before. Telling me stuff I didn't want to hear. But I've thought about it a lot over the past few days. Been more . . . well, critical, I guess you'd say – of everything John said. I stood back, really analysed it all. And I see it. I see his bad side.'

Nina looks up to the ceiling, breathes in deeply, her nostrils flaring. Blinks rapidly. My heart goes out to her, I recognise the internal fight she's experiencing right now.

'But you're worried about the consequences of tackling him about his behaviour.' I lay my hand over hers. I let the silence hang for a few moments; the shared emotional load we've endured holding us both in our memories.

'I think you forced me out of my denial – and at first, I really didn't appreciate it, you know?'

'I understand. I honestly didn't see it for years. Or, rather, I didn't acknowledge my concerns. There was always a reason he acted a certain way, an excuse either he gave, or that I attributed to his actions. It's bullshit. I'm mad at myself that it took something so blatant, in-my-face obvious, before I allowed myself to believe John had a side to him that was so utterly deplorable.'

'At least you only let it happen the once,' she says, hanging her head and I know there's a story there, but now isn't the time to get into it. She sighs, looks up. 'I don't know what you want from me, though.' Her eyes cloud with tears. 'He's suspicious all the time, keeps me close – I can barely shit without him knowing. My parents don't know the half of it and even they're afraid of him. Being here with you now . . .'

Her breathing shallows, and she gets up, sneaking to the window. 'He probably already knows you're here again.'

'It's risky, that's for sure. I won't stay much longer. But I wanted to know if you'd help—'

'There's no way! I've got Millie to think about.'

'I know, I know. But *I'm* also thinking about you both. Do you really want to live with someone like John? Allow him to be part of Millie's life? The man's a rapist, Nina.'

The words seem to echo in the room. The knowledge weighs heavily on my shoulders and maybe I'm not only trying to alert Nina, somehow save her from John's poison, make sure she isn't sucked into the cesspool along with him – but I'm also attempting to get someone else on my side to help share the load. Spread the guilt. It's an awful thought – but if I'm holding John's behaviour up to a light, then I have to do the same myself.

'He destroyed the phone I found the incriminating evidence on, Nina. He truly believes he's invincible now, that no one will speak out for fear of the repercussions, or simply because they're made to believe their efforts will be futile and *they* will be the ones harmed by any accusations. I assumed his arrogance was banter, maybe even a cover – that he'd rather his colleagues thought he was egotistical than afraid. It's only with the benefit of hindsight I now know it's because he feels more powerful than anyone else, he's confident that no one can take him down. It's scary.'

Nina nods, silently. She doesn't attempt to jump in to defend John, doesn't argue that what I'm saying is wrong.

After another half an hour of honest talking, I'm optimistic Nina will be able to do what I cannot. Log John's movements, dig deeper into his personal activities; keep as close an eye on him as she suspects he does her. She's agreed to meet in secret on a regular basis – out of town – only if she doesn't think she's being followed. Otherwise, I'll work out another way, maybe using Hannah and Charlie, for her to deliver information.

'Any issues with the plan, contact Charlie or Hannah through the station. Probably best not to call mobiles. Especially mine,' I say. Nina's chest rises and falls rapidly. 'I know I'm asking a lot. It's really important to gain hard evidence. I need to produce a file of it – build a case against him so watertight that he's unable to wriggle out of it this time. He needs to be in prison for public protection.'

I won't rest now until John's behind bars.

Chapter 29

ISABEL

Isabel learned that if his victims attempted to bring him to the attention of police, John Lawson acted swiftly and efficiently to ensure that if there was any tangible evidence in the first place, it was destroyed. Whether that was by his hand, or via one of his internal sources, wasn't clear, but she knew he had help. At first it had only been an inkling – wondering how else he'd be getting away with the things he'd done – but with time, and an increasing pool of victims coming forward with similar stories of being threatened by John and others, Isabel became convinced the intricate web of deceit contained a number of officers and staff in the police force, maybe even those high up. Numerous allegations had been brought to light over the past couple of years, and talk of internal investigations and officers being suspended. But not John. He was being protected somehow.

Her plan had come about because of the newspaper articles that had sent her into a spiral. Though she loathed the hacks, the way they didn't care about the real people contained in their attention-grabbing, shock-value headlines, she realised the journalists might be the only ones who could highlight the corruption – although, given who owned the papers, and the no-doubt complicated inner workings of the relationship between police and journos, even that avenue would likely be a minefield.

But with a careful two-pronged attack, Isabel might well offer irrefutable evidence that could split it all wide open.

The evidence part was proving trickier than she hoped. One of the victims she'd spoken with agreed to offer verbal confirmation that they were targeted, manipulated, raped and threatened by John. Another was on the verge of adding her name to the list. Today's meeting was the one that had caused Isabel's sleepless night; had ensured she couldn't keep her breakfast down.

This one promised solid evidence.

Chapter 30

NOW

BECKY

Leaving The White Horse by the door I was dragged through only an hour ago, my cap pulled low, I jog to the bus stop at Lymworth Cross. The next service is a few minutes away. A sense of being watched creeps over my skin. There aren't many people around, I note as I scan my surroundings. A few people exit the Sainsbury's Local and give me a passing glance, then move on. Following the meeting with Nina and with thoughts of Tamsin on my mind, feeling vulnerable is to be expected, I tell myself. I've taken every precaution to prevent being followed here.

I'm safe.

Unless the second I turned up at the pub, Nina's parents informed John.

I brush a hand down the back of my neck, calming the tiny bristling hairs, and slip into the shadow of the village monument. Footsteps, heavy and fast, approach from

179

behind me. I push my back against the sandstone of the cross, holding my breath. The urge to close my eyes, too, is strong. Like a child's game of hide-and-seek where you believe if you can't see the seeker, they can't see you.

If it's John, I'll be screwed. What if he causes a big fuss, hauls me in on a stalking charge? I have to get out of here, quickly. As the steps progress around the monument, I hear the unmistakable sound of a bus engine. With my heartbeat loud in my ears, I wait until the last moment to make a dart for the bus, jumping through the doors a split second before they whoosh closed.

When I try to breathe properly again, my ribs ache as though I've been thumped in the chest, and my fingers shake as I attempt to unfold the bus ticket. The driver, keen to get moving, gives it a cursory glance and returns his attention to the road. I scan the seats for anyone that looks out of place. Of the six passengers, only one is on their own and they look about fifteen and are engrossed in whatever is playing through their EarPods, so I think I'm safe to take a seat.

With my cap tilted, I chance a look out the window.

And then I see him.

I shove my bottom forward, scooting down low in the seat as my heart rate shoots up.

Fuck. *Had* Nina's parents told John I was here again? Or had Nina been put in a situation where she'd been forced to confess and tell him?

The bus leisurely swings around the corner beside the monument, and my pulse thuds in my neck. I screw my eyes closed, willing it to speed up and praying John doesn't hold out his warrant card, stop the bus and get on. Time slows almost to a stop. The bus's gear goes up one and I feel my

180

body being pushed back in the seat as it begins to accelerate.

Thank God. I pop my head just above the window in time to see John, both hands in his coat pockets, turning around on the spot, searching. It's possible he hadn't known I was there, that he was looking for someone, or something else. But I doubt that. Either I outsmarted him this time, or he wanted me to believe that I had.

The journey back to Alan's Autos takes me through Salford city centre, an area I've spent a number of hours in over the years – both professionally, and personally. It's the usual hive of activity – buzzing with people. There's so much to do here with crowds flocking to its retail stores and leisure facilities; it's jammed with businesses and packed with tourists lapping up the music, art, and theatre culture. The architectural designs are an endless fascination to me, the old red-brick buildings creating a juxtaposition among the modern shiny steel and glass structures. Greater Manchester has a lot to offer.

But, as I drive on, the scenery changes, as does the feel of the place – and my perception of my personal safety. It becomes a little 'rough around the edges' as some regard it – with areas known to be plagued by gangs, organised crime and drug dealers. My thoughts darken, echoing my surroundings, as I mull over today's events and revelations, then without conscious attention, those during the past year rear their ugly heads. I remove a hand from the wheel to massage the knot in my neck. Nina said that John is the father of her daughter, Millie. Given everything, I'm thankful we didn't have a child, but my belly still cramps with a sense of loss. The repeated claims by John that he didn't think bringing a baby into this world was fair and that it was

181

selfish, in most ways, that I'd want to. Overpopulation, increasing the effects of global warming, the state of the government, the health service, crime – all reasons he would spout. And then, there were our jobs. It was a dangerous career; he didn't want a child of his growing up without a father. Yet, he's fathered a child with another woman. Millie is four, so clearly he cheated on me.

I laugh, a guttural sound erupting, and my nose tingles with the onslaught of tears. Cheated on me. That's one way of putting it. That's how it feels with the knowledge he was seeing Nina. Sleeping with her.

But what about those women he raped?

I shudder, and my body begins to shake so much I have to switch the heater on. As the forced air gradually warms the car, my nerves settle a bit and my mind stops jumping from one panicked thought to another. There's a lot for my brain to take in. I need to share this all with Hannah. It's been five days now since I saw, or heard, from her. That in itself isn't a concern, the job is often all-consuming, and she and Charlie will, no doubt, be working to help me build a case against John under challenging circumstances. It's not easy to gain official information unofficially. Not hearing from them only means they've yet to uncover anything concrete. But, I can't help the worm of worry from growing that neither of them have even responded to my messages. A thumbs-up emoji would've done, just to let me know all was well. I'd better hope me showing up at Hannah's door in a moment, complete with backpack and without so much as an invite, is convenient.

I'm dropping the Toyota back but leaving my car at Alan's garage as arranged with him, then getting a bus to Swinton. This level of subterfuge is possibly unwarranted, but I'm not prepared to chance it. If John has got people trying to keep track of my movements, I'm not going to make it easy for them. And I don't want to lead them straight to Hannah's door. That would put her at further risk, too. I'm not sure if Hannah will be working. What if she's not at home when I get there? I hadn't conceived a plan B. My tummy rolls at the thought of having to go back to my flat tonight. I tap the steering wheel while I think. It'll be fine. If Hannah isn't there I'll find a coffee shop to sit and wait. Somewhere public.

The thought of a coffee shop brings Elijah to mind. I cut him off when he called out of the blue the other night, confused as to how he'd got my number, and also the timing of his phone call. I can't quite let go of the underlying concern he's not just some guy working as a barista – as though he could be undercover, or someone John is paying to keep an eye on me. Pressure builds in my head as the potential scenarios of what John might be capable of mount up. A few years ago I'd have dismissed these as quickly as they'd entered my mind – not that they would have back then – as ridiculous and paranoid.

Sadly, they're neither of those things now.

My back aches with the weight of my rucksack by the time I walk up the pathway to Hannah's mid-terraced house. But a feeling of lightness takes over when she answers the door.

'Oh thank God. I've been worried, you haven't been returning my calls.' I stand, relief washing over me, awaiting a gushing 'come on in' from Hannah. But there's not a hint of a smile on her blank face as she regards me. While her mouth slightly opens, no sound emits from it. I shift my weight awkwardly from one foot to the other. 'What's going on?'

'Becky!' she declares, as though she's only just recalled my name – like one of those embarrassing situations where you're approached by someone in the street and they greet you loudly, confidently by name, but you've literally no clue as to who they are, so spend a few minutes talking vaguely in the hope theirs will magically spring into your mind.

'Yes. It is me,' I say, my eyebrows raising.

'Er . . . right. Yes. I guess you should come in.' She gazes at my rucksack, and I swear I see her chest heave with a deep, but silent, sigh.

'So much has happened,' I say, fighting a sudden urge to cry. 'I hadn't heard from you . . .' I step over the threshold, a smell of pine assaulting my nose from one of those plug-in air fresheners, and place my rucksack at the bottom of the stairs. Hannah side-eyes it, the atmosphere heavy with her obvious concern over why I have it. I wasn't expecting her to welcome me staying with open arms, but now I'm worried when I broach the subject and ask her, that she'll point-blank say no and tell me to find alternative accommodation.

I follow her into the first room off the hallway.

'I tried calling,' I reiterate, my voice pitiful, verging on begging. 'You and Charlie are proving hard to pin dow—' My sentence cuts off as I walk into the lounge and see a man sitting statue-like in an armchair, his scrawny legs wide, elbows resting on his knees and his balding head cupped in his hands. He doesn't look up; he hasn't made a sound on my entrance. 'Oh, sorry. I'm interrupting.' I look from the unknown male to Hannah, my eyes narrowing.

My neck pulsates as quickly as my mind works to figure out if this is a bad situation I've walked in on, whether this man is the reason behind Hannah's strange demeanour when she opened the door. Did I misread her signal – was she trying to warn me someone was here? I stay close to the door, ready to bolt into the hallway and back out of the house if need be.

'Hannah?' I look to her for reassurance. 'Everything okay?'

'Sorry, Becky,' she says, avoiding my gaze.

Fight or flight?

Chapter 31

NOW

BECKY

'What are you sorry for?' I ask Hannah, keeping my eyes trained on the man, who still hasn't moved.

'You've caught me at a . . . well,' she says, her hands splaying, 'a difficult time.'

Hannah's face is ashen. I wonder if she's expecting me to say I'll go then, leave her to it. But my instinct is to stay to make sure whatever I've walked into doesn't turn into a situation I'll later regret walking away from.

'What's going on?' I ask again. The direct route is the easiest. I search Hannah's expression for clues, but as is often the case with Hannah, she doesn't give much away. Great in operational terms, always looks calm under pressure and suspects get no hint of what she's thinking or planning. Not so great in this type of situation though as I'm unable to read the room.

'Oh, just a bit of a family crisis,' Hannah says with a

forced smile. 'You remember my brother, Danny, don't you?'

Oh, my God. If it's possible, I feel myself relax and tense up at the same moment. My legs tingle and weaken, but my chest tightens. The man, Danny, is no threat to me, and I don't believe he is to Hannah, either. My shock, however, is surely plain to see, because he's a shadow of the man I met before. Last time I saw him must've been a few years ago, but his appearance has altered due to loss of weight and hair. My immediate thought is it's cancer. Hannah had spoken of her fear of it being hereditary when she'd learned of her mother's diagnosis. I clear my throat.

'Hey, Danny. It's been a while.' He lifts his head slightly, his hollowed eyes dark, dead like a shark's.

'Oh . . . hey,' he says, slowly. His lips are so cracked and dry they seem glued to his teeth. 'Rebecca, isn't it?'

'Becky, yeah. We've met a couple times.' I shoot Hannah a questioning glance. She jerks her head towards the kitchen as Danny lowers his back into his hands.

'What the hell?' I whisper when she's closed the door between the rooms.

'I know.' Hannah rubs her hands over her cheeks. 'He's not good.'

'I can see that. Is it . . .' The word sticks in my throat.

Hannah purses her lips, nods her head. 'He's my little brother,' she says, her eyes glazing over.

My heart aches, assuming she's about to tell me the worst thing. 'I'm so sorry, Hannah. I had no idea you were going through a family issue. And here I am, asking more of you.' Guilt surges through my body. I'm so absorbed with my mission, and my personal problems, I've forgotten other people have their own traumas to deal with.

She turns, walks to the counter top. 'Cup of tea, then?'

'Nothing stronger?' I half laugh, but Hannah shrugs, then moves to the fridge and pulls out a bottle of wine.

'I can only have one. I need to drive Danny—' she sucks in a lungful of air '—to get his treatment.'

'Okay. I'm sorry, again. Dropping in on you unannounced. But if I can help, in any way . . . '

'Yes, actually you can. I need a distraction. I have a feeling you can help with that.'

'Well, I do have some significant developments.' I raise one brow at my understatement.

'Sounds promising.' She takes a few sips from her glass, then places it down and opens the door to the lounge. 'Make yourself at home. I'll be about an hour.'

'Oh . . . yeah. Thanks.' I fluster, surprised at the suddenness of her departure. I watch as she helps Danny out of the armchair, and they head out.

While Hannah's gone, I walk from room to room, inadvertently treating it like a crime scene. With a pen in hand, I touch the tip to various items, lifting them, and then, with my sleeve over my fingers, pick up photos, a few pieces of paperwork and flick through her vinyl collection, surprised at some of the rare albums she has.

Hannah isn't someone I'd have naturally gravitated to for friendship – our life at work started out very much separate from our lives outside of the force, but the thing with police work, the intensity of it, is that bonds form, relationships grow, and even the unlikeliest friendships can form over shared experiences. The culture of going to the pub after work enabled us to grow closer. We've been through a lot together.

I consider now, as I observe a lonely existence in the house she once shared with her parents and Danny, that she

188

might miss me, crave our camaraderie. I took the piss out of her a lot, in a light-hearted way, as did Charlie, really. We ripped into her about how she spent far more hours than we did on writing up reports, how she was quick to pull us up on inaccuracies, questioning us on everything to make sure we were following procedures and protocols. We were an interesting trio – our personalities and skills complemented each other. The dynamic after I'd gone would've altered dramatically and impacted them both. I've never really talked about it with Hannah; the rare times since I left that we've spent time together have been taken up with my obsession of bringing John to justice.

You've always been selfish, John's voice whispers inside my skull.

I guess not everything he told me was a lie.

Chapter 32

NOW

BECKY

Having sunk as low as to breach Hannah's privacy by wandering around her home, I unpack my rucksack and begin spreading the content from my investigation wall on the round table in the kitchen. I remove the three deepfake photos, placing them back in the zipped compartment of the rucksack without focusing on the grossly morbid nature of them, and not wishing to see the inane grin on my fake face as a hand containing a knife slits Tamsin's throat. Sharing these images feels a step too far at this point.

A nagging twist of my gut reminds me how deep in the shit I am. If I'm unable to prove I had nothing to do with Tamsin's disappearance and she isn't merely holed up safe somewhere awaiting rescue, and if I've no alibi and Vince runs his mouth off about how I assaulted him, stole their cat and interfered in Tamsin's life, things are going to be extremely awkward for me.

Ironically, evidence isn't something in short supply in this case. If me or my car have been picked up on ANPR at the same point that Tamsin supposedly met her death at my hands, then my claim of innocence might wash. But, if it's my car that's been clocked, I can't immediately prove I didn't have Tamsin stashed in my boot – the lack of her DNA will be a while coming through. Bile swills around in the pit of my empty stomach, acid burning my oesophagus. This development with Tamsin is troubling, but I mustn't let it sidetrack me entirely. That's the exact result John was going for. I can't allow his actions to distract me from the task of compiling evidence against him. I glance up at the wall clock – it's almost seven, and I can't remember when I last ate. Hannah won't mind me tucking into her snacks. I grab a packet from the cupboard, groaning as I unwrap one of the chocolate footballs inside.

'Ugh. There's no getting away from you, is there.' I stare at the familiar packaging as the memory of the night I last ate one of these needles my brain. 'I will get you,' I say as I roll up the foil, bin it and take another. He might think he's a step ahead, but what I hope he doesn't know is that I now have an insider. My secret weapon is Nina, and her being on my side will be the last thing he's expecting, even though he knows I've seen her. John isn't used to his manipulation tactics failing. They worked on me for five years, and no doubt he'll believe he has Nina, and her family, under his thumb.

'Unsuspecting' is the best play I've got. With Hannah and Charlie's help as they cautiously seek evidence on the inside, Nina, and together with my planned visit to Barbara Thomson, I should gain valuable information to add to the evidence file. Justice is within reach; I can almost taste it.

191

The front door slams and I look up from the table to see Hannah walk in, a white carrier in hand.

'Couldn't face cooking. Been to the chippy,' she says, lifting the carrier. The smell of fish and chips and curry sauce fills the air and starts my digestive juices off again, the chocolate balls barely having registered in my stomach.

'No complaints from me. How much do I owe you?' It's an automatic question, but I screw my eyes up, realising I have a card, but no cash. And my bank balance isn't exactly healthy because I'm forever taking and not replacing.

'Don't be daft,' Hannah says, unwrapping the paper and sharing the contents between two plates. I'd have been happy eating straight from the paper, but Hannah is more civilised. 'Besides, it's heavily discounted.'

'Really?' I pinch a chip from my plate before she's finished dishing it up and she slaps my hand away. 'Don't remember this particular perk of the job!'

'There's probably a lot of perks you didn't get around to exploiting.'

I stand back, staring at Hannah with mock surprise. 'No way. The Hannah I knew would not take advantage of other people to benefit herself in any way!'

'We've all had to adapt,' she says, coyly. 'Now, let's eat.'

She turns, holding a plate in either hand, then stops abruptly. 'Oh.' She looks at the table. 'When I said make yourself at home . . . '

'Ah, yes – sorry. While you were gone I transformed it to an investigation table. Thought you might freak out if I stuck this all to your wall.' I offer an apologetic smile.

'Trays it is then.'

Once we finish eating, my stomach aching from fullness, I suggest Hannah peruses my 'Operation Lawless'.

192

She hunches over the table, offering intermittent sighs as she peruses each index card, each image and clipping. I chew on the inside of my cheek, observing her facial expressions, trying to decipher her thoughts. Is this all information she and the team already know about from when they were originally investigating my report against John? For obvious reasons I wasn't allowed anywhere near that case. Am I offering up anything new? A dozen questions jostle inside my mind as I await her appraisal.

'Who's Tamsin?' she asks, finally, her finger pressed against the index card. 'And how is she connected to any of this?'

A frisson of excitement, mixed with anxiety, shoots through me. Her question reassures me that this contact is unknown to the team, so it's covering new ground. However, it also means I'm going to have to go into detail about how I came across Tamsin, and how she's linked to the case. And if Hannah begins asking too many questions, I'll be forced into a corner. On a more positive note, if I can convince Hannah, she could use her position to search for traces of Tamsin. I just need to make sure I don't divulge the fact I have photos of Tamsin's supposed murder . . . carried out by me.

Chapter 33

NOW

BECKY

With careful wording, I bring Hannah up to speed – or, as up to speed as I'm able to. My original confidence that Tamsin is alive and well, and that this whole charade is a way for John to keep me in check, rises and dips like a boat in a storm. If, by omitting the information I have, I'm putting her life in danger, how am I ever going to reconcile that? But it's the only way I can remain focused. Surely even John wouldn't go as low as to have someone killed merely as a warning to me?

'Okay, so that's your flat friend taken care of,' Hannah says. I wince at her choice of words as she shifts her attention across the table. 'What's this about Nina?' Hannah's querying tone changes as realisation dawns. 'You've *spoken* to John's new partner?' Her eyes widen to an almost comical degree. 'Are you mad?'

I swallow, wait a beat before responding. 'I did tell you,' I say, indignance still colouring my tone. But then I remember that I hadn't spoken about it and all I'd done was hammer out a vague text. 'Well, I tried. You never picked up my calls or returned my texts.' I also take this as an opportunity to explain how, when I'd called Charlie, a woman answered and denied it was even his phone. She agrees it's odd but bats away my suspicions of a cloned phone.

'Honestly, we both know Charlie's reputation – he's never at his own place. He probably told his latest *friend* to pretend it wasn't his because he was . . . busy at the time.'

'Then surely she'd have used those words!'

Hannah's shoulders visibly lower a few inches. 'I'm not being funny, but although we agreed to help you . . . it was with some reluctance.'

'Oh, thanks.'

'You can't dispute, it places us in an awkward position.'

'Yeah, I know. And I appreciate it. But if I'm being that much of a pain in the arse, why didn't you both just fob me off and let me get on with it my way?'

'Because I wouldn't forgive myself if you got in over your head and something bad happened.'

Her words suspend in the air before the weight of them crashes down on me.

'Anyway, as I was saying,' I say, transferring the focus of the conversation back to more comfortable ground. 'Nina must've had an inkling about John's past, maybe even what he's up to now, and finally pushed aside her sense of loyalty.'

Hannah pouts, then crosses her arms. She's not buying it. Is her police experience preventing her from believing this evaluation? She doesn't trust that Nina would be that quick to flip sides and help his supposed stalker ex-wife. I mean, she has a point.

195

'There's something else,' I add. 'Nina's kid, Millie. She's John's daughter.'

Hannah doesn't flinch. 'Shit, that must've stung,' she says, without looking at me.

'In a way,' I admit, giving a half-shrug. 'He did me a favour, though – in the long run. But, I expect Millie was the driving force behind Nina's decision to act. I imagine protecting her will be the number-one priority.'

'We've seen it before, though, Becky. It doesn't always follow that the partner keeps their side of the deal. Fear is a strong motivator, but it depends which side poses the greatest threat.'

I can't deny this is a fact. Not only have I seen it before, but I've also *been* that partner.

'I'll be careful.'

'You've got to let us know dates, times, locations of any future meet-ups. Got it?'

I nod.

'I'm serious, Becky. I know you aren't seeing results as quickly as you'd like from us, but you got me and Charlie into this, the least you can do now is act with some degree of responsibility.'

Hannah's lectures were legendary in CID. For someone only five years my senior, she comes across very much like a stern headmistress. The kind you were always afraid of and would make sure you handed in your completed homework to for fear of the repercussions.

'Yes. I will.' I give a salute. 'And will you be able to conduct a bit of checking when you go in tomorrow?'

'I'll try. But I have a suspected homicide to deal with. I do work you know.'

Charlie's words come back to me now, about Hannah

196

staying behind at work due to a homicide.

'Only suspected? Charlie mentioned something about a homicide last week. Same case?'

'Yes, same one. At first it looked unremarkable. A suicide. Things aren't adding up, though. No doubt it'll get passed to the MIT.' She shrugs it off, but I remember the frustration of cases being passed over to another team. The hint of the suicide being a staged one sparks my curiosity.

'In what way isn't the evidence stacking up?' I ask. 'Who is the victim?'

'I hope you're not expecting me to discuss an active case, Becky.'

'Old habits.'

Hannah's mouth tightens slightly, but perceivably. 'All I will say is – our vic was an ex-cop.'

My heartbeat slams wildly against my ribs. It's never good to hear there've been murders on our patch, but harder to digest when it's one of your own. And for some reason, the news that Hannah's latest suspected homicide victim used to be on the force, feels especially concerning. I wonder who it was?

Chapter 34

THEN

FRAN

<u>Voice recording of phone conversation.</u>

'Can you come over? I need your help.'

'We agreed you wouldn't call anymore. Not after the way you spoke to me last time.'

'I'm sorry about that. I want to see you.'

'I don't think that's a good idea.'

'Please. I don't have anyone else I can turn to.'

'And whose fault is that? [sighs] You at the house?'

'Yeah, I haven't left for days.'

'What do you expect me to do?'

'Help me get Oakley back. I can't bear it . . . knowing he's with a family that's not his.'

'Not this again! Look, you know there's nothing I can do. You had your chance and you blew it. Up your fucking nose mostly.'

[Crying]

'Crying isn't of any use, is it?'

'I'm sorry.'

'I knock off soon. Be there in . . . an hour or so. Be ready.'

'Ready? Are you going to take me to see him?'

'Don't be stupid, of course not. You know what *ready* means by now, no?'

'Oh. Yeah, right. But I don't . . . please I don't want to—'

'Want my help or not? Don't bite the hand that feeds you.'

Chapter 35

NOW

BECKY

Staying at Hannah's is like having an extended sleepover at the nerdy kid's place when you were at school. The kid you were desperate to 'get in with' because they'd help with your homework, but who was no fun to hang out with because they were too geeky to even contemplate breaking any rules. Although I am very grateful that Hannah is, albeit aversely, doing just that. Adamant I should avoid my flat for a bit longer as a precaution, she even popped there yesterday to check it was secure and to leave more food for Agatha. Her comment of still not liking the 'mangy thing' when she returned makes me smile now as I think of it. I'm sure she only said it to ensure I didn't think she was going soft.

With adrenaline continually pumping since I rocked up here, I barely slept for the third night in a row – my mind running over what's happened together with all the possible current and future scenarios – and in the short bursts of time when I did doze off, I awoke panicked and sweating from nightmarish visions of Tamsin begging for her life only for her to meet her death via the knife in my hand.

In the garish pink bathroom, a sad relic of the original suite installation of the Sixties housing estate, I take one of my tablets as a precaution, cupping water from the sink tap in my hand to swallow it down. Then I stand in the bath to take a quick shower, staring at the worn dial of the electric monstrosity, which was an addition installed by Hannah's dad rather than an engineer in an attempt to keep costs down. As I spend several minutes attempting to control the temperature, I wonder why Hannah hasn't had it replaced, but then remember the conversation we'd had three years ago, at the time she inherited the family home. She'd said she couldn't bring herself to rip it out as her dad – now in a residential home following the death of her mum from bowel cancer – still talks about the day he accidentally electrocuted himself when he installed it live, and the story makes her smile each morning she comes in here. The story doesn't give me much confidence in the electrics, though, and I gingerly twiddle the controls, wary of the same fate.

It's the quickest shower I've had in a while.

I can hear Hannah in the kitchen – a clatter of china, banging of cupboards as she puts the dried dishes from last night's meal back in their place. The noises are comforting, reassuring, and a far cry from those of loud music, yelling and door slamming I've become accustomed to in my block of hell. I put my hand on my chest, closing my eyes and taking a deep breath as I make a silent wish that Tamsin *is* safe and well. And then another that Agatha is coping without me. Mentally, the past twelve days have felt as if a tornado had swirled through my head, destroying everything in its path.

If I can gain the evidence I need though, it'll lead to John's demise and it'll be worth the chaos.

While slipping into my now three-day-worn jeans and sweatshirt, my thoughts turn to the officer who – from the little info that Hannah's divulged – was more than likely killed in a premeditated manner by someone with insider knowledge. The motive remains unclear. Or, at least, that's what Hannah has shared with me. Charlie still hasn't been in contact, which is beginning to irk me, so I've been unable to extract more detailed information. I unplug my phone from the charger and check for new messages. Nothing.

'Keep calm,' I tell myself. I stand in the centre of the spare bedroom, rotating my neck, rolling my shoulders, breathing slowly and deeply. 'Remember what it's like to be a detective.'

'First sign of madness.' I startle at Hannah's voice outside the door. 'You need to watch that.'

'Thanks for your insight,' I call. I listen as her footsteps descend the stairs, then I hear the door open. I hang over the banister as she's pulling her coat from the hook in the hallway. 'Be careful today.'

Hannah stops and looks up at me. 'You too, Becky.'

The arranged meeting point for Nina to give me any information about John's movements and/or suspicious activity is, aptly, the John Lewis café, located in the Trafford Centre. It's far enough out for her to not be recognised, but if she is, it's easy to cover as it's a massive shopping centre and not at all strange for her to be there.

Hannah is aware I'm meeting Nina, but I didn't disclose where – only me and Nina know – as I felt that added a safety net for her and was needed to gain her trust. Surprisingly, Hannah agreed without resistance. Once I've obtained intel, if of course Nina has managed to collect any, I'll pass it on to Hannah to dig into. She'll then attempt to cross-reference it with reported stalking, sexual abuse, violent attacks and rape. She said she'd liaise with Charlie, as he has a contact in the Lymworth division so could check more recent details like if John was in the office, when he was out investigating, whether he went alone or with other members of the team and so on.

Last night I asked Hannah if she would also put feelers out regarding Tamsin's whereabouts, reiterating I was worried about her safety and needed reassurance. She took this on board, albeit reluctantly. Although she'd been interested in the link between Tamsin and the Moods club when it was discussed on Tuesday evening, I had moved the direction of the discussion swiftly on to the situation with Nina due to my fear of accidentally blabbing about the faked photos.

My insides squirm now as Hannah's words echo inside my skull. 'I'll look into your concerns about Tamsin, Becky. But may I remind you of the enormity of the things you're asking me and Charlie to do?'

It's for the greater good, I'd told her, before thanking her again for putting her job and reputation on the line.

A nervous tingle radiates through my intestines as I hover close to the John Lewis store. It's only a minute past ten now, but already the undercover Trafford Centre, with two entire levels dedicated to shops and restaurants, is bustling with people. It is a Friday, I guess. We chose this time and location because it gives Nina time to drop Millie at nursery and get here. She can easily meet me and get back home without really being missed. If asked, her parents would say she'd run an errand for them. It would make sense now she was working at the pub rather than the café.

I glance at my phone: 10.05.

The tingle becomes a twinge. She hasn't walked past me, I know she's not already inside. I move away from John Lewis's entrance and head to the bookstore just along the level. Browsing books is better than pretending to look at homeware I can no longer afford or have room for. She's only five minutes late, nothing to stress about, I tell myself.

She'll be here soon.

Picking up the closest book from the round table near the entrance, I half-heartedly flick through it, my focus on the people walking by and willing Nina to come into view. I put the paperback down, then run my fingertips over the covers of the others. I can't recall the last novel I read. The ones I own are still in one of the boxes I've yet to unpack; I must get them out when I return to the flat.

If I return.

An icy chill tracks down my spine. Most of the dark thoughts I've had I've managed to quash, or compartmentalise, in order to maintain actual functioning. If I allow them to take root, spreading their doom-filled prophecies, I'd lie down and give up.

I check the time: 10.13. Has she bottled it?

I tut, berating myself for even thinking this. It's nothing to do with not being brave enough, not having the courage – I know that. It's way more complicated. People like John make sure of that.

As I head back to John Lewis, I spot Nina swooping past one of the large pillars on the opposite side to me, her dark-grey trench coat flapping out behind her, her face flushed red and set in a stern expression. I move a little faster and we both cross the threshold into the store at the same time.

Our gazes meet fleetingly, but no words are spoken as we make our way to The Place to Eat café. She reaches it first and heads for the far side. I see she's grabbed a table, so I queue to order drinks and snacks.

With a sense of relief she's here, together with trepidation about what information she has, or has not gained, I shuffle forwards in the queue, unconsciously pushing the tray along while possibilities run through my mind. God, I wish they'd be quicker. My nerves can't take the suspense any longer. I'm next to be served when I see Nina talking on her mobile, her posture stiff. Angry words drift in my direction and my entire body freezes. Shit. Is it John she's speaking to? I guess I don't know if I can actually trust her.

'What can I get you?' a voice asks, then I feel a gentle nudge against my back.

'Oh, sorry.' I force my legs to move and rattle off a few things, my gaze fixed on Nina. The call has ended and she's still sitting. That's something, at least she hasn't run off. Yet. *Hurry up*.

'Going as quick as I can, love,' the voice says. My head snaps to look at the woman. Did I say that out loud? Judging by her face I obviously did. I mutter an apology and thank her with gusto as I order and pay, then rush myself and the tray to Nina's table.

Nina doesn't waste time. Without so much as a greeting, she withdraws an envelope from inside her coat and pushes it towards me, takes the mug of coffee off the tray and starts drinking.

'That for me?' She nods to one of the random pastries I picked up.

'Yes. Go for it.' I put my hand on the envelope, draw it closer to me, and seeing it's unsealed, peep inside.

'Don't open it now,' Nina whispers. 'It's a list of dates. Look later.'

I wasn't going to fully open it anyway, but now, seeing her anxiety-ridden expression, I remove it from the tabletop and stand it against the leg to try to reassure her that I can be covert. She must be feeling on edge – just being here with me is taking a huge risk.

'Who was on the phone?'

'Jesus. Have to answer to you now as well, do I?' She tears off a segment of the pastry and eats it – it reminds me of how my mum used to eat a Chelsea bun – carefully unravelling the spiral roll with her fingers before tearing off a piece and popping it into her mouth. I remember watching her long, painted nails as she worked on deconstructing it before devouring it. Some memories of my parents are beginning to blur at the edges; even their faces aren't as sharp as they once were. I find myself smiling at this one popping into my head. Then I see Nina's narrowed eyes glaring at me, bringing me back to the here and now.

'No. Of course not. Sorry, it just appeared like it was heated and I was worried it was him.'

'He doesn't call me when he's at work,' she says, her words clogged with food. She finishes eating, swallows down some more coffee. 'I know it's not a lot to go on, but it's a start.' She tilts her head towards where I put the envelope. 'I have to be careful. He's been really agitated since you showed up.'

'But he doesn't know you're with me now?'

Nina looks cautiously around at the people in the restaurant. 'Let's hope not. For both our sakes.'

'As far as he's concerned, though, you think everything he's told you about me is the truth. That *I'm* the stalker, that

I'm the one who ruined his career?'

'Yeah, he thinks I'm still on his side. I've hated you for long enough, it's second nature to me now. He absolutely believes that I believe!'

'Okay, that's good. Well, not the hating me part . . . '

'If it turns out you're right about him, I'll reconsider.'

I smile and lift my coffee to hers. 'Deal.' The mugs clink together and it feels like we've made a pact.

'Will you be able to check the list of dates and times with your ex-colleagues?'

'That's the plan. But it would be really helpful if you could continue to monitor his movements, and . . . ' I scratch at my neck, knowing what I'm about to ask Nina will be awkward and potentially awful. 'And, given the extent of his offences—'

'Alleged offences,' Nina corrects. I let it slide.

'Yes, and the likelihood he's in way deeper than we could even contemplate, you need to be looking for particular behaviour patterns.'

'Like?' Nina's eyebrows draw together.

'Secrecy. Not answering his phone in front of you, excusing himself a lot. Evidence of another mobile, odd pieces of equipment that don't seem linked to his work. A regular place he visits, or somewhere in your home or close by that he goes to a lot.' I could go on, but her eyes are wide, her lips parted. 'What is it?'

'Nothing.' A look of horror is clear on her face, the colour drained. She puts her hand to her mouth and I think she's going to vomit. 'I've got to go,' she says, the words muted. Before I can even say anything, she gets up and rushes back through the restaurant, her trench coat trailing behind her.

I give it a minute, then pick up the envelope and slump

back in the chair. It was a lot for her to come here and meet me and I've sent her away with more to do. Riskier things to look out for. Have I done the right thing? If I endanger her and Millie by roping her in to do my detective work for me, I might get the opposite of what I'm hoping for.

Instead of saving her, I could have just set her up to become John's next victim.

Chapter 36

NOW

BECKY

The second I set foot onto Hannah's path, I hear the slamming of a car door and turn to see Charlie leaping from his Audi like he's about to bust me. For a split second, my face frozen in what must be a shocked expression, I wonder if he actually is going to arrest me.

Has Tamsin's dead body been found? Were the photos left at my flat only copies and another set have been sent to detectives at CID?

'We need to talk,' he says, jogging up to me.

'You don't say,' I retort. 'It's been over a week! Why the hell haven't you called, or at least messaged?'

But instead of answering, he takes me by the elbow and begins leading me up the path. I want to shrug him off, I was walking this way anyway, I don't need manhandling, but the urgency with which he's doing it makes my skin prickle. I find that I can't object, instead allowing myself to be guided to the front door. With shaking hands, I find the key Hannah gave me and let us in.

'What's the cloak and dagger approach in aid of?' I say, laughing to cover my nerves. Charlie ignores my question putting his forefinger to his lips which makes me snap mine closed. Then, while I stand transfixed, he begins going from room to room. My initial unease slips into curiosity as he exits the lounge and climbs the stairs. I hear the opening and closing of doors. He's conducting a sweep – but what for? I stay in the hallway, waiting for him to complete this task, questions racking up.

'Right,' he says, slightly out of breath when he reappears at the bottom of the stairs again. 'All clear.'

'What, or who, were you expecting?' I ask, shaking my head while I stomp past him. With a cursory glance at the table filled with my Operation Lawless material, I head to the kettle. 'Tea?'

Charlie stops at the table, scratching his head as he peruses it. 'Yeah, go on then,' he says, absently.

I take the envelope from my bag and open it while waiting for the kettle to boil. I flick through the pieces of paper containing dates and times, like Nina said. Then I stand next to Charlie and slide them under his nose. His eyebrows raise as he scans the pages.

'How did you get these?'

'Haven't you seen Hannah?'

'Yeah, she mentioned all of this . . . ' Charlie sweeps a hand above the evidence table. Though, evidence is a slight exaggeration at this stage. 'But there wasn't time for thorough discussion. She didn't say anything about this intel.' He waves the paper at me.

'Nina's helping.'

Charlie visibly inhales. 'I see.' He seems to take some moments to take this on board and is about to say something when the kettle clicks, and I go to make the drinks.

'Why were you sweeping the house?' I hand him the cream-coloured mug – everything is plain and simple in this kitchen in contrast to the rest of the house's decor – and pull out a chair to sit.

'Because when Hannah said you'd called me and a woman answered telling you it wasn't my phone, it got me thinking.'

'I knew it,' I say, jerking my arm and spilling hot liquid onto my jeans. 'Shit.' I rub at it, making it worse. 'It's been cloned, hasn't it? You've no idea who's listening in.'

'Hold on, hold on,' he says with a heavy sigh. 'I mean, there's always that possibility, but it's far more likely there's a simple explanation – you know, like I left my mobile unattended while I showered after a one-night stand, or something,' he offers a coy look. 'But the thought was enough to put me on edge if I'm honest. And then, following other alarm bells, I just wanted to make sure Hannah's place is secure before we talked, that's all.'

I narrow my eyes at him. I'm not sure I buy the one-night stand version. Would he be this riled if it was something so simple? 'This is all happening because of me. I've dragged you into this.' It's close to an apology without saying the word.

'I need to be in it. The more that comes to light about what John, and probably others, have done, the more I know they need bringing down, Becks.' He takes a slurp of his tea.

'Others?'

Charlie sits down too, now, his eyes heavy; sad looking. 'Yes, back to the alarm bells I mentioned. Of the case files

211

I searched from around the timeframe you first highlighted before you were pushed out . . . Weirdly—' he shakes his head '—or maybe not so – every single one that was relevant to the time and type of offence we were focusing on had been heavily redacted.'

I slam back against the chair. 'Wow. And I wonder why that was.'

'That's not all,' Charlie says, clearly getting into this role, 'some of the related evidence that had been logged at the time was missing from the electronic file and I'm almost certain some details of the reports were actually falsified.'

The enormity of what Charlie's saying hits home. My head feels too heavy to hold up, too fuzzy. Of course I suspected there were those on the force who would help John out – maybe even offer him an alibi for the assaults I brought to their attention a year ago. Mates. Officers who would not in any way, shape or form believe John was capable of anything so heinous. But redacted reports, falsified records and possibly missing evidence doesn't bear thinking about. Corruption at the top-brass level.

'Which means, we don't have a clue who we can trust.'

'Exactly that. And that goes for Nina, too, Becks.' Charlie flicks through the list she provided. 'How do we know for sure that she hasn't just given you precisely what John wants you to have?'

'You think she could be knowingly handing me a load of rubbish? What would be the point?'

'Get you running around on a false trail? And let's face it – if you go at it like you did before, then all of the stuff you've collected proves to be unfounded . . . for a second time . . . you'll be the one who is completely discredited—'

'Again,' I say before he does. 'Clever.'

'Once was enough to get you discharged and add credence to his side of events. Twice . . . Becks, if you go off on his wild goose chase, you'll be playing directly into his hands.'

The hot ball of rage starts growing in my belly and I have a burning desire to punch something. I slam down my mug and push up, pacing the kitchen, my fists clenched.

'I fucking *hate* him.' The words spit from my mouth like lava.

'That's the problem. You're allowing your personal emotions to get in the way.'

'What? Oh, come on, Charlie.' I want to be angry at him now too, but deep down, I know he's got a point.

'You have to be a detective – look at it logically, never fully trust a source until they're proven to be trustworthy. You're so desperate to trap John you aren't looking at Nina with the same caution as you would with a case you don't have a personal connection with.'

He's right. I used to be top notch at analysing not only data, but people. My investigation skills were good. Not clouded by personal feelings. I've been approaching this all wrong. The weekend is coming up – time to pay Barbara, Marcus's wife a visit. I'd forgotten about the way he'd hinted about seeing me outside of the work environment. Maybe he doesn't feel safe to speak freely because he knows something about the corruption within his own division. Or, further up, even. I need to follow that up.

213

Chapter 37

NOW

BECKY

'It's so kind of you to visit, Becky,' Barbara says as she leads me through the house to the back and out to the conservatory. It's familiar to me – it's where her and Marcus would set up the large table and seat their guests when Barbara insisted on entertaining. I recall the last one I was invited to was almost three years ago now – an autumnal-themed dinner party which Marcus referred to as 'a light supper'.

'Oh, not at all. I saw Marcus the other day and he mentioned you were—'

'He likely exaggerated,' Barbara cuts in, and I stop speaking to look at her. Her skin tone has a dark-yellow-almost-orange tinge to it, her eyes are sunken and circled with dark patches and her cheeks, once plump, are hollowed, the bones jutting out at sharp angles. I offer what I hope is a warm smile, realising she knows he didn't, but that she doesn't care to dwell on it. She takes the lid off a biscuit tin and gives it a little shake in my direction. 'Do have a digestive, won't you? If Marcus had told me you were coming, I'd have made a tart, or muffins at least.'

'A biscuit is perfect, thank you.' I reach into the tin. 'Marcus playing golf today?' I didn't see any sign of him when I arrived, but his car was on the drive.

'He went off early this morning, but he'll be back shortly. Now, tell me, Becky love – how are things going for you? Marcus tells me you've got a new job lined up.'

The conversation hovers around safe topics for a while, with me enthusiastically speaking about my application and how grateful I am to Marcus for offering a reference. She seems a little puzzled by this, but doesn't verbalise it and I try to pretend I didn't notice her frown. Marcus not mentioning it to his wife isn't cause for alarm, I reassure myself, why would he mention a reference to her?

'Ah, here he is now,' Barbara says, pushing up from the wicker chair. I hear mumbled words coming from the kitchen, then Marcus strides into the conservatory.

'Lovely to see you, Becky.' He's dressed in casual cord trousers and a polo shirt. Not sure it's golf attire, but maybe people don't wear plus fours, chequered V-necks and long socks after all. I stand to greet him and he embraces me the way he usually does. It feels fatherly, and as far as I can remember, it was after a heart-to-heart here one evening with him and Barbara where I spoke of my parents' fate, that this moment of affection began. Of course, he's never done it while in a work environment as that would be deemed inappropriate, and it's not something I've ever felt awkward about or wished he wouldn't do. There's something comforting about it, and if I'm honest, Marcus is the closest person to a father I have – it's also the reason

215

I found it so hard when I was dismissed, I was so hurt that he didn't save me. It was like a knife to the heart that John was chosen over me.

He likely didn't have the power I imagined him to have in order to keep me after the allegations were made – then not substantiated. When he said, 'my hands are tied', I took that to mean he was only one cog in the rather large wheel. But what he said on Monday indicated a change in his thinking, or he'd been given food for thought. Whatever it was I'm sure I'd been correct in my sense that he was hinting for me to come here to see Barbara so that he could also tell me something.

'Barbara's been treating me to biscuits,' I say, looking around Marcus to see where she is.

'She's gone for a lie-down,' he says, his voice heavy with sadness. With Barbara's avoidance and the palpable pain coming off Marcus in waves, I suspect her cancer is terminal. I squeeze his arm.

'I'm sorry,' I say, surprised to feel tears prick at my eyes.

'I see she's made enough tea for an army. Let's have another, eh?' he says.

Stoic as ever. I wonder if my dad would have been like this in the circumstances.

Once the cups are filled again, Marcus sits back and peruses me, his drink perched on his knee. 'It's not been an easy time for you, I know,' he says, his eyes boring into mine. 'I'm truly sorry you weren't backed up. You should've been.' The hairs along my forearms stand up. I thought there might be some preamble, some small talk, but it seems we're going right in. A good thing, given the situation I'm in. I don't respond, keen for him to keep talking. 'You know there are always people to answer to in this job, however high up you think you are; you'll always be someone's puppet.'

My heart rate picks up, a genuine fear that he's about to confess he himself is involved in a large-scale cover-up or something equally horrifying. Despite the second cup of tea, my mouth is dry, my tongue like cloth. I stare at him, adrenaline spiking so much I can't stay still, my knees bobbing, thumbs twiddling.

'It's not something I'm proud of,' he says.

My left eye twitches furiously. I don't trust myself to speak now, but at the same time I feel I may burst if I don't.

'What do you mean?' My voice is little, weak.

'It's worse than even you thought. You believed John to be abusing his power, well, I'm afraid it's rather bigger than him, Becky.'

I knew it. Charlie knows it, too. It's no wonder he was avoiding contact with me, and I suspect it's why Hannah's been reluctant to tell me too much. God, have I put Charlie and Hannah in danger?

I look directly into Marcus's eyes. 'How much bigger are we talking?'

'Let's just say, John Lawson isn't the only bad apple.'

Chapter 38

NOW

ISABEL

It was coming together. Wasn't it? Isabel remained in the car long after her new contact left. She sat still, growing colder by the minute, her skin erupting with goose bumps which she idly rubbed. Did she dare to hope this time? Yes, she'd gained new information, gathered more names. It was certainly an interesting development, albeit such a tragic one. Isabel had tried to speak with Francesca Withers before but failed. With a question mark by her name and a note to try again in another month, Isabel moved to the next, assuming she'd get another opportunity.

It was Francesca's mother who then contacted Isabel through Gransnet online chat forum, and it set her heart racing, thinking about the prospect of getting Francesca on board. As she read the message, though, the light of hope flickered and extinguished.

'My Fran took her own life,' the mother said.

The wish that it was entirely unrelated to John Lawson crashed too, when she went on to explain the circumstances. Social services had stepped in and removed Fran's son, placing him into emergency foster care due to her alcohol abuse and, it appeared, subsequent drug use. Fran's mother was devastated she couldn't take him on herself – failing health meant she wasn't suitable. Oakley had been adopted.

She'd lost everything.

She was determined any assistance she could give to help Isabel gain evidence against the man who drove her daughter to suicide, was the least she could do.

Chapter 39

NOW

BECKY

The light filters through the beige curtains and I close my eyes again, not overly eager to join the day. A leaden feeling settled in my stomach after seeing Marcus yesterday and has remained there since. Along with the deep, soul-sucking sadness – which feels very much like the way my depression began after losing Mum and Dad – my limbs are too heavy to move.

A soft knocking on the bedroom door is followed by a creak of it being opened a crack and Hannah's voice, quiet and enquiring. 'You awake?'

My eyes stay shut. It's even too much energy to make my mouth work.

'I'll bring you a coffee.' The door closes again.

When I returned here after the meeting, I relayed some of what Marcus told me. It was met, quite understandably, by shock. While we'd already been discussing how John had seemingly been protected by some people inside the force, hearing it from such a trusted and high-up source was undeniably worrying and Hannah took it as badly as expected, but also insisted those involved would be brought to justice. Every last one of them.

As I sink into my pillow, bone-weary from it all, I only wish I shared her optimism. One step forward, two back. That's how it feels right now where John is concerned. And I can't seem to stop the negative thoughts now I know that whatever went on, and is likely still going on, will go unchallenged, and unpunished.

'Charlie and I had a chat,' Hannah says. I open one eye as she places a mug on the bedside table. 'There's been no report of a missing person, or anything else untoward regarding a Tamsin . . . that's good, isn't it?' Her tone is bright and cheerful, and I know she's trying to jolly me up. 'Come on, Becky, mate.' My body shifts slightly as a pillow is pulled from beneath me. 'Are you sure she's not lying low in the flat? Or, maybe she just left him and went to a refuge?' Becky pulls at me, while trying to place the pillows against the headboard. I open my eyes fully – they feel gritty as I blink away the lingering fatigue. Hannah is fully dressed, but her face, inches from mine as she encourages me to sit up, is bare of make-up and displays the same creases of concern I imagine mine does. I wonder how much of that is due to Danny. She wasn't forthcoming with information when I asked how he was doing, and a shadow passed over her face when I mentioned cancer. She's always been so strong, holding everything together for her family – and her work colleagues. My gut twists. I'm adding more to her list of worries and it's really not fair. I allow her to position me upright, arms to the sides

221

above the duvet – just how she might a doll at a tea party – then she hands me the mug.

'Get this in you. Might perk you up a bit.'

She's mothering me. And the thought is comforting, but disconcerting. This isn't her job.

'I'll go back to the flat today,' I say, my voice hoarse. 'Get out of your hair.'

'No, Becky.' She shakes her head and sits down on the edge of the bed. 'It's too dangerous for you to be there.'

I shrug, then take a sip of coffee. The hot liquid burns my lips, but it tastes good.

'No more so than here,' I say. 'If John wants to get at me, Hannah, he will know exactly where, or who, to target, won't he? Even Charlie seemed a bit on edge on Friday.'

Hannah's eyebrows draw together. 'Charlie did?'

'Yep. I think it was because he'd uncovered the redacted files and stuff – and then finding out I was seeing Nina, that she'd given us that list, didn't help his unease. I understand I'm causing some . . . anxiety . . . among the CID lot.' I try to laugh, but have a coughing fit instead. Hannah jumps up and slaps me on the back as if I'm choking on food. I wave my hand to let her know I'm fine.

'You might be right about John knowing where to look for you, but at least I'm here some of the time. That flat . . . well – Christ, Becky, it's not like you've made friends *there* is it!'

'Well, there is Agatha.'

'That bloody cat? Please.'

'Seriously though. I've had *five* days away and you said yourself after you went there, the flat was secure, with no signs of anyone having been inside. Trust me, I appreciate your hospitality – and your food – but you've got enough on your plate with Danny. You'll need this room for him.'

'If he comes home,' she says. My heart aches for her. Although she still hasn't said as much, I fear the prognosis isn't good. I want to be a friend to her, support her with this. Yet all I'm managing to do is rope her into something that could jeopardise her job. Her life. What kind of friend does that make me?

It's another hour before I pull myself from the slump and I take my last shower at Hannah's. With some space, and a different environment for several nights, to contemplate the situation and what I should do about it, I've concluded I will not be forced from my own place. I refuse to be bullied anymore. John is a very dangerous individual, that is a fact, but ultimately, he's also a coward. Using others to do his bidding, threatening women, manipulating people, and abusing his position – and all the while he wholeheartedly believes he can get away with all of this behaviour. It makes me sick to my stomach. *He* makes me sick. This establishment does too. It all sucks.

We're in the twenty-first century, it shouldn't be the case that women don't know if it's safe to trust the police. A few years ago, in the wake of an attack on a female in London by an off-duty officer, it was suggested that if a woman was stopped by a lone officer they should simply challenge their legitimacy, or if they didn't trust them, to run to a nearby house, or yell for help, or flag down the nearest bus. It was advice that had been embarrassing back then, even before I knew what I do now. As a female CID officer I cringed; as a woman, I was gobsmacked, outraged that 'tips' to handle being stopped by police were being given. Not reassurances that serving police would be thoroughly vetted, pulled up on inappropriate language, treatment of female victims and the like. Why wasn't 'how to stop male violence' high on the agenda?

It's the rising anger these thoughts create that snaps me into action and with my heart pounding, I begin stuffing my clothes into my rucksack.

'These yours?' Hannah comes into the bedroom, holding out a small brown bottle. My face burns as I take it from her.

'Yeah. Started them again, a precaution, you know? It's been a tough two weeks,' I say, not quite catching her eye. I know I shouldn't be embarrassed. Hannah had been aware of my medication use following the first round with John, but not that long ago I'd told her I was managing without them.

'I'm glad you're being sensible,' she says with a smile.

I leave Hannah's, retrieve my car, drive to Pendlebury and park in my garage. Speed-walking with my rucksack banging against my back, I march towards the block of hell. Each step reinforces my resolution that I'm not letting the bastard win. Utilising this momentum, when I reach the building I go straight to the steps to get to the second level, and without any hesitation head to Vince and Tamsin's flat. My knuckles rap on the wood, the sound echoing across the walkway. My breaths are ragged, but my shoulders are back, head held high as I wait to face Vince – and I'm hoping by some miracle that Tamsin will be there, too. Maybe she'll have been wondering where I've been.

After a few minutes of me banging, I hear someone hollering. But the voice is above me, coming from the third floor.

'Isn't it fuckin' obvious they ain't in?'

I take a few steps towards the balcony, hang over so I can look up. 'Have you seen either of them?' I shout back.

'You feds?'

'No. I live in this block. They have something of mine.'

'Well good luck to ya. That arsewipe ain't likely gonna give it back.'

'Have you seen the woman?' I know I'm on borrowed time with the upstairs neighbour; I'm surprised I've kept them in conversation this long. 'She's called Tamsin.'

There's no response. I haven't heard the slamming of a door, though, so assume they're still there. I'm tempted to rush up to the next level, but it's unlikely I'll reach the flat before they disappear back inside, and I doubt they'll answer to my knocking.

'The arsewipe was giving it some the other night,' I say, going along with their appraisal of Vince, 'maybe she's left him.'

'Nah. They left together, didn't they.' The voice tells me – it's not a question.

My heart leaps and I have to quickly pull myself back in from overhanging the balcony as the blood leaves my head. They left together? That's either really good news, or really bad, and for the moment, I can't decide which.

'Oh, really?' I call. Then, pushing my luck, I ask if they know which way they went, whether they were with other people and if they had any bags with them. After telling me in no uncertain terms what I should do with my questions, the upstairs neighbour divulges that the pair of them got into a dark car – into the rear seats – and it sped off like it was a getaway car. My luck runs out when I attempt to pin them down on the day and time of this occurrence. I swear I actually feel the concrete beneath my feet shift with the force of the person's door banging.

Where are they? Have they both been taken – or is Vince

the one who's holding her somewhere on someone else's instructions? I'd love to believe the refuge theory Hannah came up with, I really would, but if she knew the full story, she likely wouldn't believe that either. I fight the urge to read too much into the third-floor flat person's retelling of events because without knowing all the details, my mind is currently presenting it as evidence that Tamsin is alive and well. I sweep the hair from my face where it's become plastered against my forehead with beads of sweat. What a tangled mess this is. And it's five days before I'm due to see Nina again. I'm not sure I can wait that long to find out if she's uncovered anything more that could shine a light on what's happening.

When I reach my own flat, breathing fast from exertion, I give it the once-over before attempting to go inside. Hannah was right. Everything looks as it did when I left on Monday evening – and so, with my lower lip partially clamped between my teeth, I stick the key in the lock, and pray it's the same story inside. The mat is clogged with mail, mostly junk, and I have to force the door over the pile. How the hell does this much accumulate in a matter of a few days? I drop my rucksack, gather it all up and begin to rifle through it. Takeaway menus, funeral plan leaflets, and then I stop, my breath catching as I get to a cream envelope with just 'Rebecca Lawson' written on it. Someone knew to deliver it here, but chose not to post it. The writing is neat; rightly, or wrongly, I'm presuming it was penned by a female.

After a few seconds of pondering, I slip my thumb underneath the flap and tear at it. A furball knocks against my shins, and I take a moment to make a fuss of Agatha. A warm sensation builds inside me just having her here to greet me. She purrs loudly, like a tank. And while I appreciate she would probably exhibit the same behaviour

226

with anyone if she thought they were here to feed her, I lap up this attention before resuming the task in hand. With my focus back on the envelope, I pull the folded letter from it – the same neat writing adorns a single piece of pretty, patterned notepaper – and begin to read it out to Agatha.

'To Rebecca. You don't know me, but from the limited information I've managed to find out about you, I think we have some things in common. Or, more to the point . . . a person.'

I stop talking, swallowing down the obstruction in my throat. The writing blurs and becomes wavy, my vision acting like it does prior to a migraine. Or an anxiety attack. I half expect my mobile to ring, as it did before when I was going through a similar thing and Elijah, again, coming to the rescue – but it stays silent. After sitting and focusing on my breathing, determined not to reach for the tablets this time, it passes and I carry on reading. And when I finish, I get my phone and dial the number contained within it.

'Rebecca? Thank you for calling me, I know it can't have been easy.'

The voice is silky smooth, she would make a great voiceover artist.

'Call me Becky,' I squeak – my larynx needs oiling.

'We need to talk about your husband—'

'*Ex*-husband,' I correct.

'As I say in my letter . . . there are a few of us who, well . . . want justice served.'

'Go on,' I say, warming to this unknown woman.

'Will you meet me?'

I know I'm going to agree, of course I am, because this is huge. Having someone else who's after John will make this process faster. Won't it?

If she's genuine.

Ignoring my warning thought could lead to a fall. 'Why should I trust you?' I say.

There's an audible intake of breath, then after a few seconds, she responds. 'Before he walked away from me, leaving me naked, vulnerable, hollowed out – he told me that no one that *could* do anything *would*. I have to believe that's not true, Becky. You should trust me, because I'm placing mine in you.'

Tears spring to my eyes, her words piercing through me like shards of glass.

After agreeing where and when to meet, I sit and swipe the cuff of my sleeve at the seemingly limitless outpour of tears. This is the first time I've spoken with one of John's victims. I finally don't believe I'm crazy. Her words resonated with me. She's genuine. So, without bothering to unpack my rucksack, I add a few other items to it, then restock Agatha's food dishes and clean out the litter tray. Apologising for abandoning her again, I leave my flat. This time, there's hope firing every nerve ending and I refuse to quell it. This is it. I can feel it.

Chapter 40

NOW

BECKY

The intensity of her gaze as she watches me approach sends an ice-cold shock wave up my back. She looks to be in her early twenties, petite – around five feet, with silky chestnut hair that frames her heart-shaped face. We stand for a few seconds, as though weighing each other up. Trust is something we are both apparently lacking, despite the fact we're here as agreed.

'I'm Isabel,' she says, coolly.

'Becky Gooding.'

'You're not what I was expecting. You were a detective?' she says, narrowing her eyes as I widen mine. I run a nail along the side of my mouth, unsure what to make of her assessment of me. She flusters. 'I mean, I thought you'd be older, somehow. The stuff I found out online made it seem as though you'd been on the force for years.'

'Five,' I say. 'I went in direct, through the degree

programme. Anyway . . . shall we?' I point to the house we're standing outside of. 'Is this her place?'

'Yep,' Isabel says, looking up at the mid-terraced property. 'Fran's mum kindly gave me a key.'

'How did you find her?' I ask as we make our way to the front door.

'I put posts up on social media, asked online in groups like Mumsnet, Gransnet, and every other one I could think of, even placed an ad in the local paper.'

'Wow. How did you even word it?' My thoughts swiftly go to libel. As much as I'm quite sure whatever Isabel has on John is true, proving that, as I know, is much trickier. Easier for John to sue if he insists his 'good name' is being publicly dragged through the mud.

'Carefully,' she says. 'Anyone reading them would identify with what I wrote. Was a case of if you know, you know. I had to weed out some irrelevant info, and, depressingly, I needed to forward a lot of women onto an appropriate service as they were victims of something, or someone, different.'

'Oh, God. That's awful.' In this moment, I'm shrouded in a shawl of guilt. Both personally and professionally, I've let a lot of people down. Somehow, the very act of marrying an evil predator feels very much like I've contributed to his victims' pain.

None so more than the woman whose place we're about to walk into.

'So, let's do something about it,' Isabel says as the key turns. It takes several firm pushes before the door opens; the wood's swelled and, judging by the huge pile of post, I guess no one's been here for a while. Isabel bends to gather it all, and I follow her inside.

The musty, not-lived-in smell makes my eyes water

within seconds. Or, maybe it's merely contributing to my teary eyes. The first room we enter is filled with dust-layered furniture, knick-knacks and discarded toys.

'I thought you said her child had been placed in foster care?' I direct my frown at Isabel.

'I assume Fran left Oakley's things out as a reminder of her son.'

My eyes cast around, taking in the chunky plastic toys, wooden blocks and teddy bears still strewn around the room. 'Or as a punishment,' I whisper, my lower lip wobbling.

'And Fran's mum did likewise.' Isabel lightly touches the sweater that's been thrown over the back of the sofa before lowering her head, putting chin to chest. I turn away, to allow her a moment of quiet contemplation. I'd seen so much over the past five years, in some ways I've become desensitised, hardened to the horrors some people have suffered. The cases which tended to break through the barrier were road traffic deaths caused by drunk drivers, child abuse, and – particularly during the final year of my time at the CID – violence against women. Each of those felt like a blow to the head, a stabbing sensation inside my gut, or a crushing of my ribcage.

This right here, this feels as though I'm experiencing all of those things at once. I sniff, shake my shoulders and blink rapidly to regain composure. Falling apart won't help anyone.

'Are you ready?' I ask, going to Isabel and laying my hand on her shoulder. She inhales a juddering breath.

'Yep. Let's do this.'

Together we begin the search. We take a methodical approach, with me suggesting that Isabel begins in the kitchen while I take the lounge before we both move to the upstairs bedrooms. These are the most likely spots we'll find anything useful. Once we've completed those, we'll move on to the smaller spaces.

With as much speed as possible, while also trying to be careful, I sift through the content of the Ikea unit that takes up the length of one wall. I hear Isabel rummaging in the drawers in the kitchen. Apart from those sounds, there's a deathly silence. Speaking would feel wrong as I rifle through a dead person's belongings. I try to imagine I'm working a crime scene, that I'm searching for evidence. Which, in many ways I am. I think John will have been inside here. *Raped Fran here.* I push that thought from my mind.

'Focus.' I close my eyes and recall the forensic team talking about how they approach crime scenes. And I hear the voice of the coroner as they undertake a postmortem. Both fields of expertise analyse evidence in different ways, both piece together the event, whether that's a crime or accident, to ascertain the timeline and the way it occurred. Though Fran officially died from suicide, I know it isn't cut and dried. The evidence from the postmortem, Isabel informed me, was that she'd taken a lethal amount of prescribed sleeping pills with paracetamol. Case closed according to the inquest.

But Isabel and I are here now to backtrack. The cause of death was ultimately because everything had been taken from her. We have to piece together what Fran had been trying to do – her message to John's burner seems as though it was a last-ditch attempt to bring him down before she ended her pain. She's left a legacy for us to continue.

I know in my heart that Fran would've left something incriminating. Something John wasn't able to find and destroy as easily as he did with his phone and the content on it. Would John have come here afterwards though and removed what we're looking for? My head throbs. That's the worry. He was aware she'd sent the screenshot, maybe had more besides. It's clear, especially now Marcus has added weight to it, that John has the 'support' of other officers – possibly detectives, or even people he employs to do some of the dirty work for him. Wouldn't they have cleaned up the mess he left? Tied up loose ends?

I'm a loose end, too.

These thoughts begin to bring down my energy levels, and I step away from the unit and slump down on the sofa – a puff of dust whooshing into the air.

'That's where she was, you know.' Isabel stands in the doorway, her hands on her hips. 'Where her poor mother found her,' she adds with a deep sigh.

'I can't imagine how traumatic that was.' It's a bit disconcerting knowing Fran's life ended on this very sofa. I don't move though. For the moment, I want to sit here quietly and place myself in Fran's shoes. She was at a point of no return, having lost the most important person in her life, her little boy. There was no coming back from the edge, no one to pull her to safety. How did it start with John? Did he pick her because of her vulnerabilities or was it random? Did he stalk her for a while? Wait for the perfect moment – then pounce? Her message, or screenshot of messages, hinted at him abusing her more than once. He made her think he would help her, I bet. Offered her a way out . . . if she did something in return. My stomach churns; I press both hands into it, then close my eyes and lie back.

A flash of a memory shoots into my mind's eye. John pushing me down on our sofa, having rough and hurried sex with me before he headed off for work. I remember making excuses for it at the time, blaming myself for him hurting me because *I'd* asked for it. That night is imprinted – it's when my world began to unravel. Finding the burner down the back of the sofa was the start. My eyes spring open and I sit up straight.

'I wonder?' I spread my hands each side of me, the material of the sofa scratchy against my palms. Pulling apart the fixed sofa cushions, I check the cracks, removing bits of old food, fluff, and a five-pence piece. Then I face the back of the sofa and kneel on the cushions to make the gap large enough to slip my hand down.

After a few sweeps and not finding anything, disappointment kicks in and I sit back on my calves. When I found the burner, though, it had accidentally found its way into the sofa, it hadn't been purposely secreted there. If Fran was intending to *hide* it . . . With a new-found enthusiasm I dig deeper, pushing my arm in up to my elbow to check the depths of the furniture inch by inch.

My fingertips touch a solid object and I freeze. Please, please be something.

With a little patient manoeuvring, I pull out the item, excitement-induced nausea twisting my stomach.

'Isabel . . . *Isabel*,' I call. She comes rushing in, and I hold out my hand. 'I'm scared to get my hopes up, but . . . '

'Shit. Her phone?'

'I think so.' I turn the dusky-pink mobile over in my hands. 'Battery is dead, obviously.'

'Let's see,' Isabel says, striding over to me. 'Oh, sod it. Not the same connector as mine. Yours?'

'It looks the same as mine. I'll take it,' I say, reaching for Fran's phone. Isabel is hesitant, giving me a questioning glare. I understand she probably doesn't want to relinquish control – she's done that for too long *and* she's the one who has managed to bring together the women who could provide the much-needed evidence to finally ensure John is punished. It must feel like I'm taking her case away from her. Similar to when the MIT swoop in and take command of a situation you've been working on for weeks. It's frustrating, and sometimes difficult to let go. You've taken ownership of the case and want to be the one who secures the right outcome. It's what you feel you owe the victim and their family.

'Haven't you got it in your car?'

'I'm not that organised.' I hold my hand out. 'I want this as bad as you do,' I say. Isabel purses her lips, then slaps the phone onto my palm. Our gazes meet and I inhale sharply as the hurt and sorrow in her deep-brown eyes spills out. 'I'm so sorry. For what he did to you and the others.'

'Do you know how long I believed I deserved it?' She sniffs loudly then sits down beside me. I put my hand on her arm and give a shake of my head. 'He said he'd help me. And even when I got that gut-wrenching sensation it was going to mean something bad – because I let him do it – I'd *asked* for it.'

John had watched her, approached her, 'helped' her, then raped her. That was his MO. Isabel tells me how she went from an outgoing, fun and exuberant person to someone afraid of her own shadow. Not trusting anyone – even herself. Something snapped and after feeling like she had no other way out and considering suicide, she decided if she was going down that route, she may as well cause a shitstorm for John first. That's how she came to where she is today. And I'm so thankful she found me.

'I wonder if Fran left anything else? I mean, if she was

235

in a similar position to you, it's conceivable she thought similarly?'

Isabel shrugs. 'What, though? The phone could be all there is.'

'What did her mum say when she met with you?'

'Fran hadn't even told her the truth, Becky. I get the impression her mum had got to the end of her tether with her.'

'That would've worked out well for John, then.' A sadness presses down onto both of us; I can sense it in the room, in the space between us. *Enveloping* us. I know where this feeling leads. 'Come on,' I say, getting up from the sofa. 'We need to keep going.' Isabel's cheeks puff out with air, and she expels it forcefully.

'Right,' she says. 'Bedroom next.'

We ascend the stairs, the wood beneath the carpet creaking in response to each step; it's likely the first weight they've experienced in months. I'm first up and go to what looks most likely to be the double room. Fran's. I pause, turning to face Isabel.

'Shall we do this one together?'

We step inside the teal-coloured bedroom and the first thing that's striking is how tidy it is. Compared to the disarray of the downstairs, this is a picture of orderliness – everything perfectly placed and organised. The duvet on the bed is taut, not a wrinkle visible in the cream cover and teal throw.

'Do you think her mum's been in here? Tidied?' Isabel says, echoing my own thoughts.

'It's a stark contrast to the chaos of the lounge that's for sure. There's something deeply personal about a bedroom though, isn't there? Maybe a mother would want to somehow preserve what was left of her daughter's privacy and dignity.'

We both fall silent again. Searching in here, messing up the perfection, feels wrong.

'It's necessary,' Isabel says, quietly, like she read my mind.

The wardrobe is the usual place people tend to hide things. False back, false bottom, high shelf, cardboard box buried beneath piles of shoes or clothes. We start there, but there's nothing. Trying not to lose hope yet, we move on to the bed, checking under the mattress, in the drawers of the base unit, the headboard. We shift the bed to under the window and silently walk over the floor hoping to feel an uneven board. Nothing.

'Are we wasting our time in here?'

I don't answer, walking instead towards the dressing table. It's antique-looking, mismatched to all of the other furniture in the house. The drawers are still filled with Fran's clothes, and, like everything else in the room, they're neat. The clothes folded.

'It's all just a bit too tidy,' I say. 'Like someone's been here, but didn't want it to appear like they'd conducted a search.'

'Would police have searched when they found her?'

'Not if there were no suspicious circumstances. Are you able to call her mum and ask her?'

Isabel nods and leaves the room. I hear some muffled talking, and when she returns, she tells me that the police didn't mention a search, and Fran's mum hasn't stepped foot inside the bedroom because she hadn't found the strength yet. It's either a case of Fran keeping this room immaculate, or someone was here looking for incriminating evidence but didn't want to leave a trace.

'So, even if Fran left something, you think *they* found it?'

With an exasperated groan, I sit down heavily on the dressing table stool, kicking out my right foot, frustration getting the better of me. The thud against the wooden leg of the dresser is hollow. Frowns pass between Isabel and myself and I push back on the stool and get to my hands and knees to inspect the leg. My fingertips dance over the ridges in the wood, then, just above the leg I find a lip and dig my nails in and pull. I wince as they slip out, several bending back. Maybe I'm imagining a secret compartment because I'm so desperate.

'Here, let me try.' Isabel, now on her knees beside me, moves forwards. She takes out her keys which have a tiny penknife attached. I raise my eyebrows but say nothing as she teases the tip into the ridge and slides the blade along the length of the plinth. I suck in a lungful of air as something clicks and a drawer pops open. Like a magician withdrawing the rabbit from the hat, Isabel retrieves a small brown, leather-bound notebook. We both stare at it, unmoving. A shiver of anticipation breaks the spell and I stand up.

'You do it,' I say, barely able to stay still. Pins and needles from kneeling are spreading from my feet to my calves as I shift my weight from one leg to the other, while still hovering over Isabel. Her trembling fingers unravel the lace that is wrapped around the leaf-embossed book. She slowly opens it, revealing the deckle-edged pages – it's a beautifully crafted vintage-style journal. And from what I can see as Isabel does a quick flick through it, there is writing on almost every page.

'Oh, God,' Isabel says.

'What is it?' My throat constricts with the fear that this is from Fran's childhood, a *Dear Diary* affair where she relays in minute-by-minute detail how she fancies the boy next door. Is it jam-packed with teenage angst and hatred for school, her parents? Does it even belong to her? My heart slams against my chest. It's an antique dressing table. This might belong to someone who died fifty years ago or something.

'Look . . . ' Isabel turns to face me, her eyes wet with tears as she holds up the journal. I take it. And I read the first page. Then the next. Then I flick past a few entries and stop at a page where she's written a bunch of initials, and nicknames.

'Shit, this could be gold,' I say as my eyes scan the page. My mind is too jittery to figure out if any are familiar, or stand out. I pass it back. 'Do you think they could be names of other victims . . . or?' I hardly dare to hope the details relate to those responsible for helping John cover this all up. Isabel studies it.

'One of these nicknames—' she points to the middle of the page '—I'm fairly sure rings a bell. Misty.' She stands up, her brow furrowed as she concentrates on recalling a memory. 'I swear I've spoken to someone of that name.' She paces, then her eyes widen, and she looks up from the journal. 'Yes, of course. Moods club.'

My pulse skips. That place is what links Tamsin to this, too. 'When did you go there?'

'One of the first places I tried. I'd seen John going in there. Officially, of course, but I just had a feeling.'

'Young women. Those he felt most comfortable manipulating.' Hatred oozes from my words. He has so much to answer for.

'I wish she'd been supported.' Isabel slumps onto the bed. 'If I'd reached out to her before. I might've been able to stop her.'

'Don't do that. There's only one person to blame for all of this, and that's the perpetrator. The predator . . . ' Heat flashes in my cheeks, then a burning sensation fills my gut. 'The *monster*. The person whose actions created the hurt. He's the cause. He's the manipulator. He's the one who needs to be punished.' My breath runs out. The anger never will.

A slight smile plays on Isabel's lips. 'Quite the motivational speaker,' she says.

The room grows dim, and I switch on a light to continue reading.

'We'd best crack on,' Isabel says, getting up to look out of the window. 'I get the feeling we should wrap this up before nightfall.'

'We've got the phone and now this.' I lift the journal.

'Yep. But there could be more. And I want to be the one to find it. Not him.'

Chapter 41

NOW

BECKY

After searching for another hour in the dying light of Sunday evening, Isabel and I called it a night. We hadn't come across anything else that seemed significant. With further reassurances from me that I'd immediately share any findings from Fran's mobile with her, I took it and the journal, and we went our separate ways. As soon as I got back to my flat, I plugged the phone in to charge on the kitchen worktop and sat down in my armchair to read the journal cover to cover.

And that's exactly where I wake up – slumped in the chair, stiff from another unrested night. The room is light, and I can hear the thrum of steady traffic. Shit. What time is it? My eyes are bleary, but my mind sharpens quickly. Agatha stares at me from her position on the back of the futon, her twitching whiskers a sign of contempt. Poor cat never gets fed on time. I'm surprised she didn't jump all over me to jolt me into action.

My stomach lurches. Fran's mobile.

Eager to see, hesitant to know, I fling myself from the chair, stride to the kitchen and with my hands clenched and my breath held, I peek at the display. Every muscle fibre is taut, the voice in my head pleading for incriminating evidence against John to be contained within this six-inch piece of technology.

My hand hovers above the screen – I envisage swiping my finger up and the home screen coming to life. Deep down, I know it's unlikely. It'll be password protected and I'll have to get Charlie or Hannah to take it to the techies – although quite how that'll work I don't know. The fact it was *hidden* gets my hopes up, though. Fran had wanted someone like me, or Isabel to find it. In which case, she'd possibly made it easier for us.

'Procrastination is the thief of time.' I take a breath and touch the screen.

The loud ringing tone momentarily confuses me.

Then I realise it's *my* mobile.

'Jesus!' I scramble around the kitchen trying to locate mine, then rush into the lounge, finding it perched on a box. 'Hello,' I snap, annoyed at the caller's timing.

'Get out on the wrong side of the bed?'

'Not even close,' I retort to Hannah's sarcasm.

'Just a quick request,' she says. My shoulders dip – anything that's going to take me away from Fran's phone isn't to be welcomed. 'I forgot to bring Nina's list of dates and times into work. Can you go and get them from mine and meet me at the front of the CID building at 1 p.m.?' She goes on to say that she wants me to 'surreptitiously' hand them to her and carry on walking. I want to tell her it's not an episode of *Bosch* but my mind is already onto the next thought: Didn't Charlie take it? I don't recall seeing the list when I was packing up my investigation table. But Hannah wouldn't be asking now if Charlie was already in possession of it. With my mind in shards when I left, I might have even stuffed it into my rucksack along with everything else. Lack of sleep combined with a ton of worry has messed with my head to such a degree that I can't one-hundred per cent trust my memory. I obviously wanted Hannah and Charlie to work through the list and highlight any dates where John was working, where and with whom, or if he was off-duty on any or all of the dates, so surely I *did* leave it there.

As I'm talking, I find my rucksack and rummage through it just to be sure. I wonder if now is a good time to tell her about Isabel. And that we found a mobile belonging to one of John's victims. The decision is made for me when Hannah delivers a harsh whisper of 'Got to go,' presumably having been rumbled being on a private call. I hadn't had the chance to agree to visit her place and pick up the list, but I guess seeing as it's *not* in my rucksack and I've asked for so much from Hannah, I need to do as she asked. And, given it's for the benefit of the investigation, I unplug Fran's phone from the charger and shove it in my tote bag, grab my coat and keys and head out.

Maybe it's related to Charlie's actions the day he swept the place and what he said afterwards, or maybe it's a sixth sense, but a stab of unease overcomes me as soon as I open the door to Hannah's and step inside.

Someone's here.

The noise I've made entering will have alerted the

occupant to my arrival, and my head tells me to make a swift exit. Not take any chances. My gut, however, is having none of it. I'm not running. If the person here wishes to harm me, I'll put up a bloody good fight. I'm on high alert as I tread cautiously through the hallway, clutching the tote bag tightly. My hearing is heightened, preparing me to respond to any sudden movement. All the warning signs I get prior to an anxiety episode assault me all at once, but it's as though my mind and body are working in symbiosis and instead of creating a full-blown attack, I'm emboldened, just like I used to be in dangerous situations prior to finding out about my ex-husband's crimes.

The sound of coughing stops me in my tracks. It's coming from the lounge. When it continues, I decide to use it as cover to make my move. I take quick steps and push the already ajar door open enough to see inside. With my eyes wide, I take in all I can. Relief relaxes my posture, but my heart muscle continues to contract strongly and rapidly even though the immediate threat of danger is over.

'Christ, Danny. You gave me a fright; Hannah didn't say you would be here.' I put my hand to my chest, feeling the thudding against my palm begin to lessen.

Danny recovers from his coughing fit and runs his bare forearm along under his nose, leaving a trail of slimy residue.

'She don't know I'm 'ere.'

I reach into my pocket and get my mobile.

'Don't. Please don't tell 'er,' he pleads with me. He appears even paler than the other night. Grey even – the colour I've seen people prior to death.

'Why not, Danny?' The tiny hairs on my neck stand up. Something's not right here. Hannah took him to his appointment – for treatment, that's what she'd said when she left me here last week. Was he meant to be in hospital?

''Cos she'll worry. May as well give 'er a few more hours, eh?' He offers a weak smile.

'Are you . . .' I struggle to find the right word '. . . er . . . okay? I mean, you look pretty sick.'

'I'll survive. For now.'

I need to get the list and get going if I'm to meet Hannah outside CID for one o'clock as she instructed. Looking at Danny, though, I'm compelled to stay a little longer.

'Can I make you a brew? When did you last eat?'

'Tea would be good thanks. Make it strong.' He collapses back on the chair, his long, thin arms loosely draped over each side, resembling an orangutan. I go into the kitchen. While waiting for the kettle to boil, I check around the worktops, the table and inside all the drawers for the list that Nina gave me. But there's no sign. Where the hell is it?

I pour a tea for Danny, squishing the teabag between the back of two spoons to develop the tone to a burnt toffee colour, while contemplating where else I should look.

'Here you are.' I hand the mug to Danny, waiting to be sure he has proper hold before letting go. 'You haven't seen some A4-sized papers clipped together have you?' He squints at me through the puff of steam from his tea. Shakes his head. 'I'll be back in a min,' I say, and go upstairs to check the room I stayed in, then Hannah's. The list isn't there. I've half a mind to go and pat Danny down, in case he has it on his person. But why would he?

He hasn't shifted from the chair when I return to the lounge and take a seat opposite him, scrutinising his face. His leg bounces. I hadn't noticed it on any previous meetings, so I don't think it's a tic. Maybe it's related to whatever illness he has. Or I'm making him anxious.

245

'Danny, look this is really important. Have you seen any paperwork or picked it up, maybe?'

He avoids my gaze, shuffles in the chair. Then the leg bouncing continues. I've seen this kind of physical manifestation during interviews before. When the person is stressed, and usually that stress is because they're lying. I must remember I'm not interrogating a suspect here, though. This is Hannah's ill little brother. And if he were to relay my actions to her, I'm pretty sure I'd lose my inside allies because of it.

'If I 'ad I'd have said when you asked the first time.'

'What time did you get here?' I look around, wondering if anything has been disturbed, like someone was searching for something.

''Bout ten minutes before you showed up. Got a taxi 'ere if you need to check,' he says, glaring at me now.

'Okay, sorry. I'm not . . . I'm just asking.'

'Once a fed, always a fed. Even if you were thrown out.' He smirks. 'How come you got that flat in Pendlebury? Bit of a comedown from your place with John.'

I try to hide my shock at his question – at his knowledge of my living arrangements past and present. He must hear things second-hand from Hannah. My eye twitches.

'Beggars can't be choosers, eh?' I flash Danny a smile, but ensure it signals that I'm saying no more than that.

'But, I mean why that block, why that flat?' The tables being turned and now me being under some form of interrogation flusters me and I want the conversation over. I get up, readying myself to leave.

'It was obviously meant to be,' I say. Although I don't believe it could really have been serendipitous – there are better places. 'A simple case of right time, right place.'

'Yeah. Meant to be,' he says, in a way that's weighted with a meaning I'm not sure I want to understand. Then it clicks. He just wants to change the subject – stop me from asking him questions.

'Let's get back to why I'm here, shall we?' I say, firmly. 'I need to find the papers I came here for—' Danny thrusts his hand up towards me, then shakes his head.

'You don't want to keep looking,' he says in a way that sends a chill down my spine. *You don't want to keep looking* . . . I've heard that before. The phone call I received that first day I went to Lymworth in search of John. I was in Maccies. The person on the phone echoed a near identical phrase.

'Why would you say that, Danny?'

'Bad things happen to them that know too much.'

The urge to get out speeds up my exit. Has John got to Danny? How the hell do I tell Hannah I suspect her brother of being behind some of the threats. He looks like he's at death's door – from the way Hannah was talking the other night, I get the feeling he's not long for this world.

Dying people don't need to be afraid of the consequences. Unless they're religious, of course. That makes Danny a perfect candidate to do some of John's bidding. When I'm back in my car, I text Hannah to let her know I have nothing to hand over, asking if she's sure she didn't already give it to Charlie. Because if she didn't and none of us has it, then who does? I push that awful thought away, and instead I find myself battling my conscience as to whether I should tell her Danny is home. I type out another text, then delete it. I drag a hand through my hair, irritated by my own indecision. She'll find out herself shortly; I guess there's no reason to say anything right this minute. Had she not asked me to pop in, neither of us would be any the wiser. Plus, Danny asked

247

me not to tell her, so maybe I shouldn't interfere. As I begin the drive back to my flat, Danny's question: why that block, why that flat – plays on my mind.

Is John behind every move I make? When I think, believe, I'm the one making decisions and taking control of my life, is he there, behind the scenes like a ghostly puppeteer pulling my strings so I only do what he wants, or needs me to? My pulse thuds in my ears. Maybe Danny knows more than he should. And he's probably right with his assumption . . . Bad things *do* happen to those who know too much. Especially those around John Lawson.

Chapter 42

NOW

BECKY

When I arrive back at my flat, the majority of the journey having been completed on autopilot, I get Fran's mobile from my tote bag and sit with it on my lap, gearing myself up to swipe the homepage properly this time. Isabel will be waiting for the update I promised her. I'm surprised she hasn't already been badgering me for it given it's almost twenty-four hours ago we found it. She has more patience than me, that's for sure.

With a few quick gulps of air, I do it – my fingertip slides upwards, and a clicking noise follows. I look with eyes wide at the home screen. 'Yes!' I mentally thank Fran for not having it password protected, then a shadow looms over my moment of elation when it's clear the photo is of her and her son, Oakley. What a waste. Poor kid growing up without his birth mother. My throat tightens seeing the young mum and son together, smiling and seemingly carefree. I can't dwell. I start scrolling until I find messenger and WhatsApp.

The messages, texts and screenshots are from the original source this time, not on a burner phone I only had access to for a short time. But, my elation is brief, a surge of disappointment quickly replacing it as I scroll, noting the use of initials or what appear to be nicknames for all her listed contacts. I'd forgotten only JL had been visible on the screenshot message I found on John's secret phone. Not one here states *John*, or better, *John Lawson*. And of course, I doubt he'll have ever used a mobile or landline that could be traced back to him anyway, so without his original I can't match these up. I attach Fran's phone to my computer and begin downloading the entire content anyway – there's a fair bit here to go through and something might yield a result if the tech guys can take a proper look.

I try to be positive, telling myself this is progress, allowing myself a small victory punch to the air. It's great evidence. Something physical at last. But realistically, only if it's accompanied by something stronger. The reality is, having messages like this, with limited ability to actually prove it's John sending them – means there aren't enough defining details, and a good solicitor would be able to brush them off. Still, it's the best so far and my spirits are lifted. I tap the mobile and smile. Fran tried really hard to get him. And now, even if John were to destroy *this* phone, there'll be copies of everything it contains on my hard drive. Once it's transferred, I'll see if I can match up any of the names and initials to those she wrote down in her journal.

To pass the time while it downloads, I raid the fridge for anything remotely passable as a snack. Agatha shared some of my food when she first came into my possession and now, looking at the content with my lip curled, I come to the conclusion she'll have to return the favour and share some of hers with me. I give a snorting laugh at the thought and slam it closed. Agatha pads in and shoots me a concerned look.

'It's not come to it yet, Agatha,' I say, petting her. My phone pings. It's a text from Charlie.

Can you call me?

I contemplate his request, but erring on the side of caution, text back a random comment first to check it's really him. Moments later, the phone vibrates in my hand as a call from an unknown number comes through. I hesitate, dread filling me. This at least shows a number, though, it's not been blocked by the caller. I accept.

'Hello?' I say, tentatively.

'It's me, Becks. This is secure, it's my friend's,' Charlie says.

My muscles relax. 'Hey. Everything okay?'

'Our contact has been in touch.' I note his vagueness and assume it's to avoid leaking sensitive information to those within earshot. 'They looked me up after you said not to call you. They were in a phone box, so don't worry . . .'

Charlie tells me the meeting has to be brought forward. Same time and place as before, but tomorrow, then hangs up before I get the chance to ask if he's in possession of Nina's list, much less that I'm in possession of a possible lead. I lean back heavily against the worktop, almost as though I've been pushed. It's only been a few days and if Nina can't wait until Friday, does that mean she's uncovered new information about John?

251

Chapter 43

NOW

BECKY

Nina fidgets: her fingers pull at the sugar sachets arranged in the bowl, then drum the table, before going to her hair and tugging at the longer strands near the crown of her head. But all the while her lips are tightly pursed – her facial features all stone-like. I feel the weight of her glare and I sense she's carrying a heavy burden.

'Why did you drag me into this?' she hisses through clamped teeth. I shiver. She's definitely found something. Controlling my urge to demand to know what, I offer a sympathetic smile and keep my own voice low when I apologise. It seems the right thing to do in this moment. After all, I did seek her out. I did, on three occasions, go to her. It was her choice to help, though. No one forced her into that decision.

'Has something happened?' I ask.

Nina scratches her thumbnail with her index nail, the

annoying scraping noise cutting through me. I place my hand over hers to stop it. She pulls her hand out from under mine and starts biting the nail instead, her focus faltering and shifting to look outside the café. She's more anxious than I've see her. This must be big.

'Happened? Yeah. You could say that.'

'What did you find, Nina?'

Her head shakes from side to side as she mumbles something I don't catch. Guilt vies for position against the sheer hope that whatever it is means trouble for John and any other corrupt officers he's got under his spell.

'It's . . . I couldn't. Fuck! I don't want to believe it. How could I miss it?'

I blink rapidly, drawing in a shuddering breath. 'You're asking the wrong person,' I say. 'I lived with him; I married him. I thought I knew him. And for five years I trusted him. *Loved* the man. And unwittingly I gave him an excellent cover. Maybe even alibis.' Nausea swirls in my stomach, dredging it all up again is like reliving all the hurt and pain. And the guilt. So much guilt. 'It was going on right under my nose. I married a monster, now I'm afraid you've taken up where I left off.'

Nina leans in closer to me, puts her mouth next to my ear. 'He's *kept* things.'

Icy tentacles slither around my body, embracing it tightly as the words sink in. Does she mean trophies? As awful as the thought is, this could be the break needed. I try to contain a surge of elation – showing any excitement right now would be inappropriate – Nina is clearly distraught by what she's uncovered. As I was when I found the burner phone. I must remember how shocked I was. Despite my earlier warnings she'll be feeling the same. It's one thing being told something, or suspecting wrongdoing, but facing that evidence yourself – irrefutable proof you're living with a serial rapist – is a hard pill to swallow. I count to five, take a breath.

'What kind of things? Where?'

'Photos. Of . . . Oh, God.' She moves away from me slightly, gives a furtive glance around the café, then continues. 'Some of them, they're so young. And there was *hair*.'

My pulse quickens as my mind screams, *DNA*. But of course, having locks of hair doesn't tie you to rape. If he'd murdered the women, then maybe. I mentally chastise myself for even thinking that.

'When you say there were photos . . . '

'I think he must've had a camera on a tripod,' Nina says. 'Because they're of them . . . together.' Her face contorts. 'Having *sex*.'

'Can you see them clearly. John's face? Are they tied or—'

'Stop. Please stop speaking.' She buries her face in her hands. 'Don't ask me that stuff.'

'I'm sorry, Nina. But if you've found trophies he's kept that show him committing rape, that's the best evidence yet. But if the images merely look like two people engaged in consensual sexual intercourse . . .' I sit back so hard the front chair legs lift from the floor, then slam down noisily, resulting in a few looks from other customers darting in my direction. I don't finish my sentence, the implied 'we have absolutely nothing' remains unspoken.

'There were USB memory sticks with each photo.'

Bingo. 'Did you photograph them?'

'No, Sorry. I didn't have time. He almost caught me. I couldn't chance him finding me looking through his private stuff. The last bloke I was with didn't take kindly to that

254

kind of thing either.' Nina lifts the edge of her top, revealing burn scars. 'I really thought I'd picked well with John. Was going to be protected.'

'I'm so sorry, Nina. John senses vulnerability. It's like he has a magnetic force drawing us to him.' She looks unconvinced.

'You don't strike me as vulnerable.'

'Maybe not outwardly. Inner trauma doesn't always seep through. But it's there all the same, not far beneath the surface.'

Nina puts her hand on mine – solidarity uniting us. 'I know where they are now, though. His disgusting souvenirs. To think they're in *my* house. Where my Millie lives.' Nina's eyes widen, she swallows repeatedly, like she's trying to prevent bile spewing from her mouth. She's genuinely horrified and the emotions she's experiencing I've been through too. Bar one. I don't know what it's like to have a child involved in this awful situation. I don't want to imagine how it feels to know your daughter is the offspring of a rapist. A part of me wonders if Millie was the result of John's manipulative tactics. Whether he forced himself onto Nina but she's blocked it out. My musings will stay as just that – there's nothing to gain from questioning her about it, and everything for her to lose if I did. Looking at her crestfallen face, she's already lost so much.

I can't stop shaking my head in astonishment that John would risk holding on to items that could provide DNA and a clear link between himself and rape victims. Nina gives me a questioning glance, so I share my contempt for the complete arrogance John's behaviour exhibits.

'He absolutely believes he's above reproach,' I say, my jaw tight. 'But no one is untouchable.'

255

'So, what should I do next?' Nina asks.

'Nothing for the moment.' Now it's my turn to drum my fingers on the table – a release of the nervous tension I've been holding on to. 'Carry on normally, acting the way you have been. Try not to alert him to a change.'

She snorts. 'How the hell do I do that?'

'I'll talk with my colleagues, let them know there's potential evidence in your house. Make a plan. In the meantime, keep track as you were doing. If, and I mean *if*, there's a chance for you to take photos of some of the images, then do. But you mustn't put yourself in danger.'

'I should've slipped one of the memory sticks into my pocket.'

'No. You were absolutely right not to take anything, disturb his treasure chest. He'd notice. Straightaway, he would know it was you.'

Nina's face is pale and drawn. Her fidgeting starts up again and she looks towards the exit. She wants to escape. Who can blame her?

'I'm scared,' she says, looking me directly in the eye. 'I'm thinking I should take Millie and stay at my parents' pub for a bit.'

'You could. But wouldn't he know where you were straightaway? Although, Millie could have a sleepover with her grandparents, I suppose – that's not out of the ordinary, is it?'

Nina brightens. 'Yeah, that's a good idea. Wouldn't start alarm bells ringing 'cos my mum's always going on about having Millie overnight, give us some space. Time to have a date night or something.'

'Okay, good. Try not to worry. You're able to contact Charlie again if you're at all concerned?'

'Yeah – I thought it best to go through him, like you suggested.'

'Definitely better not using mine. I don't trust he's not somehow listening in to my calls. And remember, use a landline, not your mobile.'

Nina nods and gets up. 'I'm sorry. For not believing you straightaway, I'm such a fool for being taken in by his lies.'

'You're not a fool, Nina. It'll take you a while to forgive yourself, but you will.'

After she's gone, I sit awhile, stirring the dregs of my coffee with the long, silver teaspoon. She's escaped this café, me and the conversation from hell, but gone right back to him. I have to pray I can help her escape him, too.

Chapter 44

NOW

BECKY

After leaving the Trafford Centre, I pop into the supermarket to grab some essentials. I don't want too much as my weary muscles won't cope with lumping more than two carrier bags from the car to home. Pleased with my minimal items – I can stretch this stuff to make at least five meals – I dump the bags in the boot and get behind the wheel. Spots of rain begin to appear on the windscreen. I hadn't even noticed the building clouds. I snort. This could easily be a metaphor for my life.

As I set off, tutting at my squeaking wipers, I try to imagine my life without the drama. Without the secret meetings, the covert – or, more accurately in my case, overt – surveillance, and the thrill of the chase. When this is all over, what will I do with my life? Will a job in psychological services really satisfy me? Or am I enjoying the resumption of playing detective too much for that to be a realistic goal?

The rain has passed by the time I reach the garage. Thank

heavens for small mercies because in my eagerness to leave to meet Nina, I didn't grab my jacket. I zigzag along the puddle-ridden pavements, walking as briskly as I can with a bulging carrier bag in each hand. The block looms ahead – the upper part and side even darker now it's been coated with rain. A flutter of apprehension in my stomach causes me to slow. Every time I spend time out of the flat, I expect to return to something . . . *different*. Graffiti, a smashed window, a break-in, or something else my ex-husband has deemed is warranted and instructed whoever he has watching me to carry out. From the things Marcus confided, I'm convinced John will have eyes and ears everywhere.

Before letting myself back into the flat, I put the shopping down, check the exterior for any signs that someone's paid me a visit while I've been with Nina. The lock is intact, no obvious forced entry there or at the window. The back courtyard is only accessible from inside, there is no rear access – well, I guess if someone was really desperate they could maybe lower themselves down to it from a higher level. I allow this sudden realisation to unnerve me, then try to brush it off. It is worth noting, though, and I should at least check for its likelihood and take responsible measures to reduce the possibility or, at the very least, put in some kind of alert system if such a play was attempted.

With my boldness returning, I plunge the key in the lock and turn it. I push the door open and take my shopping inside. After a minute or so scanning each room and finding nothing out of place, nor anything 'extra', I feel the tension in my tummy ease. Maybe John thinks he's done enough to scare me off and so doesn't want to waste his time stalking me, threatening me with calls and breaking in. Is he done with me because he thinks I'm done with him?

The ringing comes so closely after my thought, I'm afraid I've manifested it – that John's calling me to tell me not to be so stupid. Of course he isn't done with me. He's got all the time in the world to ensure my life is brought down. Ruined. I shake my head to snap myself out of my doomsday thoughts and check the display. It's a local number I vaguely recognise.

'Rebecca . . . '

My heart plummets hearing the male voice speaking my full name. This can't be another warning call, surely?

'Ms Gooding? Just a quick call in relation to your recent application.'

My short, sharp laugh isn't exactly appropriate, but the relief means I can't hold it back. I've yet to hear someone call me by my maiden name, I like the sound of it again. 'Yes, sorry. It's Becky Gooding. How can I help?'

After a brief intro, I'm informed they've yet to receive the reference they need to move forward. I grit my teeth, silently cursing myself. Over two weeks have passed and my enthusiasm for the role has been taken over by current events. Created by the same person that got me into the mess I'm in. With a sickly sweet, measured voice, I apologise for the non-receival of the glowing recommendation from Detective Chief Inspector Marcus Thomson, citing an issue with communications as being the hold-up. He seems to buy it, and with my assurance that I'll get the reference to him by next Monday at the latest, he hangs up. I mustn't allow this investigation into John to ruin the next chapter in my life, too. Without this job, I'll be on the street within four months – the meagre savings left from my parents' wills and my small share of the sale from mine and John's house are running critically low and there's no other backup plan.

While putting the shopping away, my mind conjures up a best-case scenario that the items Nina found, together with the information I hope is contained within Fran's phone combined with the journal, will make the evidence against John so compelling that he's locked up for life.

Fran's phone. It must've finished downloading by now.

I slam the cupboard door closed and rush to the computer, silently begging the universe to deliver the goods. I pick the mobile up, but nothing seems to be different. The connection lead is attached but the computer doesn't spring into life when I jiggle the mouse. Then I note the absence of the usual humming it makes, and there's no green light blinking away.

'For fuck's sake.' I fall to my knees, crawling under the desk. 'No!' I yell, grasping the detached power lead. How has that happened? A gentle nudge to my arm, followed by the appearance of Agatha joining me in the small space, provides the answer. She reaches a paw up, dapping at the other cables, tugging them with her claws. 'You little monkey.' I back out from under the desk, coaxing Agatha away too. Then I reconnect the power and start it up again. The heavy weight of disappointment when it becomes clear the power disruption occurred as the download reached just forty per cent, quickly intensifies and my thoughts spiral. Why isn't anything panning out? Is everything and everyone against me? I'd better let Isabel know there's a delay, I don't want her to think I've forgotten about the phone when I was the one who'd suggested holding onto it.

My body aches: tension in my back, shoulders and neck all knotted up, making me wince as I climb into bed and attempt to get into a comfortable position. To anyone witnessing this, I'd look as though I were in my nineties, not thirties. Probably as well I'm single. I sit up with a sigh, whack the centre of the pillow with the edge of my hand and cradle my head in it, then turn to look at the expanse of space next to me. It's not a conscious decision to be alone. I can't deny company would be nice.

After fantasising about Elijah and then concluding that: one, he really is a bit young for me and two, that due to my failure to contact him after my abruptness more than a week ago, I imagine the ship has already sailed – my mind strays to Operation Lawless, and today's meeting with Nina.

It's all dangerous. Really dangerous. But if it comes to fruition, what Nina mentioned seeing would make the best kind of evidence. Huge. With any luck, she'll be the one to help secure us the ultimate catch.

The darkness closes in, but my eyes remain stubbornly open. I fight with my duvet, pulling it up over my shoulders, then pushing it down again when I become as hot as a crab boiling in a pot. An hour passes with sleep still evading me and with a sense of nakedness, I grab the duvet again and cocoon myself in it. After a few minutes of frustration and my eyes burning with exhaustion, I kick it off me and the bed entirely. Insomnia sucks.

Reaching an arm to my bedside drawer, I fumble around to find my tablets. One might be enough to settle my thoughts. After I take it, I turn onto my stomach, punch the pillow into a different shape to support my neck in this new position and close my eyes. Maybe my mind just isn't ready to shut down, so I allow the questions, worries and hopes surrounding the ongoing situation to swirl around uninhibited.

The noises are faint at first, almost passing me by as my thoughts are focused on Fran and Nina. Then they slowly filter into my consciousness and my eyes fly open. They're coming from upstairs. Proper thuds, not the building creaking or outside sounds. Footsteps? It's the first noise I've heard from up there since they disappeared. It's been eleven days since I came back to find Tamsin and Vince gone. I reach an arm across to grab my mobile from the bedside table. The backlight glares brightly and I squint to check the time. Almost midnight.

Is it Tamsin?

If she *is* back, I need to go to the police with her and take the deepfake photos. I've been telling myself that holding off is the only option because I can't risk going to the police too early and implicating myself in the process. If I'm locked up, accused of Tamsin's murder, I won't be able to gather all the evidence needed. I push my palms into the mattress to lift my shoulders and chest, pausing for a moment in this cobra-like yoga pose to listen. Somebody's definitely in the flat above. I get out of bed, pull on the discarded tracksuit bottoms off the floor, put my mobile in the pocket, then snatch a sweatshirt from the chair and rush to the kitchen to get my keys. The cold air takes my breath away as I stride to the end of the building. It's then that I become aware of blue flashing lights. My pulse picks up, increasing even more as I race up the steps, across the corridor.

I'm stopped by a uniformed officer.

Fear paralyses me as the one thing I don't want to consider crashes into my mind.

Tamsin's dead.

Chapter 45

NOW

BECKY

The realisation that the noises I heard were the police sends a shock wave through my body – the scene in front of me blurs and wavers, and my limbs weaken. I put my hand against the wall to prop myself up. They've been inside Vince and Tamsin's flat. *Why?* I crane my head to look around the cop who's halted my passage and see more response officers moving in and out of the property. I take a few steps backwards, my mind racing to consider what could be going on here at the same time it debates whether a hasty retreat is required.

Have they found a body?

No. They can't have done. Too many uniforms here that would create scene contamination; there are no CSI in white paper suits.

Drug bust?

Possible.

Did I ask Charlie or Hannah to instigate this?

Sleep deprivation is affecting my memory; the anxiety meds have kicked in too – my thoughts are muddled, as if they've been smudged. I push the heels of my palms into my eyes, inhale and exhale slowly. Start backstepping.

'You live in this block?' The man in uniform asks. I take more backward steps. 'Excuse me. Can you give my colleague here a statement please?'

As he shifts his attention to speak with said colleague, I turn, slip away and dash down the steps, pleased my reaction to this situation hasn't pushed me into an anxiety attack. I have to be anywhere else but here. I try to order my thoughts as I go: I need to get back to my flat, grab my rucksack, Fran's mobile and any other evidence and disappear for a few hours until I know what's going on. As I'm about to turn the corner of the building, I hear radios and voices. I peek around to see a couple of uniforms close to my front door. *Shit.* I flatten myself up against the wall, look to the sky as my heartbeat thuds. Maybe they'll walk away in a minute and I'll have a clear run to my flat. Is it coincidence they're outside mine? While I feel confident there's no dead body upstairs, that's not to say there's no other incriminating evidence in there. Something that points to me being involved in illegal activity. If I've got photos of Fran's apparent murder, there could be similar images inside their flat too.

None of the scenarios playing out in my head make walking to my front door right now a good idea. I have to decide: wait and hope I'm not spotted entering my flat, questioned and possibly arrested; or bolt, and when I'm out of the vicinity of the police activity, give Hannah a call to find out if this is bad news for me? The sound of approaching footsteps forces my hand and I whip across the grass verge and take the long way to reach the road and head towards my garage.

Once inside the car I catch my breath then make the call. 'What's going on, Hannah?'

'It's all kicking off. I can't . . . you know I can't divulge anything. But, Becky, we have to rein it in. You need to lay low for a bit.'

'Christ, have you found Tamsin?' My voice trembles almost as much as my hands are doing. While there may not be a body in the flat, that doesn't mean they haven't found her elsewhere. I don't want to hear the worst. 'Is she alive?'

'What? I don't know what you're talking about.'

'The police? They're here, at my block of flats. At Tamsin's – you know, the woman who I asked you to—'

'That's not what I'm talking about, Becky.'

There's an element of relief following this statement, but it's short-lived.

'What is it? Give me something. What's this all about?'

Hannah takes several breaths, and my heart beats like a bass drum in the seconds before she speaks again. 'We think he knows.'

I swallow hard. 'He? John? Knows what? Which part?' The panic rises and erupts too quickly for me to control and my breathing shallows.

'Yes, him. I'm really sorry, Becky . . .' Hannah's speech is so slow it's stretching this moment of suspense to unbearable levels.

'Just say it!'

'We think he knows that Nina's helping you.' Her hushed, whispered words almost stop my heart. My vision dims, like a curtain is lowering over my eyes. Shit.

What have I done?

Chapter 46

NOW

BECKY

With Hannah unable to give details and our conversation being cut short by someone on her end, I've been left hanging. I blink rapidly to regain normal sight, then sit staring at the condensation on the inside of my windscreen, a numbness creeping up from my feet. It's one in the morning now, the temperature is low and my ability to generate warmth lacking – my thoughts are permeated by violent judders and teeth chattering. Everything that's happening is connected, I'm certain of it. But how?

What I do know, though, is that if John thinks his ex-wife and new girlfriend are working together to catch him out, trap him, he'll have been forced to up his game. Whatever is going on at my block right now is very likely something related to him. He's going to try to discredit me again, like he did before. And he'll do the same to Nina. No doubt he has a contingency plan for every challenge.

My initial idea of staying in the car in my garage until sunrise doesn't seem the best bet. To my knowledge, John hasn't been pushed quite this far before, and I don't know the full extent of his web of deceit and how far-reaching or high up it goes, but from what Marcus hinted at, and based on the redacted files Charlie spoke of, it's kept him safe up until now. But if several sources come forward with evidence, it might not be enough protection this time. If he's feeling threatened from multiple angles all at once, he may well be sensing the walls closing in on him. And that's when people who've committed crimes are at their most dangerous. Like a cornered animal, the desperation to get away can mean they fight viciously in an attempt to escape. Suddenly, being in a car in an enclosed space feels foolish. It's somewhere John could conceivably know about; it's as good as serving myself up to him on a platter.

I rub my hands up and down my thighs, the thin material of the tracksuit bottoms not sufficient to hold in any heat. I jiggle my feet to circulate some blood, then start the car. I drive close enough to the block to see the eerie, flashing blue glow casting pulsating shadows on the side of the wall. It's not a good idea to return to the flat yet so I head in the opposite direction. I cruise around for a bit, heater on full blast to bring some warmth back into my cold body and the radio on in case I hear something on the local news. When I've passed some time doing that, I park up close to Alan's Autos to gather my thoughts.

There have been two big developments over the past few hours. I'm not yet sure if the police activity at Tamsin's is good or bad, but the other is most definitely bad. Nina's pale, frightened face takes up residence in my mind. It's my like-a-dog-with-a-bone attitude that's kept me digging,

268

refusing to give up my attempts to bring John to justice by seeking Nina out, coercing her to help – shit – I'm not much better than he is. Did I learn this stuff from him? Even with the small car interior filled with warm air, I shiver.

Like attracts like. That's the saying, isn't it? Me and John were attracted to each other. What does that say about me? When I think about other couples with hideous shared crimes, the names Bonnie and Clyde, Myra Hindley and Ian Brady, Fred and Rose West, spring immediately to mind. While I haven't had direct involvement with the awful things John has done – is that because I'm a good person? Or simply because he hadn't had the chance to manipulate or coerce me further? He managed to keep me under his control for five years without me even realising that's what he was doing.

Rather than run out of petrol, I park up in a 24-hour supermarket and go inside to warm up – grabbing a bacon roll from the reduced section and wandering around as slowly as possible without looking as though I'm trying to shoplift. There's only so much time I can conceivably kill in here, though. Eventually, I also get a drink from the machine, and go to pay. I dig into my tracksuit pocket to check if there's any cash, but instead pull out a folded photo, my stomach lurching as I realise what it is. Without needing to look, I shove it back. I don't have any memory of placing one of the deepfake photos inside my pocket. With my heart skipping along at a rate of knots I hold my phone up to the terminal to pay via Google Wallet instead, and then go back to the car, lock myself in and tuck into my roll, watching the time tick by.

The text notification wakes me. Seems I *can* fall asleep despite what's going on *and* in an awkward position. The message from Charlie is short and to the point.

Same place as before. 8 a.m.

At first I'm reassured by its brevity, and that it didn't mention the café name. Even if someone had cloned his phone, this doesn't give away the location, so, at face value, the interaction feels safe. But my cautious mind throws up an inevitable counter: if Charlie even suspected he'd been hacked, why didn't he ditch the phone and get another? But then I recall his assurances that it was a one-night stand of his answering my call. And that it was *my* suggestion it could've been cloned, my possible over reaction.

All of a sudden, my thoughts muddle, my recollections of conversations and events occurring over these past two weeks becoming blurry and mashed up. Starting to take the anxiety meds again now seems like it was a bad idea. Clarity of mind is something I need to get through all of this. Regardless of my concerns, I have to trust Charlie knows what he's doing because what other choice do I have? I hold my head with both hands, gently putting pressure against my skull as though that'll stop memories from spilling out. I'm woozy with tiredness, my body rocking in the seat.

A nap before driving might be a good idea.

Fifteen minutes ahead of the agreed time, and feeling better after some sleep, I drive slowly by Hamley's café, peering in the large window to see if anyone is sitting inside. The morning is still breaking, though, so it's too dark to make out individual figures. I do however, spot Elijah placing the café's chalkboard on the pavement and my pulse begins to pound that bit harder. I swipe some strands of hair away from my face and carry on past, feeling the heat of a blush.

'God's sake. What are you, fifteen?' I push my chin up in

270

the air in a moment of self-indignation and start looking for a good place to park. Luckily, I find a space up a nearby side street, then do another sweep past the café by foot. As I'm standing looking at the flowers on display outside the florist a few shops down, I feel a hand on my shoulder.

'I'd prefer some tinnies, mate.'

I shake my head, but the relief it's Charlie must be evident as he then squeezes my arm and offers reassurance it'll be okay. We probably don't need to go into the café, we could say what's needed to be said right here, but I begin to walk in its direction. Charlie gives me a knowing look.

'What?'

'Nothing. I'm not judging.'

'I don't know what you're talking about. Honestly, a woman doesn't *need* a bloke you know.'

'If you say so.'

I stop and turn sharply to look at him. 'No. Really. Sometimes, they're an add-on – you know, like an app, or tool that could help improve the system – possibly – but they're not required for it to work well, it's merely an enhancement.'

Charlie presses his lips together, like he's stifling a laugh. Idiot. I walk on.

It's warm inside the café, and together with the comforting smell of fresh coffee, I find myself relaxing my shoulders an inch. Daren't fully let my guard down, and not sure I could even if I tried. Too much is going on for that. I tell Charlie I'll order the drinks, then I stand waiting to be served, my eyes darting around, checking out each of the five other customers – analysing their faces, movements, seeing if anything stands out as strange. Is anyone showing an interest in me or Charlie? Their gazes lingering a few seconds too long? Or, conversely, is anyone blatantly not taking notice? Nose seemingly in a newspaper, or staring out the window so I can't see them fully?

'What would you like?' the voice cuts in, lifting me from my deep scrutiny.

'Two lattes, please.' I smile at the female barista. She takes my payment, and turns to relay the order to the other person. It's Elijah. I take a new loyalty card from the holder, then with my upper body leaning over the counter, I make the point that I've clocked him, but he doesn't look in my direction. The woman is talking to the next customer, so I take this opportunity to speak.

'Oh, hey. Here's my card,' I say loudly, holding it out towards Elijah. The hissing of the steamer must drown out my voice because he doesn't acknowledge me. With my fingers drumming on the countertop, I gaze at Charlie while I wait. He looks almost as awkward as I feel. A thud makes me turn back. Elijah's put both glasses down hard. He pushes them towards me, then pulls the loyalty card from my grasp. I open my mouth, but surprise renders me mute. He stamps it once, leaves it by the side of the lattes then moves on to the next order – all without a word spoken or any eye contact. Heat rises up my neck and I lower my head. I don't blame him after I didn't ever get back to him. Still, he's acting like a spurned teenager. I give a 'hmph' and leave the stupid card on the counter. I've more important things to deal with right now.

Charlie tells me they got an anonymous tip about my upstairs neighbour. Nothing there when cops arrived. Hoax call, seemingly. A mix of relief and disappointment swoops in first, followed by the thought it was definitely another warning aimed at me from John.

'To frighten the shit out of me, I suspect.'

'It's not all about you, you know.' He smirks.

'So it's safe for me to return to my delightful abode, then?'

Charlie makes a face. 'Not sure I'd class it as safe, Becks. Why would you think it wasn't though? The police weren't in your flat.'

'Hmm. I know, but . . . ' I think of the photo I found in my joggers earlier. Should I show Charlie? With a deep sigh, I pull the photo from my pocket, unfold it. My heart flutters wildly. He's going to be mad I kept this from him and Hannah. Especially as I promised them I wouldn't withhold information. 'There's a complicating factor, Charlie. But you can't report it, okay?'

His features contort as I slide it across the table. I don't say anything. Just wait for his response.

'Where did this come from?'

'It was left on my investigation board in my bedroom.'

'Fuck's sake, Becks. When?'

I rapidly explain the timeline of events. That last night I thought perhaps police had found something significant in Tamsin's flat. Panicked it was a body until I realised no CSI were on site. Couldn't rule out John had someone plant something like this inside though. Thought I'd be arrested. Was too afraid to tell anyone until I figured out how to prove they were fake. I run out of breath and sit back. Charlie's staring at the photo, silently twisting it this way and that as my blood pressure rises. I wish I could hear what he's thinking. Is any part of him querying if it's real? That I did harm Tamsin?

'He's really upped his game. Shit.' He leans back. 'This isn't good.'

273

I blow air from my cheeks, his words offering some reassurance. The fact he's said that John's upped his game makes it seem to me that Charlie believes it to be a fake, too.

'No, not good at all,' I agree. 'And Hannah told me it's kicking off. That you guys think John knows Nina's helping me?'

'Yep. It looks that way.' He leans in now, a worried expression crossing his face. 'Nina's house – John's current residence – was broken into last night.'

'What? You're just telling me this now? Is she okay?' A crushing sensation spreads through my chest.

'I was building up to it,' he says. 'She's pretty shook up. She's being . . . looked after.'

I nod my understanding, assuming she's been taken into protective custody.

'Are things finally happening then? Have you got enough to arrest John?'

Charlie puts his head in his hands and my heart immediately sinks. 'Nina found evidence, Charlie. Proper, hard evidence. You've got it, right?' I ask desperately. I swallow hard as a sense of dread rises. 'Charlie?' He looks up, his expression despondent.

'Nina said when she got back to the property after taking Millie to her parents' pub, it'd been ransacked. From top to bottom,' he says.

Tears fall freely down my face. I don't need to ask the question, but I do anyway.

'All the evidence was stolen?'

'I'm afraid so.'

Air leaves my body, my shoulders folding in on themselves and I sink lower in the chair, deflated. My stomach twists thinking about Nina and Millie – the danger I put them in.

And for what? I can't let it be for nothing. I sit up, planting my palms down on the table.

'If he had those trophies, there'll be more. And they have to be somewhere, I doubt he'd destroy them all. We'll find them. And what about the dates and times on Nina's list – anything link up there?'

'I thought Hannah told you?' he says, frowning. 'God, Becks, that list vanished into thin air. She thought it was at hers, apparently you thought you might've had it?'

'This is great,' I say. 'What good detectives.' I shake my head. But I know it's not down to us. Heat rushes to my face. 'I'm not giving up, Charlie. *We're* not giving up. That's just what he wants.'

Charlie's eyes meet mine and I know he sees it in me. The absolute grit and determination that I cannot fail these women. He offers a sympathetic smile.

'I know,' he says. 'Come on then, Miss Marple. Lay it on me – what else have you got?'

I tell him about the club, Moods – that I'm sure there's a link there. Then about Isabel, giving a brief explanation of her role so far and that we found evidence at a known victim of John's. Charlie's expression remains neutral throughout my run-down, but his silence unnerves me, and I know it's because I've kept this from him.

'It's not like I didn't want to tell you any of this, Charlie. It's all happened so fast.'

He nods. 'Yeah. And I haven't been exactly on hand. You do know I've been busy behind the scenes though?'

'Of course,' I say, quickly continuing. 'Before Tamsin er . . . disappeared, she said she remembered one time last year, someone had been there asking questions. I thought it was Isabel, but maybe not. The initials, nicknames in the journal she found – I'm wondering if any relate to Moods.'

'I can drop by there, that's not a problem.'

'Thanks, Charlie. I'd appreciate it. Seriously, John can't control everything!'

'Not alone, he can't, no.' Charlie's face becomes serious. 'But it does look as though he's turning up the heat. Like he's coordinating his attacks.'

'Like last night,' I ponder. 'Like we'd do when working a case – target several areas at the same time so no one can be pre-warned . . . ' I put my hand to my chest, feel the bashing of my heart. 'Oh, shit!' I push up from my chair.

'What?' Charlie stands too, looking to me for an answer. My throat's so tight I can't speak. I crash into the next table in my need to get out. I'm aware of eyes on me as I right myself, but I fail to stop a chair toppling to the floor with a crash. Charlie's voice grows muted as I reach the exit.

Chapter 47

NOW

BECKY

I feel a weight pressing down on my chest as I flee the café, running like my life depends on it, my legs pumping so fast and hard I'm light-headed by the time I reach the flat and my entire body trembles with exertion.

But I'm too late.

'No! No, no, no,' I cry. The door is already wide open; the new lock was clearly better than the last as they haven't picked it. The wood is splintered, like a battering ram was used on it. I step gingerly inside. Whoever was here has left a trail of destruction in their wake. 'Fuck!' I yell. There's a space where my computer once sat. There's also a space atop the futon where Agatha usually lays. Hot tears bubble and cascade over my burning cheeks. I bet the hoax call about upstairs was a way to ensure I disappeared for long enough for them to break in. My rucksack is not where I remember leaving it – and is turned inside out. Why not take that, too?

I call Charlie to explain. He doesn't pick up. I try Hannah. To get away with the computer, surely a vehicle would've been needed. Maybe she can get nearby CCTV checked.

After several rings, I hear Hannah's voice. 'Hello.' Her tone is flat.

'Hannah. Christ, Hannah.'

'I know,' she says. Then she breaks down. My breath hitches. Why would she be crying about a break-in at my flat?

'Hannah? Hey, Hannah. Are you okay?'

'No. I'm really not. I can't believe he's gone.'

What is she talking about? 'You mean, you can't believe the evidence has gone? No, me neither.'

'No, Rebecca,' she snaps. 'My little brother has gone.'

All the blood drains from my head, pooling in my feet like I've just plummeted from the top floor of a building to the ground in a millisecond.

'Gone where?' I rasp, all moisture disappearing along with my ability to make sense of anything.

'I came home . . .' Her voice cracks.

Of course, given the past few days' events, I forgot I'd decided not to tell Hannah that when I visited her place, Danny was there. 'Oh, Christ, I *knew* I should've mentioned this to you on Monday, but—'

'I . . . went upstairs to . . . change, and I—' Her words come out in between huge sobs. 'I found him, Becky. I found him.'

The words I want to hear now are: *I found him, and now he's in hospital where he should be*. But the hideous realisation comes at last, and I hold my breath for it.

'Dead!' Hannah sobs. 'Dead in that bloody shower. It's

278

my fault, it's all my fault . . . '

My lungs burn and my breath rushes out. It's as I feared.
Coordinated attacks.

Chapter 48

NOW

BECKY

From what Hannah says she, as well as the attending services, believes the dodgy wiring in the shower killed Danny. That it was an accident waiting to happen.

I'm almost certain they're wrong.

My final conversation with him – his assertion that bad things happen to those who know too much – was like he knew it was coming. A premonition of sorts. And he was warning me that my fate was likely to be similar. It seems likely now, that Danny was responsible for the missing list of names. Probably destroyed it not long before I arrived at the house. John – via someone else, or by his own hand – has reached another level of criminality. His world is collapsing, and he is fighting to save himself. No matter the cost to others.

Once I got hold of Charlie, he was able to fill in the gaps that Hannah was too upset to manage. By all accounts, thirty-seven-year-old Daniel Martin died from electrocution. No suspicious circumstances.

Another win for John.

I refuse to allow him any further ones. He must be stopped. With virtually zero evidence, yet again, it's going to prove difficult. I need to get hold of Isabel, let her know we've hit a stumbling block. A massive one. But I'm determined to knock it down.

My heart races as I scramble through my memories as to where I put the journal. Had it been inside the rucksack that's been emptied?

Retrace your steps.

When I came home from being at Fran's house, the first thing I did was . . . I screw up my eyes, envisaging Sunday night. 'I plugged in the phone,' I say. Then what? 'I sat there . . . ' I walk to the armchair, amazingly still in its original position, not like the boxes that were upended and emptied everywhere. 'I woke up in the chair and remembered about the mobile. Jumped up . . .' Had I fallen asleep reading the journal? I get down on my hands and knees to look underneath the furniture. Something is visible. Lifting the chair up an inch with one hand, I'm able to grasp it with the other. I press it to my chest, relief at having something left bringing tears to my eyes.

I still have the journal. Whoever broke in here targeted the computer and Fran's mobile phone, made a general mess looking in other places, but maybe they didn't know to search for Fran's diary with the pages inside containing lists of initials and names.

John appears to know my every move. But he doesn't know about the journal. Or at least that's the positive take from this. Is Isabel the only one who should be trusted? I

281

need to get what little evidence there is left, to her. I secrete the journal in the waistband of my tracksuit bottoms and pull my sweatshirt over to cover it. Then put my coat on for good measure. I send Isabel a four-word text: I'm coming to you. Then, hood up, I leave the flat and walk towards my garage.

Chapter 49

NOW

BECKY

A sense of urgency increases my pace as well as my heart rate, the pound of my feet on the pavement almost matching the thudding in my chest. I glance behind me every few seconds, checking for a tail. Part of me feels safe in the knowledge John's got what he wanted – the evidence stolen and in his hands now – but another part doesn't want to be lulled into a false sense of security. I'm *assuming* John doesn't know about the journal I currently have tucked in my joggers. But what if he does?

Would he still have someone watching me, just in case, to see what I do next?

I press a hand to the concealed evidence as I break into a jog, making a slight detour so that I'm not taking my usual route to my car. I roll my eyes as I'm about to pass Hamley's café. I keep facing forwards, not even glancing in. I can't be distracted by seeing Elijah now. I make a mental note to pop in again at some point, because even though he was the one being rude, I feel the need to smooth things over.

I slow down as I approach the garage block, my lungs burning. The noise of a car engine draws closer, then levels off. Turning the corner I see the stationary vehicle. The driver is revving it to the max, like they're about to begin the biggest race of their life. The headlamp's glare blinds me, despite being daylight, and I shield my eyes with my hand. What are they playing at?

My thought that it's just a boy-racer, or possibly I've happened across a carjack in progress, is fleeting. With a sinking feeling I realise I'd been so concerned someone would follow me, I hadn't considered they'd already be here waiting. I'm in trouble.

Fight or flight?

Me against a car.

Instinct is to run. But my legs don't move; I'm frozen to the spot.

'Who are you?' I mutter. Marcus said there were other corrupt officers. I want to know who they are – if this is one about to drive at me.

I pull my mobile from my pocket and fumble to open my video app – the revving so loud it's unnerving. I tap to record and hold the phone up. It shakes violently in my trembling hand as the tyres screech and the car hurtles towards me. Too late, I think maybe a 999 call might've been better. I try to keep the phone aimed at the windscreen, hoping I'll capture a face as it gets closer. My own face screws up, turns away from the ear-deafening engine noise, the fear of what's to come all too much.

Is anyone else around? I shout to what I think is a figure of a person, but get no response. I'm on my own. I'm going

284

to be hit.

Run, Becky, for fuck's sake, run.

When I come to, I don't feel any pain. Nothing. I'm aware of my breathing. That's good. I'm not dead then. Why can't I feel my limbs, though?

Charcoal blobs scud across my field of vision. I'm on the ground, staring up at the sky. I try to move my head, turn it to look at my body. I can't. My brain isn't sending the right signals. Why?

The car hit you. You're paralysed.

A replay of the car, its tyres screeching as it hurtles towards me, slams into my mind.

Did it smash into me?

There's no noise of sirens. No people rushing to my aid.

All I can hear is a high-pitched whining – a ringing – that's taking up space in my head. Filling it.

A face looms over me, blocking the cloudy sky. Lips are moving, but I don't hear any words.

'You're on mute, mate.' Do I say those words, or just think them? I laugh anyway.

Then as though they've pressed the unmute button, their voice booms, my eyes squinting in response to the suddenness of the audio assault. It takes a beat to realise they're saying my name.

'Stay still, Becky. An ambulance is on its way.'

I can't do anything but stay still, it seems. Only my eyelids move. They flitter and I struggle to keep them from closing.

'Stay awake, you have to stay with me.'

The man's tone is edged with concern. Maybe panic. And when I open my eyes as instructed, the familiar face comes into focus.

'Does this mean . . . I'll get . . . double stamps again?'

I don't hear anything else. Even the ringing stops when I close my eyes this time.

Chapter 50

NOW

BECKY

'Where . . . is it? I have to . . . '

'Hello, Rebecca.'

My head splits with a sharp pain as I push up into a sitting position.

Rebecca.

I blink hard, then attempt to see who spoke my name.

'It's okay. You're okay.'

I'm not. Nothing is.

'You're in the hospital, love. Lie back down or you'll have the headache from hell for even longer.'

They're right about the headache. I've never experienced this pain before. 'Where is *it*?'

'What are you looking for?'

'The . . . the erm . . . ' Oh, my God. What's going on? I can't find the word.

'You were very lucky to get away with a concussion.

Things'll be a little hazy. Odd for a bit. Try to relax.' I'm guided to a supine position again by the nurse, then she makes some notes on what looks to be an iPad.

'Who brought me in?'

'An ambulance was called, love. A man – um, let me see . . . ' She fusses around the cabinet that's beside my bed. 'Left you this.' She passes it to me.

A loyalty card.

'Your boyfriend, is it? Ahh. It's like he left a calling card.' She laughs, begins to walk away. But her words send a chill so deep I swear it hits the bone.

Hannah stands to the side of the hospital bed, an air of distress surrounding her like she has a shadowy aura. Her skin is sallow, her eyes tired; black. She looks like the Grim Reaper. My initial confusion as to why she appears this way is displaced by the terrible recollection of our last conversation. Danny is dead.

'I'm so sorry, Hannah,' I say, my throat tight. Her silence sends a ripple of dread through my sore body. 'Hannah?' Is she even here? Or am I imagining it? My pulse pounds and I prop myself up on my elbows, squinting in the hope I can determine if she's really here, in this room with me.

'You need to come with me,' she says, finally breaking the spell. 'You're not safe here.'

In a replay of events, like watching a silent movie sped up, I see the police swarming at Tamsin's place, my ransacked flat, the car hurtling towards me. Christ. I was targeted just like Danny was. Does Hannah now realise her brother's accident was more than likely a murder?

Am I next?

'Was it him?' I ask Hannah as she assists me getting

288

out of the bed. I wince as I shuffle towards the edge of the mattress, and press my hand to my aching ribs. 'Shit.'

'I'm taking you somewhere safe.'

'You didn't answer the question.'

'Of course it's him, Becky. Not necessarily by his own hand, but he's behind it.' Tears make her voice thick. I don't want to cause more pain for her by asking if she means Danny too. But when I look into her eyes, it's there to see. 'All of it,' she adds quietly, before looking away. I've still got an IV line attached to me, which presumably means Hannah hasn't cleared this abrupt discharge with the medical team.

'Pass that.' I point to the sterile pack on a silver trolley in the corner of the room as I peel the tape from the back of my hand. I open the packet, pressing the cotton swab against the cannula and gently sliding the tube out, then I stick the gauze down on the tiny puncture wound it's left. 'Okay. Clothes.'

It takes me a few minutes to dress back into the tracksuit bottoms and sweatshirt. As I'm doing it, there's a nagging voice inside my head, a sense of something missing, but I can't decipher what; it's too disjointed. I remember the nurse saying I've got concussion. The fuzziness is likely due to that. I take Hannah's arm to steady me and we leave the room. At the nurses' station I sign a self-discharge form. The doctor repeats that it's against medical advice, and I repeat that I'm aware of the risks.

With nausea building in my stomach, I grab a couple of cardboard kidney dishes from a trolley on my exit of the ward. They come in useful as I vomit three times in the car because Hannah drives like she's involved in a high-speed chase. Between retches, I beg her to slow down.

'Sorry. No time to waste.'

We go over a speedbump and I'm sick again. Bile sloshes in the papier-mâché-type container. I stare at it, the smell burning my nostrils. I've no clue where Hannah is taking me, I can barely hold my head up long enough to gain my bearings. It feels like another ten minutes or so before she takes her foot off the gas a bit and we travel at a more comfortable speed, and I'm finally able to lift my head.

After taking a few slow, deep breaths to recover, I turn to look at Hannah. 'I'm sorry to inform you, Miss Martin, you did not reach the required standard to pass your advanced driver qualification.'

'We're here.' Hannah swings the car into a long, sweeping driveway. It's secluded, surrounded by well-established trees and high walls.

'Where's here?' I try to get a good look around, but the movement of my head causes everything to spin, like I'm having the worst vertigo attack.

'It's a safe house. You don't need to worry about where.'

So why do her words have the opposite effect?

With my fingers trembling, I set the vomit bowls down in the footwell and wait for Hannah to open my door. The nerves in my legs jump and I rub both hands up and down my thighs in an attempt to still them. I'm guided down the side of a large, Victorian-style house and ushered through a patio door at the rear of the property. She seems to have walked right on in – no key. The pain in my head pulses and all I can think about is sitting down.

'Here, drink.' Hannah thrusts a glass of water into my hands and I gulp it down greedily. 'Sip it!' she demands.

Once I've allowed the water to settle, I start asking questions about the latest intel on John, Nina, Tamsin and every other name that rolls off my tongue. Hannah slumps in a chair opposite me, eyeing me intently as I rattle them off. But she doesn't even begin to answer any of my questions. Am I making sense? The words do sound a bit muddled; slurred. I feel as though I'm falling backwards into a pit of despair.

'I need to lie down.'

Next thing I know, I'm in a darkened room lying on top of a luxurious thick duvet, my head sinking into a soft pillow. And my eyes flutter closed.

What time is it?

Where the fuck am I?

I sit up, my heart racing like a rabbit caught in a trap. I strain to hear any sounds, but there's only a high-pitched ringing noise that I know is in my own head. The room I'm in is unfamiliar – far too pretty and cosy for it to be mine or belonging to anyone else I know. Apart from Marcus's place – I imagine his and Barbara's room might be like this.

Am I at Marcus's? I swing my legs off the bed, watching them with interest – the knowledge that these are the same trousers I've worn for days already in my mind. But the rest of my memory is gappy at best. A sharp pain in my side steals my breath as I try to stand.

A car. An accident. Hospital.

Fragmented images burst like a firework display inside my head. My eyes are drawn to the glass of water and tablets beside the bed. My anxiety meds. Or maybe painkillers from the hospital? I take two for good measure.

With some calm breathing and relaxing my neck, shoulders, then working my way down my body, I remember that it was Hannah who brought me here. But why?

A safe house. She said it was to keep me safe from John.

291

Ah yes, John. And my flat.

Oh, God. I collapse back onto the bed, neither my body nor mind able to deal with the realisation.

All the evidence is gone.

Chapter 51

NOW

BECKY

It takes a few minutes to get my body working in conjunction with my brain, but I manage to pull everything together. I've slept – it's now Friday – and I gingerly walk out of the bedroom and find my way downstairs.

'Whose place is this?' I ask the second I enter the large, farmhouse-style kitchen and see Hannah leaning against the worktop, nursing a mug, her gaze somewhere off in the distance.

'Good morning to you, too,' Hannah responds flatly, without looking my way.

'Sorry. My mind's on fast-forward. Now it's done with the catching up. How long have I been out?'

'You obviously needed the sleep. Coffee?' She doesn't wait for my response just turns and starts preparing me a drink, her movements sluggish. Like she hasn't slept. A pang of guilt pierces through me. She must be going through hell, yet here she is, helping me. I sit at the unknown homeowner's table, silently taking in the detail of my surroundings. There aren't any personal items like photos or trinkets anywhere that offer any clues to its usual residents. It could be that this house is purposely set up for such situations, but from my limited experience of an official safe house, they aren't generally this well furnished, or this luxurious. This feels more like a family home where the occupants have merely left for a holiday.

Hannah brings over the coffee and sits down. My chest tightens. Seeing the pain in her eyes close up brings my own to the surface. Grief has a habit of knocking on the door again, I've found. Just when you think you've come through it, you hear of another's loss and it's like reliving it all over again. Even if that person isn't known to you. It's the weirdest thing – like experiencing an echo of what's been before.

'Where's Nina? I need to see her.'

'Charlie assures me she's safe for now. He's seeing to that while I keep an eye on you.'

My tummy twists with anxiety. I'm not entirely happy about not being able to see Nina. I'd rather know first-hand that she's okay. But now John has possibly rumbled her involvement with us that would cause more issues than it solves.

'Are you okay babysitting me? I mean, with Danny—'

'I don't want to talk about him. I'll deal with it another time.'

It doesn't seem particularly healthy to put off the grieving process. I know that all too well. But Hannah's snappiness accompanied by her glare, leaves no room for misinterpretation – she'll cope in her own way in her own time. And for now, me, and my safety, seem to be her current focus.

Isabel.

'Shit. I've just remembered where I was going when the car drove at me.' I push up from the table and begin pacing, a rush of images and snippets of conversations flooding my mind. They hadn't taken the journal when my flat was broken into. *I* was taking it to Isabel. 'Did I have a journal on me? When you collected me from the hospital?'

'No. You didn't have any possessions. The police only retrieved your crushed mobile from the scene. What journal?'

I can't answer because the nurse's words come back to me like a bolt of lightning: *Your boyfriend, is it? Ahh. It's like he left a calling card.* Did Elijah take it? He was the only person I recall seeing after I leapt out of the path of the car.

Did he push me out of its way?

Or was *he* the driver of the car?

I collapse on the huge sofa that runs the length of one wall in the TV room, every muscle screaming in response to my frantic pacing.

'Hannah, when I saw Danny he said a few . . . strange things to me.'

She looks up from her phone, frown lines like deep crevices forming on her forehead.

'He wasn't himself,' she says. 'He'd been through a rough time of late. Lots of things he said didn't make sense to me.'

'Yeah, maybe. But this was about why I chose to live in my particular block of flats. I came away feeling unsettled by it, like he was implying I hadn't had any agency – that I got that place for a reason.'

'I don't understand,' she says, sighing heavily. 'It was

literally the last place there was, Becky. Sadly, he was probably confused because of the medication—'

'No. It was more than that.' I don't dare suggest he was in on anything with John – although I now fully believe he was – because saying that while she's still in the earliest stages of grief would be inappropriate. But I do need her to acknowledge that her brother knew more than she realises. 'Had Danny seen John – like after me and him split up?'

'Why would Danny know him? Or are you really asking if *I'd* seen John. Is that what you're trying to get at?'

'No. God, no. Obviously you still worked with him, though. It wouldn't be out of the ordinary to see him; like at the pub or something? It is possible Danny met him through you?'

'Yeah, now you mention it . . .' Hannah looks up, thinking. 'Danny might have been around on the odd occasion when John was.' She shrugs, like it's no big deal. Which, had he not said what he did to me, then been killed in his own shower, might not be. I rub my hands over my face.

'I think John used him, Hannah. Like he uses everyone – especially those who appear vulnerable. And if Danny was ill, that would be all John would've needed to hook him.'

Hannah's face pales. I've gone too far. Nothing can be gained now from unearthing a link between him and Danny: the damage has already been done.

'We'll sort it, Becky. And besides, Danny is gone now. The only way of gaining justice for everyone is to create a trap for John – get him to confess everything. And I've already started the ball rolling.'

After an uncomfortable shower, I dress in the clean clothes Hannah sorted for me. With fresh coffees and a stack of

296

crisps, we spend the next few hours going over the plan, making arrangements and mentally preparing to meet John in person. Now the evidence we'd spent weeks gathering has all gone, this will be our last-ditch, final opportunity to lure him in and get him once and for all. Hannah said she'd been in contact with Charlie, and through him, Marcus, who was apparently brought up to speed while I was sleeping off my concussion. The four of us are the only ones to know the full details.

My muscles feel tight, seized up from being hunched over the table. I stretch, my back clicking in protest, then stifle a yawn. Hannah looks up.

'Get some rest, Becky. Tomorrow's a big day.' She reaches over and pats me on the shoulder. 'I'm so sorry this is all happening.'

An uneasy, shaky feeling flutters around in my stomach and I press my hands into it. She's saying sorry like she started this when I know it's all because of me. Her brother is dead in part because of my refusal to give up trying to bring my rapist ex-husband to justice. The fact she's still willing to help either means she doesn't believe that and assumes his death was accidental, or she does, and she too now wants revenge on John Lawson.

We've both got a score to settle.

Chapter 52

NOW

BECKY

Now, almost three weeks after receiving the threat of an injunction and Marcus informing me of John's upcoming promotion, the day of reckoning has come. Hannah's driving me to the meeting place to confront John. Trap him. Force him to make a move that will reveal his true nature and uncover his heinous acts. I've been sick twice this morning, and my insides burn with nerves. Although the plan is engraved into my brain, I can't stop the negative thoughts, or the worry from twisting my gut.

What if this doesn't work?

What if he gets away scot-free yet again?

What if he really does kill me to save himself from facing justice?

At least this time I have people that believe me. Not just any people, but a DCI and two detectives. They have my back. I glance at Hannah now – her strength is astounding.

She's resolute and in control; nothing shakes her for long. Or, if it does, she doesn't often let it show. Her features are set as she stares dead ahead, her hands gripping the wheel so tight her knuckles blanch.

'Thank you, Hannah. Having you all onside is what's giving me the strength to do this.'

She nods.

Sometimes nerves render me mute. Today, I can't stop talking and ramble on and on – like a stream of consciousness that I'm sure Hannah doesn't understand as she remains silent on the journey. I stop to take a breath, and ready myself to begin again. Hannah puts a hand firmly on my thigh.

'It's okay, Becky. Relax.'

I laugh. 'Yeah, sure. Nothing to worry about. He's already failed to kill me once. He'll fail again. Right?'

'You know this is risky, I'd be stupid to persuade you otherwise. But we've got this. I'll be close by.'

'And so will backup, yes, I know. Won't he be expecting that, though? Have planned for it?'

'He believes you've alienated everyone. He's made sure you have no physical evidence. He is so fucking sure of himself, I highly doubt he'll consider you've managed to gain help from *any* source, let alone officers. He thinks he's got the monopoly on bent cops.'

It's a good point. His unwavering confidence will be his downfall this time. He truly believes he's untouchable. It's how he got away with raping and abusing his victims in the past, and has, so far, managed to escape any real consequences since. I shudder as I consider just how many people have been hurt by him over his lifetime. I don't think we'll ever learn the full extent of his crimes.

Hannah stops the car after turning off the main road.

'Okay. Ready?' She locks eyes with me.

'Oh, yes.' I feel a surge of adrenaline quicken my pulse. This is a showdown that's more than a year overdue.

Hannah gives me the directions to the location, and gets out of the car. She says it's only a few minutes' walk away for her. I shuffle across to the driver's seat and take a few seconds to settle. I know I need to ensure I'm seen driving into the warehouse grounds alone, but doing it will expose me – physically and psychologically. The plan is Hannah will hang back for five minutes once I drive off, then follow and covertly enter the warehouse via the back to secretly record John's actions. Getting him on tape threatening me, maybe even attempting to kill me, will be gold – but if I can get him to own up to everything else, too, that'll help replace the lost evidence. We've got a codeword for when I feel it's time for help, but Hannah insisted it should be left to her discretion when she'll make the call for the backup to enter the premises. If she thinks there's danger to life, she wants to make the decision. Either way, the team will hear John confess to at least some of his crimes and it'll add extra weight to what she captures on camera.

And there'll be no deepfake trickery required for that.

John will be seen for what he really is. No wriggling out of it.

I give Hannah an affirming smile, turn my head to focus on the road, puff air from my cheeks and put the car into first. My legs tremble as I drive towards John.

When the tyres crunch over the gravel my respiration rate doubles. Hyperventilating could well cause me to faint, so I consciously slow my breaths – holding each one for the count of three, then releasing. I reverse and park to the side

300

of the large unused warehouse – positioning myself for a quick getaway if things go pear-shaped.

There's no other vehicle here. Has he been dropped off by someone? Is he also hanging back to see if I'm really alone before coming here? Maybe he's bottled it. This last theory is the most unlikely. My mouth is so dry, my tongue feels like a piece of sandpaper. I push my hand into the side pocket of the car door and pull out a half-drunk bottle of diet lemonade. It's warm and flat, foul-tasting, but it does at least offer some lubrication. While remaining in the car, I observe the immediate area, check the perimeter and turn in my seat to locate any CCTV.

Hannah was careful to choose this place. It's not covered by cameras. Although it would be good to have that safety net, John of course wouldn't show if he got wind of anything like that. Which is why I'm counting on Hannah.

I've easily been five minutes sitting here. Should be okay to move out now. She can't be far away. I need to be inside, with John, before she can position herself. After another mouthful of lemonade and knocking back an anxiety tablet, I mentally motivate myself and then confidently exit the car in one swift movement. I stand beside the car for a couple of seconds, all my senses on high alert. As sure as I can be that I'm doing the right thing, I enter the warehouse and ready myself for what lies ahead.

It takes several seconds for my eyes to adjust to the dim, shadowy light inside the building and I strain to see exactly what's contained within it. Hannah assured me it was disused, but there is some kind of industrial machinery in here. Boxes too. My pulse begins to whoosh in my ears, making it harder to decipher sounds. I roll my neck, push my shoulders down, interlock my fingers and stretch both arms out – a ritual I used to do all the time in preparation for raiding a house, or before conducting interviews. Then I slow my breathing right down, as if I'm about to meditate. Finally, my heart rate settles, and the noises in my ears disappear.

'You couldn't let it go, could you?'

I jump hearing his voice. It comes from behind me, loud and echoey in this huge warehouse, and sends a judder of repulsion up my spine. It's been a while since I've heard it directed at me and now I'm standing here, in his presence, my tenacity wavers.

Hannah is close. I'm not alone. I repeat in my mind.

I sense his body, large, hot and firm against my back and have to clamp a hand over my mouth to stifle a yelp. With my eyes wide and tears immediately threatening, I take a few quick steps forward to maintain some distance. Then, my breath measured, I turn to confront him. He cocks his head to one side, and I note some flecks of white in his once purely sandy-coloured hair. Even in the short space of time since I've been this close to him, I can see that his face carries a few more wrinkles. A little bit more weight. Things I couldn't perceive on the occasions I saw him in Lymworth. But the menacing expression is just as familiar. His nostrils flare as he takes deep, angry breaths.

'Shoulda listened, *babe.*' He makes a tutting sound while smiling – he looks like a freaky clown in a horror film. If only this were fiction. 'I warned you not to come within three miles of me.'

He's just a man. A bully. Like Vince. You can take him down like you did him.

'Where's Tamsin?' This isn't the opening I'd planned in

my head, but it's high on my list of priorities and I'm pleased to hear the steadiness of my voice – its clarity. I don't want him to hear or see my fear. He'll feed off of it, like a vulture picking clean the bones of its meal.

'You should know, Becky.' He laughs. He's in control. I need to knock him from his perch. But he's holding all the cards for now. He will know I don't have any evidence because he's made sure of that. He's only agreed to come here because he thinks I'm giving up – he wants to see my face as he declares it a win for him. Again. He wants the pleasure of gloating, demonstrating his invincibility. This bastard. What does he want – a fucking red cape?

'If you think a bunch of faked photos is going to fool anyone—'

'Oh, come on. If you didn't think that was possible, you'd have gone squealing to the cops straightaway. Nah. You know they look the real deal. Even digital forensics will be hard pushed to prove they're fake.'

Please let Hannah be in place and already recording. I have an urge to look around, see if I can spot her, but that would be fatal – I can't give away her location, or the fact I didn't come alone as agreed.

'So? Where did you get that creep, Vince, to hide her?'

'Oh, bless you. You really think she's alive, don't you? God, you're pathetic.'

My heartbeat reverberates inside my ribcage; I press my palm on my breastbone, feeling it pulsating against it. At least it's still beating. *Don't rise to it. He's lying.*

I don't want to play this game anymore.

'Okay. So what now? Where do we go from here, John?'

He sniffs loudly. Steps towards me. 'You see, I've worked real hard to get where I am today. Despite your attempts to bring everything crashing down.'

'You have Francesca Withers to thank for that – I mean, if we're assigning gratitude to the correct people. Because, had she not been brave enough to send that message to your burner, I'd never have found out you're a rapist.'

'Oh, now, now. Don't be modest. You were more worthy of thanks than you are comfortable recalling. You shouldn't pretend you didn't see the signs.'

'Don't be ridiculous. You were careful to hide your true self. No one suspected you for the repulsive things you did. Are still doing.'

'You saw what you wanted to see. Ignored what you didn't want to face. That makes you implicit.'

'That makes half the Salford CID and beyond implicit. Some more so than others.' Blood rushes to my face, the burning hurts my cheeks and makes me realise how cold the rest of me has become.

'If that's how you sleep at night, babe.'

I flinch. The way he's saying 'babe' is grating on my nerves. My fists clench by my sides. I could get one hit in before he launches himself at me. But before I push him to the brink, I need him to admit to what he's done. All Hannah needs is him bragging about his crimes, how he's raped multiple women, abused and attacked them, manipulated and coerced them. How he is part of a wider group of corrupt members of the force, that he and others have covered up what he's done . . . and I don't want to think about what each of those people has done in addition to clearing up John's messes. People capable of that are likely to be neck-deep in their own shit too.

John begins to circle me, like a shark breaking down its prey's defences before it goes in for the kill. My stomach bubbles with anticipation. He doesn't seem to be armed, but he could easily be concealing a weapon. Just as I am. Very slowly, I begin to take a step back with each loop he makes around me, gradually steering us towards the back of the warehouse. My foot snags the corner of a large box and I falter. John's hand shoots out to grab hold of me, preventing my fall.

'Steady on. Can't have you having an accident now, can we?' he sneers. 'Not prematurely.'

'Ruin your big plan, would it?' I pull my arm from his grasp, but we're still too close. I can smell the sourness of his breath and screw up my nose, turning away sharply. 'Jesus. Heard of a toothbrush?' I say, knowing the simple, disparaging comment will irk him.

'Why don't you just fuck off, Becky!' He lunges, and both my arms are suddenly in a vice-like grip, his face is in mine; we're nose to nose. 'Always thought you were something special, eh? Coming up here, all high and mighty. You're nothing. Just a kid of dead fishermen.'

'You've always been good at dishing it out, never could stomach being on the receiving end.'

'Whatever. I've had enough of the games now.' He shoves me, my back hitting against a stack of boxes. I try to shuffle sideways, so I'm not trapped, but John slams his hand into the centre of my chest, pinning me in place. My instinct is to go on the attack, get out of this, but I know I need it to look convincing for the recording. What if Hannah isn't even here? *No! Don't think like that.* I have to trust she is and give the performance of my life. Vulnerability is what John enjoys, what he feeds off, and I need to give him just that. No self-defence, no heroics – this evidence has to be strong, needs to demonstrate what he's capable of. It has

305

to be enough proof to ensure he's put away for a very long time. And with luck, he won't be alone come judgement day. If I shake the apple tree violently enough, I'll watch all the bad ones fall. And I'll relish each and every one.

God, I hope Hannah has a clear view. She said she'd done a reccy prior to us luring John here, and from what she said, I assumed it had no blind spots. But now, in this position, I'm not confident that's the case. I should move us out into the open more, away from the shield of these boxes.

'If you've had enough of games, why did you come here?'

'For you, Becky.' He pushes his groin into me and moves one hand to my throat. 'You always did like it rough,' he whispers into my neck, then scrapes his teeth across my skin. I gasp.

'Get off me.' I wriggle my arms to get them closer to my chest and ready to push him.

'Come on. For old times' sake. One. Last. Time.' He releases the hand from my throat, unzips his trousers.

'No! I said get off me John, you're disgusting.' I push him with all my might and manage to unbalance him. I use this brief interlude to move away from the boxes. I cast my gaze around quickly, but can't see any evidence of Hannah. She's here, though. I can sense her. She's just doing a good job of covert observation. Better than I could ever do.

But, I have my role to play. And as John strides towards me, I know it's not over yet.

'Playing hard to get?' He shrugs. 'I like it. Adds a bit of spice.'

'Say that to all the women you've raped?'

He snorts. 'Oh, Becky. I realise your jealousy was always an issue. I tried so hard to make you feel special. Like you were the only one for me – all I ever needed. But, truth be told, you were a necessity. You ensured I always stayed under the radar, was seen as a respectable serving officer. You *helped* me become the man I am today. And people say women are only good for *one* thing.' He clasps my cheeks between his thumb and fingers, his fingertips digging in hard. Pain sears through muscle, teeth and bone, triggering tears to spring to my eyes. His tongue licks at them, like a cat lapping up spilt milk.

'You won't get away with hurting me, John.' I force the words between my contorted lips, through the agony of his grip.

'I'm pretty sure I will.' He smiles as he pushes me backwards using the hand on my face, the other is rummaging around in his trousers. Dread sits heavy inside my body, a scream building as he begins tearing at my clothes. I swallow my terror back down. In my weakened state following the concussion, I hadn't considered he would rape me before going in for the kill. The plan was to film him in the act of attempted murder. I'm going to have to go through a sexual assault before Hannah calls for the backup to storm this place.

My strength leaks from every muscle; my arms hang uselessly by my side and my legs wobble. And then I feel the cold, hard blade against my skin and it reverses, everything tensing back up. I narrow my eyes as my mind struggles to comprehend what's happening.

He is armed with a knife, that's what he was retrieving from his trousers. My own weapon is unreachable.

'I mean, it's not a flawless plan,' he says, tracing the point of the knife along my jawline, then lowering it to my throat. He pauses, the tip resting above where I imagine my jugular vein is, and I freeze. I feel my bounding pulse and I'm scared that if I so much as breathe, the knife will pierce my vein. 'My DNA will inevitably be on your body, vice versa – but you know – you were so desperate for a reconciliation after the trouble you caused me, that you came to my place looking to hook up. Whatever evidence can't be explained will . . .' he smiles, 'simply disappear. Puff.'

Here we go. This is the stuff I need from him. Implicating other corrupt cops is perfect.

But do I want to *die* on this hill in the process of extricating it?

The images of Fran, her child's discarded toys, left to crumble like old headstones in a cemetery, the list of names in the journal – the many women I suspect have been abused by John – Nina and Millie, who will suffer at his hands in the future.

Yes. I'm up for taking the risk. It'll all be on film at least.

Chapter 53

NOW

BECKY

John doesn't blink. He's glaring at me, waiting for me to say something. He wants me to speak; desperate for his moment to show off. And I want him to remove the knife from my throat, give me some breathing space – literally and figuratively. I lift an eyebrow, silently communicating my wishes. He rolls his eyes. The pressure of the blade disappears, but I know he's still holding it close, so I don't make a sudden movement. Just breathe at a natural pace. My lack of vocalisation even now the knife is lowered seems to annoy him.

'Cat got your tongue?' he says, then laughs. 'I would say you'd die an old spinster surrounded by a load of manky cats, but as it is, I'll be sparing you of that humiliation.'

'Meaning?' I mumble. He finally loosens his fingers on my face, drops his hand so I can speak more freely.

'I think you know what I mean, Becky.'

'All this because you couldn't let go,' I say, a flare of anger bringing heat to my face. A moment of confusion flickers behind his eyes. 'You didn't *want* me to leave you alone – couldn't bear the thought of losing my attention. Ahh, poor John. Afraid of being forgotten. Insignificant. You revelled in the spotlight *I* shone on you. Without it, you were merely in the shadows – boring, steadfast John Lawson.'

'Shut up.' He holds the knife up again. 'I know what you're doing. And it's sad.'

'Sad?' I have to show some guts now, try to turn the tables, so I push the arm holding the knife away and begin stepping forwards, telling him how bullying and coercing women is the saddest thing – jabbing my finger in his chest with each word I speak to hammer it home.

Of course he knows I'm goading him, and there's a strong possibility he'll realise why I'm doing it, but that won't stop him from snapping. Men like him always do in the end. While not all rapists are psychopaths, I suspect John – who is a serial offender and likely does have the capacity to commit murder – is. I touched upon criminal psychology in my degree, and working for five years in Salford CID brought me into contact with a number of people displaying violent, antisocial behaviour and psychopathic traits. If I were assessing John, it would be tick after tick.

So, why didn't I recognise those traits when I was with him? Will I ever quash the anger that rises up when I think about them now, and my own actions of pushing any negatives aside? Ultimately, John's right with what he said. I shouldn't pretend I didn't see the signs. I *ignored* them. I've aided and abetted his behaviour, helped shape him into what he is. But now I have the chance to remedy it.

'Okay, you've had your moment,' he says, stopping,

counteracting my force so I can no longer push him. He grabs at my hand on his chest, squeezing my fingers then twisting them.

'That it? You're so weak, John. The inability to control yourself is astounding. How the hell did you even get into the police in the first place? Oh, wait. Of course.' I give a dramatic laugh. 'Someone on the inside helped you.' I sigh and shake my head. 'Can't do anything on your own merit. What a loser.'

His hand trembles with the effort of tightening his grasp. I clench my jaw to try and ride out the crushing pain. 'Taken a good look at yerself lately, love? Pretty grim, eh? Shithole of a flat, only a cat for company. Oh, well – until *he* left you too. And guess what? You only got that place 'cos of me. You're welcome.'

The bastard. He *had* orchestrated it and then somehow made it seem that Hannah had found the place. It's what Danny was getting at. A knot of hatred tightens in my stomach. But I can't allow my emotions to distract me. I look him in the eye as I calmly utter my comeback. 'Like I said. You couldn't let go. Needed to interfere, meddle in my life still. I feel sorry for you.'

'You won't feel anything soon.'

A cracking sound, followed by a sharp pain makes me realise he's snapped a finger or two on my right hand.

'Oh dear, sorry about that.'

His eyes light up with my involuntarily moan. Sneering, he drops my hand. I don't look at the damage, it'll make it worse if I see my deformed digits. 'You've done worse,' I say between gritted teeth.

'Not to you I haven't.'

'That's a matter of opinion.'

311

'Of course you'd say that. But, hey – you got out of the way of the bloody car, didn't you?'

My heart skips a few beats. 'You were the one who tried to run me over? Coward.'

'If it was me, there's no way I'd have fucking missed. If you want a job done, you gotta do it yourself.'

'Well, yeah – it's a real cop-out if you get others to do your dirty work. Second nature to you, though, isn't it? Surprised you didn't get your local thugs to attack the women for you, too. Or were they only reserved for officers?'

'You're trying to paint me as being a bit of a monster here, Becky. Come on, I never killed any of them slags. Just did a bit of . . . business with them. Mutual, of course.'

'There was no consent involved and you know it. *I* know it. I saw the messages, heard the evidence, read—'

'And none of that counts for shit now, does it? Because you're fuckin' useless. Lost it all. You're pathetic, incompetent. You dare to call me the loser. Hah.'

I blink with every word he spits in my face; his use of insults are his tactic, a way to demean me like he did last year after I found out what he was. For a split second, I recoil, shrinking into myself as I did then, too.

'No!' I open my eyes wide as a surge of adrenaline triggers my fight response. 'That shit won't work on me anymore, John.' I step forwards to move past him, protecting my damaged fingers with my good hand.

John puts his arm out in front of me, slides the knife under my T-shirt. 'Don't. Move.'

I freeze, my muscles immobilising. 'Why? You gonna kill me if I do?'

'I'll gut you like your dead pa used to gut his fish.'

A cold trickle of fear runs down my back. Is a threat to

kill enough? Will Hannah alert the backup team now? I'm not sure how much longer I can keep this up. Or how much longer I have to live.

'Why are you so hellbent on killing me, John? I'd have thought you'd enjoy having an intelligent adversary – keep it exciting for you. Showing off how clever you are is something you crave, isn't it? Without me around, who are you going to brag to? Nina?'

'And there it is. You're *jealous*,' he scoffs. 'You can't bear knowing I'm with another woman, can you? Bet you got into a right strop when you found out we have a kid together. Must've hurt. Knowing I didn't want one with you.' He laughs, the sound echoing. 'I knew, see, that Nina was up the duff – and I was glad. She's more of a mothering kind. You're too focused on clamouring to the top. Not good parenting material.'

'You haven't got a clue – you don't know me now. Maybe you never did. But it's you who's bitter. You never thought I'd throw you out, did you?'

'It's all by the by now, and it doesn't matter anymore. But to set the record straight, you might've got in first by evicting me from my own home, but I'd have left anyway. I wanted to be a proper family with Nina and our Millie. You were never part of my future.' He presses the knife into my side, the tip feeling as though it will push through at any second.

'Bored of raping now? Need to up the thrills to murder?'

'Yeah, I've had my fun. Let's shut you up for good, eh?' He pulls his knife-wielding hand back, readying himself to ram it in hard.

I go into survival mode. Inhaling sharply, I twist my body, sidestepping at the same time, and then duck down to retrieve my weapon from my sock. Before I can pull it out, a booted foot to my temple knocks me over and I sprawl out on the ground. The same boot propels itself into my stomach and I double up on the floor, curling my body like a baby in the womb as I lose all the air from my lungs.

'Enough,' I say in a breathy gasp. John laughs. But I'm not saying it to him. 'Enough!' I manage with more power to my voice. 'Enough,' I repeat for the third time. This is the signal – to ensure backup storm in and put a stop to John's attempted murder of me. And, in this moment, I know even though I haven't got him to confess all I'd hoped, Hannah will have enough on film to get the bastard put away.

'I say when it's enough,' John says as he pulls his foot back, ready to strike again. But just before I close my eyes so I don't have to see it coming, the foot stops its momentum – suspending in midair as though this is a TV show and the viewer has pressed pause on the remote. Tears of relief sting my face as I hear another pair of boots rushing up.

Backup has arrived.

I roll away from John, and look to the rear of the warehouse, where the footsteps originated. Hannah is coming towards John, and it looks as though her hands are raised. I squint. She can't have got a gun, but it's too dull in here to decipher. Given John stopped immediately and is now standing, shocked and silent, I guess she must have something. Maybe the camera is rolling. A twinge of concern ripples through me. Stowing it until John is safely arrested and can't damage it might've been the best option, not showing him what we've done. But it's fine. She's called for backup, and they'll be here any second.

'Thank fuck,' I say as she nears me. I struggle to get up off the ground. I need to get to Hannah's side, create a strong defensive line. 'Where are the others?'

Hannah takes my arm, and although I can't relax yet, my body slumps against hers – my adrenaline waning now I know I'm not going to die.

'You hurt?' she asks, her gaze fixed on John.

'A bit.' I hold up my oddly bent fingers.

'John Lawson,' she says. I smile, knowing what's coming. At last.

'Yeah.' He steps towards us and my heart jolts as I feel Hannah's hand leave my arm. Shit, is she going to try and launch herself at him?

'Hannah, no!' I try to grasp hold of her, but she's already pounding her fists repeatedly into John's chest. 'Please, don't—'

And then it all happens so quickly – what I see with my eyes and what registers in my brain, don't match up.

'Hannah?'

'I'm sorry.'

Chapter 54

NOW

BECKY

The events from the past few weeks flash through my mind like a film on fast-forward, but not in the right order. Images and snippets of conversations are all jumbled up as I stand facing Hannah and John trying to figure out what's just happened. She stopped hitting him in the chest. Her arms fell to her sides limply, all the fight seemingly gone. But then, as I was about to rush at her to pull her away, John took hold of her. And she let him. Uttering an apology to *me*.

I've been played.

'What . . . *You're* the one?' I reel, feeling as though I've been shot in the chest and my body slammed back against the wall with the force of it. I can't catch my breath. I'm winded by the sudden realisation. 'No. No.' I shake my head. It doesn't make sense. 'You're the sensible one of us. You stick to every fucking rule. You expect me to believe you're helping John? Hannah, please, you're lying to me. Why?'

Hannah's head lolls forward, like it's too heavy for her neck to support it.

'Look at me!' I shout at her. 'Hannah. Please. Tell me this isn't right.' My voice cracks, my emotions bubbling and rising, restricting my throat like hands are wrapped around it, squeezing tightly. I don't look directly at John, but can see his smug expression from the corner of my eye.

'I tried to discourage you, Becky,' she says, the low pitch of her voice unfamiliar. 'You had to keep going. We advised you not to go after him. We warned you against it!'

'We?' I gulp down the dread. She could be talking about her and John, but I don't think she is. Does she mean her and Charlie? Marcus? All of them?

Is everyone in on this with John?

I bend over, spitting the bile from my mouth, my good hand clenching my stomach as more ejects from it.

'How does it feel, Becky? Knowing you have no backup coming.' John claps his hands together, like an excited child. 'This is quite the finale. Excellent job, Han!' He puts his arm around Hannah and hugs her. For a split second, I think she's going to hug him back, but then she pulls away, turning on him.

'Fuck off, John,' she says. I hear the dejection in her tone and the penny drops.

'Come now, mate. We made a great team.'

'I'm sorry, Becky. I didn't want to do it.' Hannah's eyes plead with mine.

My heart is heavy, a sadness filling it. 'How did he get to you? Danny?'

Hannah nods slowly, but John doesn't appear to be in the mood for any explanations. He wants to get on with it. His plan is clearly working better than my own. There's no

317

backup coming, there's no video evidence of what's gone before this. I'm going to die.

And with the help of a bunch of corrupt officers, he is going to get away with everything. I've let all of John's victims – past, present and future – down. I gaze around the warehouse, gauging how quickly I could run to either of the exits. I don't fancy my chances of outrunning both of them. Although, Hannah might not try too hard to get me. She's been coerced into this, surely she doesn't want me dead. Or is that the reason for bringing me here? Did she knowingly set this up *for* John? Was I the one lured here?

'Wow. Can almost hear those cogs turning,' John says, moving so he's behind me. 'Don't for a minute think she'll help you get away from me.' His words are breathy, filled with exhilaration. 'She's mine. She'll do what I tell her.'

I look towards Hannah. Her face is streaked with tears, but she's not disagreeing with him.

'How, Hannah? Tell me how he got to you.'

'Give over, Becky,' John says, grabbing me. 'It's simple. Her brother was a loser who gambled. Not a great combination,' he laughs. 'Stupid prick got himself in way over his head with the wrong people. But guess who came running to me to help get him out of the shit?' He points his knife at Hannah. 'Yep. Hannah here. Miss Goody-Two-Shoes – who, by the way, isn't averse to some dodgy dealings herself – begged me to step in.'

My blood boils thinking of all the time we worked together, of our shared moments at the pub, and yet she never once sought advice or shared anything about what was happening with me. Even when I dropped in the day Danny was there and she took him for treatment, she never

318

said a word. Made me think the worst, that he was dying from cancer or something. Was he even ill? Hannah just stands mute, letting John do the talking.

'Hannah?' I glare at her, shaking my head. 'Tell me he's lying.'

'I can't, Becky.' She shrugs. 'He was my little brother. I had to help him.'

'I assume it didn't stop with just one offer of help from John. He'll have smelled your weakness, worked out how you could be useful to him.'

'Hey, now – I'm right here, you know,' he says, squeezing my arm. 'I'm capable of telling the story.'

John rattles off the details of how he used his contacts to ensure Danny wasn't killed for his debts – he bought him some time with the illegal bookies, but then Danny slipped even further, getting into the drug scene. The state he was in when I saw him at Hannah's was the result of depression and drug-taking. She'd been accepting bribes to fund her brother's treatment. And once John was aware of this, he knew he could rope her in to falsify records and help cover up his movements – smooth things over so he wasn't flagged as a suspect in any of the rapes.

'Easy to do once someone's turned to the dark side,' John says. 'All I had to do was threaten to release details of Danny's gambling debts and Hannah's own involvement in taking bribes. Oh, and then when she looked to have turned on me, I upped the ante.'

'You killed Danny,' I say.

'Fucking bastard. There was no need to hurt him!' Hannah storms towards us, and for a magical moment my heart soars thinking she's going to reveal she's double-crossed him. Maybe attack him to release me from his grip.

But she stops short, letting out a pitiful cry.

'Aw, Hannah. Shame.' John sighs loudly. 'She can't help you, Becky. This is the end.'

'Hannah, please,' I say. 'You've been protecting him, but it isn't reciprocated. Once you do this last thing for him, he'll pin everything on you. Don't you see?'

Her tears intensify. I've never seen Hannah like this. He's broken her. She swipes at her face, then laughs hysterically. She stops abruptly, like a switch has been flicked, and her face returns to its stony expression.

'If only I'd seen through him right off,' she says, sadly. 'But it's too late, Becky. Danny was a warning. I'd told John I wouldn't help lure you to him and that's what happened. I have to save the only family I have left now.'

I gulp down my anger. 'Oh, John.' I twist to face him. 'You really are a lowlife.' I spit in his face. It might be the last thing I do, but my hatred for this man has to be shown somehow. He doesn't flinch, doesn't even wipe it away, just smiles. 'How could you be so callous?'

I realise even without Hannah confirming my suspicion, that John told her that if she didn't do what he said, he'd target her dad next. And now, the awful truth dawns. All the evidence I had, and everything that Nina had, was destroyed by Hannah. Every move I made, Hannah knew about it and relayed it to John. I never stood a chance of getting justice.

'I do what I do. You can't blame me for other people's actions, Becky. Hannah could've made different choices too. But I think she enjoyed playing with you almost as much as I did.' He turns to Hannah and smiles. 'Swapping her anxiety meds was particularly inspired. Bought us the time we needed to arrange this little . . . rendezvous. And—'

320

he lowers his face to mine '—your erratic and forgetful behaviour from the past weeks will add weight to my case against you.'

Oh, Hannah, what have you done? I'm not giving John the satisfaction of seeing how hurt I am, hearing the disappointment and betrayal in my voice, so I don't bite.

'This isn't what I wanted,' Hannah says, moving closer again. 'Please forgive me.' I sense a shift in the atmosphere. There's been enough talk, I suspect they want to put a full stop to their story. Write 'the end' and move on. My insides shake as John's other hand slips around my neck. Is he going to strangle me? Or make Hannah kill me? That would work better for him – keep her on his leash for even longer.

'You'll never, *ever*, escape him if you do this, Hannah.' I squirm in John's hold, panic finally setting in. My feet push against the ground, trying to drive us both back. If I could at least get him against the wall . . . maybe I'll have a chance. 'He'll shop you anyway and it'll all be for nothing.' She pauses, a frown forming as her eyes flick to John.

'You're seriously not going to listen to this bitch, are you? She's going to say anything to try and save herself. Don't fall for her shit.'

'Think about it, Hannah,' I say, knowing this is my final opportunity to get her back on my side. 'The trail leads to you. John's made sure of that. Anyone who could've backed you up will be gone. Or in his pocket. Is Charlie in on this too? Marcus? Who else?'

She looks blankly at me.

'While you think you're all in it together, safe in the knowledge you've all had a part to play – who is the weakest link? Who is the one they've chosen to take the fall? You're the real patsy, Hannah. Not me. Doesn't matter if you do as John says here, now – your life is over if you allow him to kill me.'

'Oh, fuck this,' John yells. His grip loosens from around my neck and body, and before I can react, he's pulling the knife back, about to plunge it into me. The room darkens, and before I process any pain, a sickening scream rips through the air. My body and mind go numb.

But it's not me who's screaming. My eyes snap open.

A figure lies on the floor by my feet.

I'm standing, shaking, my hands feeling for a gaping wound in my abdomen.

My mouth drops open, and I gasp for air as it becomes obvious.

Hannah jumped in front of me in the blink of an eye. She's the one who's been stabbed.

Chapter 55

NOW

BECKY

Hannah's hand is clasped to her stomach. Blood gushes through her fingers and spreads over the floor. It sounds like liquid glugging from a bottle.

'Run, Becky.' The words come out as a gurgle as they mix with the blood oozing from her mouth. I look away, then, mentally yelling at my muscles to move, begin to run towards the exit. John is inches behind, the only reason he didn't pounce on me straightaway is because even he was momentarily stunned at Hannah's action. But now he's right on me.

Please don't let us both die here . . .

The knife.

I can't outrun John. But I can reach the secreted weapon.

I pull out the penknife, turn back to John and lift it, ready to strike. But John is backing away from me.

This, together with a deafening cacophony of sound, sends me into blind confusion.

Why is John running in the opposite direction to me, past Hannah's bleeding body? More noises fill the warehouse and I turn to see Marcus, Charlie and a whole squad of people burst in.

'Oh, my God.' I look up, then back to John as he tries to make his escape. Armed police block his path. He's trapped. I fall to the ground, tears of relief racking my sore body.

John, visibly shocked, his face pale, shouts out, 'What's going on, lads?' He puts his hands up, swings around to look at Marcus and Charlie. 'You're a bit late to the party, aren't you? It's her you need to be pointing the guns at.' He nods towards me. 'She went crazy, stabbed Hannah. Good job you got here when you did, did you see the fucking knife she pulled? About to stab me, too.'

Charlie walks past me to get to John, but Marcus stops, holds out a hand. 'You okay?'

I shake my head. 'No. But never so pleased to see you!' He helps me up. John watches, his smug expression dropping from his face. Realisation seems to hit him.

'But . . . this can't be right . . . ' he protests as Charlie cuffs him. 'Hannah didn't tell anyone.'

Charlie's glance slides to his right, lingers on Hannah for a few seconds, before he pulls John around to face him. I listen as John is cautioned, noting that he's being arrested on suspicion of attempted murder. The paramedics rush to Hannah lying motionless on the ground. Tears sting my eyes as I watch them check her vitals. My chest tightens; I know it's too late. There's no emergency resuscitation. No frantic tearing open of medical supplies or the giving of oxygen.

She's bleeding out. She's gone.

The initial surge of noise, all the commotion, begins to

subside once John is removed and taken into custody. Hannah's body remains in situ, and a white tent is being erected ready for crime scene investigators to begin recovering and recording evidence. I walk over, as close as I can to where she lies, lifeless. It doesn't even look like Hannah. A cry catches in my throat and I press my hand to my mouth. This wasn't the outcome I wanted. I'd like to believe Hannah's at peace now, with her mum and brother. What she ended up being a part of was so far removed from the person I knew Hannah to be. It must've tortured her to have to choose between what was legally and morally right and what was best for her family.

My shoulders heave as I sob. Then I feel a weight on them as I'm wrapped in a blanket. Protected. Safe.

I turn to look at my friend one last time. 'I forgive you, Hannah,' I whisper.

The paramedics take me to the back of their ambulance, check me over. My fingers will need x-raying, but they strap them for now.

Charlie comes and sits with me, his face mirroring my own horror.

'Did you have any idea about Hannah?' I ask.

He bites his lip. Shakes his head. 'God, no. Not until earlier. What a fucking shitshow.'

He tells me there was an anonymous tip informing them John was at this location, that he was armed and saying he was going to kill me. He's thinks the tip probably came from Nina, as she'd been spying on John's movements for us.

'But she was already in protective custody,' I retort. 'How could she have known?'

Charlie scratches his neck. 'Is that what Hannah told you?'

'It's what she alluded to. So you weren't looking after Nina at a safe house?'

He raises his eyebrows. 'No. As you know, we were concerned she might've been compromised, especially when her house was broken into, but we didn't think she was in immediate danger . . .'

'Jesus. Hannah really pulled the wool over my eyes.'

'Well, you did have a severe concussion. We could blame that?'

'And when were you hit over the head?' I try to smile, but with the knowledge of everything that's just gone down, it's more of a grimace.

'I know. No excuses for me. But, well. *Hannah*?' Charlie gives a bewildered shake of his head. 'We worked together. Closely. We were the A Team,' he says. 'Why didn't she come to one of us earlier?'

'John is expert at finding people's weaknesses, Charlie. Believe me.' I lean in closer, and whisper, 'Did you uncover any of the other corrupt cops?'

He quietly informs me that two other male officers – one who helped John by breaking into Nina's house and one other were also arrested. The person driving the car that tried to mow me down was ID'd by a witness. It was DS Kyle Matthews. My shock lasts all of a few seconds. Should've seen that one coming. Arsehole.

'Four down.' I stare into his eyes. 'How many more are there to go, though?'

We sit, legs swinging off the back of the ambulance, in quiet reflection.

Marcus is insistent on me having a full check over at the hospital, and to show my deep gratitude to him for his support – not to mention his timing – I agree. He must've been quietly doing some investigating in the background to try and build the case I'd started against John over a year ago. He was on my side after all, and just needed me to keep reminding him of how important it was. My skin prickles with goose bumps as an unwanted thought comes into my mind. Maybe, had I left well alone and not interfered – Marcus would have slowly, but surely, built a solid case to ensure prosecutions could be brought for *all* of John's crimes. I must try not to dwell on that. Before I'm whisked off, I ask him if he knows what happened to my upstairs neighbour, Tamsin.

'There was a hoax call made so that officers would storm the flat,' Marcus says. His expression darkens. 'Now, it's looking very likely that call came from Hannah.'

My eyes flick to where Hannah's body lays, a heaviness pressing down on me. It's going to take me a long time to wrap my head around all of this. Hannah's involvement is more intricate than I can comprehend right now. But I don't think she was behind Tamsin's disappearance.

'I'm certain the man Tamsin was living with is one of John's men.'

'There's another team looking into that, rest assured.'

I raise my eyebrows, unsure I'm capable of trusting that sentiment. 'Are you stalling giving me bad news?' I ask Marcus.

'The young woman is safe.' He smiles.

'Oh, good,' I say, my relief palpable. 'I was so worried about her. Glad to know she didn't become another of John's victims.'

'We can't prove he was behind any of it at the moment . . .' Marcus's words trail off. I sense the disappointment and feel it too. Without more evidence, John won't be charged with the multiple rapes I know him to be responsible for. 'He'll get a prison sentence for murder,' Marcus adds. 'That much I feel certain of.' Marcus sucks in a large breath of air, he pulls his shoulders back, spine rod-straight. He blinks rapidly. 'We lost one of our own today,' he says. 'That's never easy. Despite what transpired here, try to remember Hannah wasn't a bad person, not really.'

'I'll try, sir.' For a fleeting moment, I feel part of the force again.

'You did a good job of not giving up, Becky. I'm proud of you.'

I attempt to smile up at him. My bottom lip quivers. I bite down on it, but the tears come anyway. Marcus gives me a pat on the back. It's just a gesture to anyone looking on, but I know what it conveys.

Chapter 56

NOW

BECKY

The doctor clears me for release from hospital, but not before giving me grief about my previous self-discharge when I was still suffering with a concussion. I allow her to reprimand me because I know she's right. I make a vow to myself to listen to advice from now on.

Well. I'll take it on board before dismissing it, anyway.

I've a few loose ends to sort out, but my first call before going back to the flat is Hamley's café. There's a certain someone who I need to thank.

Elijah's face lights up when he sees me at the counter. 'Well, hello there.' He turns to the other barista, says something I don't hear, then steps around to my side.

'Hi, Elijah,' I say, and find that I'm able to smile. It feels good.

'Am I pleased to see you.' He gives me a look up and down, wincing as he clocks my bandaged hand, the swollen

329

and bruised fingertips peeping out. 'Ow. That from the accident?'

For the moment, I don't have the energy to retell the story. Or if I will ever tell Elijah what happened exactly. 'Yeah. I guess I owe you my life.'

He frowns. 'No. You don't owe me anything, Becky. You saved your own life.'

I find myself nodding in agreement. He's right, just not in the way he thinks. He ushers me to the nearest table and pulls a seat out for me, but doesn't sit himself. I look up at him.

'Glad you've got a good memory for faces,' I say. 'Being able to identify the driver of the car was really helpful.'

'Get to know a lot of faces working in here,' he says.

'You were in the right place at the right time, that's for sure.'

'See—' he squeezes my shoulder '—had I *not* acted like a petulant teenager when you didn't call me, there'd have been no reason for me to chase after you to apologise when I saw you jogging past here that day.'

I laugh. 'Well, there is that.'

'I am sorry, you know,' Elijah says. 'My behaviour was childish. I'm so embarrassed that I ignored you.'

'We all make mistakes,' I say. He gives a nod, and turns. But I hold on to his arm. There's a burning question I have that I don't want to keep inside.

'When you came to my aid, after the car incident, did you see a journal? Or did you see it lying close by?'

Elijah pushes his lips down at the edges, and frowns. 'No. Why?'

'Oh, no worries. Maybe I didn't have it with me like I thought. The effects of concussion, eh?' He smiles, then

330

he disappears behind the counter again. I gaze out of the window, troubled by the missing journal. I know I had it. Did Kyle have time to get out of the car and take it, then flee before Elijah reached the scene?

Perhaps I'll never know now.

A couple with a toddler stroll past outside. A deep ache in my abdomen steals my breath. Everything I've been working towards for the last year has come to an end and it hits me that now this is all over, I'm mourning my life as a married woman, with the dreams of a family. I hope, at least, that Nina is now free to bring up Millie in safety, knowing she tried to do the right thing. Maybe my time will come too one day. I decided not to get back in contact with Nina. John's been arrested and charged; her part is over. As is mine where she and Millie are concerned. I got John away from them by taking him down. They need the space to recover and rebuild. My thoughts are interrupted by Elijah's excitable voice.

'Now,' he says, placing a tall glass in front of me. 'I wonder if you'd like to taste-test this new flavour for me?'

'Oh?' I look curiously at the drink, topped with cream and what appears to be caramel syrup. 'What is it?'

'I'm calling it the Becca-double-stamper. After you.'

The burst of laughter catches even me off-guard. 'That's appalling, Elijah. Can't you come up with a better name?'

'Hey. I spent all of twenty seconds coming up with that.'

I dip the tall spoon in and scoop up some of the cream as Elijah watches me. Then I sip the latte and savour the taste. 'Well, it's really good. Whatever it is.'

'Then my work here is done,' he says, standing back and smiling. 'Enjoy.' And he passes me another new loyalty card with two stamps already on it, before walking back to the counter.

The sun gleams on the side of my block of hell as I walk towards it. As I approach my flat I see that even though the door has been repaired, the slightly mismatched paint job is visible still. My pulse jumps as I recall Hannah turning up just after the graffiti had been daubed onto it. How she stared at it and said: *Good to see you've gained some new friends*. Was it her – doing it for John? Or had she been attempting to scare me off herself, aware of what was to come? I'll never know now, but I would like to think she was trying to limit the damage – to do what she could in difficult circumstances.

'Life's so complicated,' I mutter as I step inside my flat. It's a mess still, and it's lacking a cat. My skin prickles as if there's a draught, but I know it's more than that. John made sure I found this place, arranging it through Hannah so I didn't suspect he'd had a hand in it. Vince was likely already working for him and having me living below meant he could keep track of my movements and report back to John. He had eyes and ears everywhere it seemed. So many puppets, such a complex web of deceit. I doubt I'll ever get to the bottom of it.

As I turn to go into my room, I see an envelope half out the letterbox. I tear it open and begin reading it, but there's a knock on the door. I stand rooted to the spot for a few seconds, fear shooting through me. It's a response that's going to take a while to replace. I inhale deeply, then reach forward to open it.

'Hi, Becky. Thought you'd like a visitor.' I beam at Tamsin, my anxiety melting away as I see that she's holding a purring Agatha in her arms.

'Well, aren't you two a sight for sore eyes. Come in.' I apologise for the state of the place, and while I make a drink, Tamsin fills me in on what happened after Vince smuggled her out of the building, how he held her captive in the flat above the club all because she'd started talking to me. I don't dare think about what harm might've come to her had John not been stopped, had he still been hellbent on pinning a murder on me. She tells me that Vince was arrested yesterday, charged with false imprisonment. He didn't give John's name as being the one behind it – loyal to a fault. But she feels sure he'll buckle under pressure. I agree that it's very likely.

Then, moving to the lounge and sitting among the chaos, I give Tamsin a brief rundown of the past few days. She listens intently, offering the odd nod, or alarmed facial expression as I retell some of the events. I leave large chunks out, being that it's an active investigation. Exhaustion and relief are evident on Tamsin's face. Her cheeks look hollow, her eyes dark, but behind them, there's something new I haven't seen before.

Hope.

'Oh, here,' she says, digging into her pocket and retrieving some bent-up photos. 'Shall we do some kind of ritual burning?' She smiles as she passes them to me. The deepfake photos of her murder at my hand send a fresh shiver through me. 'They were inside the flat when I got back there. No idea why they weren't taken when the police raided.'

'That is strange.' I inspect them – they're a duplicate set of the ones I had and lost – apart from the single one I showed Charlie. 'They're evidence. I should hand them over.' My mind races through the possible reasons these weren't seized as part of the investigation. They prove that John was using deepfake photos and trying to frame me.

'Really? Can they be linked to John? Or even Vince?'

I think about that for a moment. 'No. Probably not. But as evidence goes . . . At least it's something. No telling what future advances in forensics might yield from them one day.'

Agatha sits atop her usual spot. She looks right at home. But the knot in my stomach reminds me that she is not, and never was, my cat.

'Can you keep living in Vince's place?' I ask.

'For now, yeah. But I got plans.' Tamsin looks at the cat, then back at me. 'Would you take care of Punch – sorry – I mean, Agatha, for me please? If you want. Don't feel you—'

'Of course. I'd love to. She's my sidekick now. But whenever you want to see her, or are in a position to take her back . . .'

There's a bleep, and Tamsin looks at her mobile.

'Oh, good to see you have one of those now,' I say, then remember that I must replace my own. Not good to live alone here without a form of communication.

'Yeah,' she says, distractedly. 'Once Vince was gone, I was able to get it back. It was at the club all this time.' She draws her eyebrows together, then shows me the screen. 'This is the woman who came to Moods. Asking to see Fran.'

The notification is the news headline about the death of DC Hannah Martin, accompanied by a small black and white photo depicting her at some crime scene from a couple of years back. A few things slot into place.

'Makes sense it would've been her. John had her running around trying to clean up after him. He had her over a barrel.'

'I'm sorry.' Tamsin looks genuinely upset for me. Even though she's been through hell herself.

'You're worth so much more than you realise, you know. I hope you can find happiness, Tamsin. You deserve it.'

'Thank you, Becky, so do you. Will you stay here?' She casts her gaze around my pokey flat. 'I mean, not necessarily *here*, but in the area?'

'Actually, they asked me to go back on the force – in fact Marcus and Charlie begged me to return, said I'm some kind of hero now. Hah. What a turnaround, eh?'

'That's great.' She doesn't sound convinced. 'You said no, didn't you?'

'Yeah. I'm done with all that. Wait a sec.' I get up and snatch the letter from on top of one of the boxes. 'I received this today.' I hand it to her, and she starts reading it.

'Oh, wow. A job offer!' She smiles. 'Good on you.'

'I think my skills might be better assigned to psychological services after all,' I say. 'I feel I've a lot to give and I'd like to help people manage their traumatic experiences. Wouldn't hurt to get a handle on my own, too.'

Tamsin says goodbye to Agatha and goes to leave. As she's at the door, she turns to me. 'Do you think he'll ever be charged with the rapes?'

'I don't know, Tamsin. I had Fran's journal on me, was on my way to take it to a safer place, when I was targeted. Woke up in the hospital without it. At least I saw the evidence, Isabel saw it. It confirmed what we knew about John.'

'Not enough, though,' she says, sadly. 'No justice for Fran.'

'No, I'm sorry,' I say, putting a hand on Tamsin's arm. 'But I do know I wasn't the only one after him. So, let's hope new charges will be brought, eventually. The evidence *we* found might be gone, but other people will be out there. I have to trust it'll come to light one day.' Charlie spoke to Isabel for me, letting her know about the stolen evidence

335

and what subsequently happened at the warehouse. Even now as I think about it, my tummy flips. I can imagine her devastation at hearing the news. I have a gut feeling Isabel will continue building her case against him, though, contacting those who are willing to go on the record and talk about their experiences. And Charlie gave her my message – that I'd call her myself once I'd recovered.

'Difficult to put a full stop after it all, isn't it?' Tamsin says, bringing my thoughts back to her.

'Yeah, it is. Sadly, I think this fight will be one among many that never really ends.'

Epilogue

She can hear the news playing on the television as she finishes loading the dishwasher. Going to the doorway, she leans against the frame and watches the report, her breaths coming faster. An image of a man flashes up on the screen while the newsreader talks about the arrest of a serving detective on suspicion of murder. When they speak it sends an icy chill down her back. 'But,' the newsreader says, 'the question has to be asked – is this just a case of one bad apple spoiling the bunch? Or are there more to be found?'

She grabs the remote, muting the TV. Then she walks into her bedroom and from the very back of her cupboard pulls out a box, lifting the lid she checks the contents for the hundredth time. It's all there. She lays the flat of her palm on the journal and lets out a long, steady breath before stowing it back in the cupboard. It'll have a new home soon.

Getting up, she walks over to the window and looks out, a swell of emotion crashing over her. She waves to the child as she happily sings while playing in the sandpit. Her precious little girl. Innocent and safe. That's all she ever really wanted. Once her eyes had been opened to what John was capable of, she couldn't close them again. She had to make sure she was in control. She turns away from the window, pulls out a burner phone and dials a number.

'I did most of what you asked,' she tells the person on the other end. Before they can respond, she says, 'I agreed to destroy it for lifelong protection . . . security. For a better future for my kid. I never wanted this, but that's what was promised. But I know now. It isn't enough, is it?

'I'm not stupid. Getting rid of all the evidence linking John to the rapes and destroying stuff showing your cover-ups, would put me in a vulnerable position. I'll be disposable – a loose end you'll eventually tie up. So, I wanted you to know . . .' She inhales . . . closes her eyes and tells herself she's doing the right thing . . . 'I kept some items. Call it my insurance policy.' She pauses now, letting the person on the other end run with a torrent of abuse, the phone held away from her ear until their anger temporarily blows out.

She had to take the power into her own hands, turn it back on them. She needs to be the one holding at least some of the cards to ensure their ongoing safety. If she's learned anything these past weeks, it's that she's involved in a deep, dark, complex web of lies, conspiracy and corruption, and although she thinks she's talking to the person sitting at the top of the food chain, they're more likely doing someone else's dirty work. There's no telling how far this goes, how high up. She just knows she did a deal with the devil and now has to cover her own back.

'The evidence is secure and stored and won't find its way

into the wrong hands. As long as me and my daughter are provided for and kept safe. Got it?'

'It seems John doesn't always choose the most vulnerable women after all, does it?' the voice states. 'But, think on this, Nina: *he's* behind bars but there are many that aren't. You'd do well to remember that.' And the line goes dead.

If you were gripped by *Bad Apple*, you'll love Alice Hunter's other twisty thrillers . . .

Every marriage has its secrets . . .

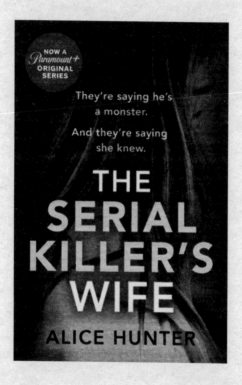

The addictive bestselling crime thriller, so shocking it should come with a warning! Read it before you watch it – now a major TV series for Paramount+.

Available from all good bookstores.

Is murder in the blood?

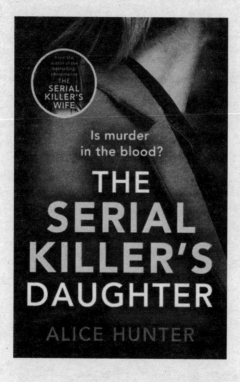

The shocking killer thriller with a breathtaking twist.

Available from all good bookstores.

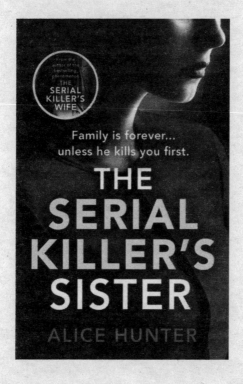